Series

Paranormal

Moons of Mystery
Sara's Moon (MF)
Charline's Solstice (MF)
Diana's Eclipse (MF)

War on Darkness
Darkness Defined (MM)
Order of Light (MM)
Knights of Nyx (MM)

Kisin Novels
Courting Death (MM)
Death, Love, & Tacos (MM)

True Mates
Truth in Exile (MM)
The Inescapable Truth (MM)
Truth in Lies (MM)

Lycan Detective Duet
Hart's Betrayal (MM)
Hart's Redemption (MM)

Contemporary

Ulwich Preparatory Academy
Our Last Fall (MM)
Our Secret Winter (MM)
Our Epic Spring (MM)

Oak Haven Romance
One Brave Thing (Enby/M)
All the Hype (MM)
The Bright Side (MM)

ALL the *Hype*

Oak Haven
Romance

S Bolanos

Contents

Chapter 1

Dylan

I STARED OUT THE window of the conference room, pretty sure my brain was leaking out of my ears. I didn't see the stellar view of uptown Charlotte. Not the glistening beauty of the Hearst Tower that I could normally stare at for hours, nor the spectacular reflection of 121 West Trade in the building adjacent to ours.

I blinked, not even registering how long I'd been standing there. Had it been seconds, minutes, hours? The last thing I'd expected after this morning's brief was for my manager, Margaret Langdon, to hand me an envelope and leave. I was fairly positive my jaw was probably still on the floor, and I'd be surprised if my eyeballs hadn't joined it.

I turned my attention back to the paper that felt like velvet promise. Unlike the skyline that I normally loved, the scrolling script captured my full attention, seeming to jump out in high relief to float off the page. I read the invitation again, still not sure I believed I was holding it.

Dylan Wells,

In recognition of your outstanding performance, Qian Wu would like to invite you to attend this year's Infinity Financial Corporate Retreat. Spouses and significant partners are welcome to join this exclusive networking opportunity and enjoy the incredible amenities of Oak Leaf Spa & Resort.

We look forward to your attendance at this week-long getaway in Oak Haven, Pennsylvania, along Lake Erie. Please reach out to Corporate Events no later than April 5th to RSVP and complete travel arrangements.

CEO of Infinity Financial Corporation

Qian Wu

IF you can dream it, we can achieve it

I carefully slid the prestigious invitation back into its luxe envelope and took a deep breath. This was actually happening. Five years of busting my ass, putting in the work, who knew how many late nights, and I was finally going to the career-making event of the year.

"Mr. Wells?"

I looked over my shoulder toward the entrance of the conference room, where the assistant of the analytics team was standing. "Yes, Simon?"

"Just wanted to let you know that the advisor meeting got moved to tomorrow."

"Okay, thanks for letting me know." My gaze flicked to the deep blue glossy envelope again, and I tightened my hold as the excitement that had been temporarily smothered by my disbelief surged.

The promotion of a lifetime was literally at my fingertips. There was only one problem. I was literally the *worst* at talking about myself or even claiming my accomplishments. A people-person I was not. But for every problem, there was a solution, and I knew exactly what I needed—a hype man. Someone charming, who knew all my best qualities, who could schmooze with the best of them, and could help me downplay any short-comings.

There was only one man for the job—James Wallace. We'd been best friends literally since diapers and inseparable from then on. If *anyone* could help me nail this opportunity, it was Jimmy. And if I remembered correctly, he had a lean schedule today.

I swiveled on the soles of my shoes, risking the slick bottom sending me down. "Simon!"

The office's shared assistant poked their head back through the opening in the glass wall. "Yes, sir?"

"Do I have any other meetings this afternoon?" I asked.

Simon shook their head, causing their short dark hair to swish over their forehead. "Not anymore. The meeting with the director was canceled yesterday due to a family emergency. And during this morning's brief, Margaret covered most of what had been planned for the afternoon meeting with the team, so that's no longer needed. Did you need me to add something to your calendar?"

"No, I'll actually be taking the rest of the day. Can you let Margaret and Sofia know?" I asked, already pulling out my cell phone.

"Sure thing. Will you be taking the rest of the week or just the afternoon?"

I glanced up from the message I was typing out. "Just today, for now. I'll let you know if that changes."

Simon nodded their head and was gone.

I stared at the screen and waited for a response to my <You free for afternoon beers? Have NEWS> as I made my way to my office to gather my things and follow up with any last-minute emails.

My impatience was about to get the best of me when a notification pinged and a message flashed on the screen.

No appointments. U buying?

I snorted and rapidly punched out a reply.

Mooch. Yeah, I'll grab our fave. Meet @ my place. Also have a favor.

Three dots appeared in the window and disappeared several times before Jimmy finally sent an eyebrow-raised emoji. Rather than respond, I focused on closing everything out for the day.

Two hours of emails, shop talk about the latest market news, and answering calls later, I was out the door. After a quick stop to pick up a case of my and Jimmy's favorite craft beer, I opted to grab Jimmy's favorite pizza, complete with all the gross bell peppers he liked. For the favor I wanted to ask, I wanted Jimmy as buttered up as possible.

Thankfully, I didn't have to wait long for Jimmy to come sauntering through the front door of my house like he lived there. Considering how much time we spent together, that would have made economic sense, but we had our own lives, and neither of us wanted to contend with bringing dates home—well, I would be bringing dates-plural. Jimmy was more of a serial monogamist. If he was dating someone, he was serious about her.

Not that I had a problem with women. They were great. Just not as sexual partners. That, and Jimmy could get pretty intense when he was in a relationship. Meanwhile, I'd somehow become the guy incapable of dating the same person for longer than a month or two. A good part of that was likely because I didn't see the big deal with long-term relationships... and my tunnel-focus on my career had led to more than a few breakups.

"Hey, man," Jimmy said after letting himself in. I stepped into a firm hug with a sharp back slap. The greeting was standard for us. We'd been through far too much together to get weird about showing each other open affection. Besides, who didn't like hugs?

When he pulled away, he brushed the dark brown strands of his hair back and smiled at me so broadly it looked like it might break his face in two. When we were teens, Jimmy had been teased mercilessly about his wide mouth, but I didn't give a shit. Jimmy's grin matched his eagerness to be bright and sunny all the time—sometimes *that* was annoying—but it was who he was.

His gaze settled on the table with the now hopefully chilled beers and pizza box. "Thank goodness you got real food and not Reid's."

"What's wrong with Reid's?" I asked with a huff.

Jimmy cracked open a beer, took a swallow, and leaned against the table, before he answered. "Uh, it's more of a convenience place. You eat there *way* too much, and they don't exactly have the diversity."

"Yeah, yeah." I dismissed the tired rebuke about my sad diet with a wave. "You want a plate?"

Jimmy gave me a thumbs up as I turned and threw open the lid of the box. "Oh, hell yes! And with the peppers? What are you trying to do, butter me up?" He laughed, but stopped with his hand inches away from a slice and turned narrowed eyes on me. "You *are* buttering me up. Just how bad is this favor?"

"Now hear me out." I grabbed a beer and took a drink for fortification. "Starting with the news. I got an invitation to the annual retreat." A beat went by where my smile slowly morphed into a grin to rival a Cheshire cat.

Jimmy blinked. Then immediately set his beer down and launched himself at me. "Holy fuck, Dill, that's incredible. Congratulations!" I struggled to prevent my beer from sloshing all over the place in the face of Jimmy's enthusiasm, but honestly, I was right there with him.

"It's gonna be at this fancy place in Pennsylvania on the lake. I looked it up—Oak Leaf Spa and Resort—and this place is incredible, plus there's this cute-ass small town nearby. For a whole week, I'll be rubbing elbows with the movers and shakers of Infinity Financial."

Jimmy stepped back to retrieve his abandoned beer. "That's freaking awesome. I'm so proud of you. You've been working for years to get here. Knew you could do it." He took a swig and considered me a second. "But what do you need me for?"

"I need you to be my hype man," I said with enough optimism to fill a lake.

"A week-long, all expenses paid trip to a fancy resort? Oh, fuck yes." Jimmy paused and cut a serious expression at me. "It is all expenses paid, right?"

I chuckled. "Yeah, it would be. Don't you have any questions?"

Jimmy hiked a shoulder and gave me a lopsided grin. "I trust you. All I need to know is when, and I'll figure out how to make it work with the clinic."

"I'm really glad you feel that way, because I can't imagine going through this without your help, but…"

"But…" he prompted.

"There's a catch."

Jimmy froze with his beer halfway to his mouth. He lowered it slowly and considered me intensely. "What kind of catch? I'm not gonna have to streak through a gym again, am I?"

"No, no, nothing like that. The invitation was pretty specific about any plus-ones. Only significant partners can join. So, we'd, uh, have to pretend to be in a long-term relationship."

To his credit, Jimmy managed to wait a whole second before he burst into laughter.

"Come on, it's not that funny."

Jimmy tried unsuccessfully to rein in his over-the-top laughter. "You? In a committed relationship?"

"Well, we've been friends for thirty-two years, and friendship is a *type* of relationship," I countered. "I need you to talk me up. You know everything about me and we wouldn't even need a BS back story. Fake dating each other will be the easiest thing we've ever done." Okay, maybe not the *easiest* considering I'd never thought of my friend romantically, but easy enough.

Jimmy scowled and crossed his arms. "What do I get out of this?"

"You mean a free vacation isn't enough?"

He shook his head. "You raised the stakes, so I am too. I'll do it on one condition."

I braced myself. Jimmy was a shit-ton of fun, and the two of us had gotten into more trouble than not over the years, but he had his serious side. The one that helped him pursue his license in mental health counseling. But it also made him hard to read, and Jimmy had an interesting way of blindsiding me at times. "Okay," I said tentatively.

"I get to ask you every weird, ridiculous, and uncomfortable question I've been keeping to myself over the years."

"Uh..." I fumbled. It wasn't as if we had any secrets from each other. We told each other everything. I knew all about Jimmy's goals, fears, and unfortunately, girlfriends. What questions could he possibly ask now that he hadn't before? Slightly reassured, I nodded. "Deal."

Jimmy's stern expression remained firmly in place. "I mean it, Dill, *any* question. And you're not allowed to evade or take a pass."

I took a moment to reconsider, intimidated by his severity, but came to the same conclusion. "Done," I said, and held out my hand to shake on it.

A wicked grin spread across Jimmy's face and sparked in his eyes. "Oh, no, that won't do. We kiss on it, or no deal."

I dropped my hand and scoffed. "You can't be serious."

"If we're gonna be fake-dating, only makes sense we seal the deal with a kiss," he said with a challenging tilt of his head.

I weighed my desire to have the ultimate hype man present for the biggest opportunity of my life, with the inevitable awkwardness of kissing my best friend. In the end, getting invited to the annual retreat was a chance I couldn't afford to squander. "Fine, you weirdo, we'll kiss over it."

We stepped in close until we were practically nose to nose. Jimmy was fighting a losing battle with keeping his grin tamped down. "What's the matter?" he asked when I hesitated. "Chicken? Afraid you'll kiss me and like it?"

"You're such an ass." Before I could well and truly psych myself out, I leaned forward, prepared to call Jimmy on his bluff. Except Jimmy didn't shy away, and our lips pressed together. Startled that I had actually kissed him, I pulled back.

Jimmy snorted. "That the best you've got? No one is going to buy that we've been in a relationship for *years* if you're kissing me like that. I mean, if you're going around kissing people like that, it's no wonder you can't hold down a boyfriend."

I growled and muttered, "I really hate you sometimes."

"Pft, you know you love me."

I glared at my smug friend. Asshole wanted a real kiss? Then he was gonna get one. Jimmy was on the verge of what was undoubtedly another flippant remark when I captured his mouth. It wasn't easy, but I pushed away all thoughts that this was my straight best friend and kissed him like I would any other guy I was really into. I barely even twitched when Jimmy met my exploring tongue with his own.

"Satisfied?" I asked huskier than I would have expected when I pulled away.

Jimmy looked back at me, his lips pinker than they had been and slightly parted, his eyes half-lidded, and his breathing edging on ragged.

I worked hard to keep my self-satisfied smirk to myself. I may not be able to maintain a steady relationship, but I could definitely fucking kiss.

Finally, Jimmy nodded and took a step back to take a drink. "Could use some work, but it'll do." And for the second time that day, my jaw dropped to the floor.

Chapter 2

Jimmy

THE ALARM ON MY phone went off, and I vaulted over my bed, un-doing my half-assed efforts of making it, to silence the intrusive sound. Right on cue a message came through from Dylan.

> Your ass better be dressed

Before I could text back a snarky reply about people supposedly dating not caring if the other was dressed, my apartment door swung open. "Back here!" I hollered.

Immediately I could make out grumbling and scrambled to shove the last of my personal hygiene supplies along with a fresh bottle of lube—because why the fuck not—into my suitcase and snapped the lid shut. The footsteps got louder, stopping right as I slid the zipper home.

"What the hell happened in here?" Dylan asked from the door-way.

I straightened up and propped my hands on my sides. I surveyed the chaos of my bedroom with the curtains half-yanked open, a half-full glass of water sitting on the nightstand, and nearly every article of clothing I owned slung over any available surface. Then I brought my attention to Dylan, standing with his arms crossed and his characteristic judgy frown. "What? It always looks like this."

Dylan snorted. "You made sure to pack at least quasi-professional clothes, right?" he asked, stepping into the room and reaching for the suitcase.

"Of course."

Dill paused with his hand around the handle and lifted an eyebrow—well, both eyebrows. Dylan never could do just the one, though he thought he could. "And a suit?"

I rolled my eyes. "You sent me a fucking itemized memo. Yeah, I got the suit." I held up a hand as Dylan opened his mouth, "*And* several button-downs. I also packed casual wear because *it's a retreat.*"

Dylan scowled at me and yanked the suitcase off the bed, grunting with the unexpected weight. "What the hell else did you pack?"

"Just the essentials," I said, slapping Dylan on the shoulder as I slipped past him. I wasn't about to tell him that a good portion of that casual wear was actually for him. I loved Dill, I really did, but man could get so wrapped up in work sometimes that he left his common sense cooling with his coffee. "You coming?" I shouted once I was at the front door.

"Don't see why I have to carry all your shit," Dylan grumbled as he maneuvered the suitcase down the short hall into the combo kitchen/dining/living space.

I lifted an eyebrow—because I actually could. "Because you took it from me."

Dylan faltered, his mouth opening and closing a few times before finally saying, "Well, you were taking too long and I don't want to be late."

I didn't bother pointing out that we were at least an hour ahead of schedule; I'd made sure of it. I knew how important this opportunity was for him and I was going to do everything in my power to make sure he killed it. And that meant being the best fucking boyfriend Dylan had ever had. Not that it was a hard task, Dill was *terrible* at relationships. I opened the door and waved for him to go through.

He glanced around the absurdly small apartment that I'd had since I'd begun training for my license. Thankfully, the lease was up later this fall and I could finally leave the shoebox place behind. "You sure?" Undoubtedly, he was referencing the dishes on the counter—all washed and scrubbed—as well as the pantry door hanging open from when I'd taken the trash out earlier this morning.

"Yep, all set."

Dylan shook his head and rolled through the door.

As he passed, I snagged the handle of the suitcase, taking it back. "Thanks, babe."

His head snapped around so fast, I couldn't help but laugh as I finished locking up. "The hell, Jimmy?"

"Just trying it out. You know, now that we're dating." I winked at Dylan and wandered a few steps before he caught up with me.

"This is gonna be so weird. Why did I think this was a good idea?"

I bumped his shoulder. "Because you need a hype man, and I'm the best one you've got. It'll be fine. But you're going to have to try a hell of a lot harder if you're going to sell this."

Dylan called the elevator, and we stepped in when the doors opened. "It can't be all that hard, right? I mean, we're the closest friends I know. We've done pretty much everything together. We're not weird about showing affection." He tugged his shirt straight, though it didn't need it. "Yeah, okay, this should be a breeze."

I internally shook my head. We may be fantastic friends with next to no personal boundaries, but dating was different. It was proximity, the way you looked at someone like they were the only person in the room who mattered, the intimacy of skin against skin just for the sake of it.

I let out a longing sigh as Dylan exited the elevator, still trying to talk himself up. I let myself indulge in how adorable it was when he got too in his own head, then pushed the feelings away just like I had every day for the last twenty years. Then I sped up to cut him off before he left the building, parking my suitcase and placing my hands on Dill's tense shoulders. "Hey, look at me."

He huffed, but dutifully looked up at me.

"You can do this. *We* can do this. We survived Mr. Harrington's class, sophomore year of college, and pretty much everything else together. We've got this." I gave him a crooked grin. "I know that you're absolute shit at having a boyfriend, but don't worry, I'll coach you through it. And I promise that I won't show up at your office after all of this and make a scene."

He snorted and pushed against my chest so that I stumbled a step back. "Fuck you. I do know *how* to date, thank you very much. I go on plenty of dates. And Carver was an isolated incident."

"Are all gay men so freaking uptight, or is it just you?" I snickered in the face of Dylan's obvious indignation. Rather than answer, he huffed—proving my point—and tried to storm out of the building. "Uh-uh," I said, catching his arm. "Any and all questions. Remember?"

Dylan's mouth worked around what I was sure were a boatload of names to call me before at last settling on a disgruntled, "I am *not* uptight."

"Whatever you say, Cameron. How's that diamond coming along by the way?" I teased.

He groaned in exaggerated agony. "Shut the fuck up. You're not going to pester me with movie quotes the whole time, are you?"

I followed Dylan to his parked car and managed to wait until my suitcase was nestled in the trunk next to Dylan's, and we were buckled before cracking. I faced him with the most serious expression I could muster. "Life moves pretty fast. You don't stop and look around once in a while, you could miss it."

"I fucking hate you," he said with a chuckle as he pulled into traffic and angled us toward Charlotte Douglas International Airport.

"You know... my best friend's sister's boyfriend's brother's girlfriend heard from this guy who knows this kid who's going with the girl who saw Ferris pass out at 31 Flavors last night. I guess it's pretty serious."

Dylan's chuckles evolved into full-on laughter.

By the time we'd made it to the airport, parked the car in extended stay, checked our luggage, and gone through security, I'd made my way through all the best quotes of Ferris Bueller's Day Off, Pretty Woman, Breakfast at Tiffany's, and The Birdcage—for flavor. The two of us were cracking up enough to make security and everyone else around us a little uncomfortable, but most importantly, Dill had noticeably relaxed.

We boarded the plane, and each of us whistled at how nice the business class seats were. "You can have the window," Dylan said, indicating for me to go first.

"Such a gentleman," I said, batting my eyelashes and sliding in front of him closer than strictly necessary.

"You are such a ham. I know you like the window."

I flashed him a smile and got settled. While the plane idled and prepared for takeoff, I explored everything within my reach. I read the emergency brochure, watched the tarmac crews scurry around like busy bees, and took out the complimentary head-phones—which I promptly abandoned to play with the vents. The whole while, Dylan checked emails on his phone, then switched to reading financial news about the current swings in the market.

We fell into a comfortable silence when the attendant called for all electronics to be placed in airplane mode. The plane wound it's way around the strip, lined up its nose, then picked up speed. Dill and I shared a happy look. We both loved the rush of takeoff, the exhilaration of leaving the earth behind, the swoop of your stomach as the plane battled gravity to gain air. When the plane leveled out, I pulled up the armrest separating us and shifted so I could rest my head on Dylan's shoulder.

"What are you doing?" he asked, looking down at me getting comfortable.

"Shh, I'm napping." I closed my eyes for emphasis and snuggled closer.

"Are you for real? It's only a two-hour flight."

"Exactly, plenty of time for a good nap. And don't forget, you're the reason I'm up this early in the first place."

He grumbled about me sleeping too late anyway, but caved like I knew he would.

I breathed in the warm scent of his cologne that always made me think of home and sighed deeper into his shoulder. Snuggling with Dylan had been a thing I'd done for as long as I could remember, and I loved that he indulged me, even though I knew he wasn't much of a cuddler. That fact only made me feel more special. That no matter who Dylan went out with or slept with, this was all mine.

When the plane jolted as its tires hit the runway in Pennsylvania, I wasn't surprised to find Dylan passed out with his cheek resting on my head. Dill liked to tease me I could sleep through the apocalypse while he was a much lighter sleeper. Maybe that was true when we were apart, but whenever we were together, he slept like the dead. I reveled in the quiet cocoon of peace we'd made until the plane hit the brakes to coast into the bay and he jerked awake.

He blinked bleary-eyed out the window and yawned wide enough to crack his jaw. "That was fast," he said, stifling another yawn.

I sat up and stretched as much as the limited space would allow. "Good naps always make time fly."

"You're a terrible influence." He undid his buckle and stood to wait for our chance to slip out.

"And yet, you haven't gotten rid of me," I teased, resting a hand on his hip so we hopefully wouldn't get separated in the rush.

He snorted, but didn't comment.

An obnoxious amount of time later, we'd managed to exit the plane, get mildly freshened up, and secure our luggage.

"There should be someone waiting for us," Dylan said as he wheeled his suitcase toward the terminal exit.

"Ooh, do you think they'll have one of those big signs? How awesome would that be?" I asked, not entirely serious, but also not entirely not. It *would* be awesome.

He shook has head and chuckled under his breath. "You watch way too many movies."

"You say that like you didn't watch all of them *with* me," I responded, leaning into him hard enough that his suitcase threatened to wheel off in the wrong direction.

A smile flashed across his face, and I imagined he was recalling some of our more memorable movie-fest sleepovers growing up. "Oh, hey, I think that's them." Dill pointed to where a couple of people were grouped around a man with a bright floral button-down and a sign that read "IF you can read this, you made it."

I barked out a laugh. I may not understand everything about the markets the way Dill did, but I certainly appreciated Infinity Financial's love of puns. I glanced at Dylan, who was trying desperately to smother a smile. "You ready for this?" I asked, sliding my hand into his and lacing our fingers. While the motion felt beyond natural to me, Dylan flinched. I could see the flicker of panic in his dark blue eyes, and I tightened my grip. "We've got this," I whispered.

He swallowed hard and nodded. "We've got this."

I leaned in to peck his cheek with a small kiss—never too early to establish the groundwork for this charade. Thankfully, he didn't flinch as noticeably this time.

"We read you," Dylan said, raising his hand in a wave and lifting his voice enough to be heard over the bustle of people.

Chapter 3

Dylan

THANK GOD FOR JIMMY. And damn him too. The smile plastered on my face hadn't moved for what felt like hours as Jimmy dragged us around to meet all the couples that had already arrived and seriously putting my peopling skills to the test. All I wanted was to go up to our room for a half hour and evaluate our game plan. Instead, I met colleagues from Wisconsin, Washington—the state and DC—Texas, South Dakota, and a few others I didn't have a prayer of remembering.

Jimmy had always been a social butterfly, a positive ray of fucking sunshine. That was why I'd known he'd blend in seamlessly. Man had never met a stranger. But why the fuck couldn't we have been like the platonic couple from Memphis? And why hadn't I thought of that *before* I'd gone along with Jimmy's version of a couple? Whenever we *did* manage to get to the room, we were gonna have words.

"Hey, Dill, do you know Marcus? He's from the New York office. His wife sadly couldn't make it because of some sensitive experiments she's working on. But how cool is that?" Jimmy gripped Marcus's shoulders from behind, his over-wide smile in full force. "This man is married to an honest-to-goodness scientist."

I chuckled and stepped forward to shake Marcus's hand. In a welcome change, I did actually know him. Marcus Abernathy was the district manager of Infinity Financial's northeastern division. We'd worked together on a number of occasions, and I was aware that Abernathy's wife was incredibly accomplished in the scientific community. "Nice to finally meet you in person. Great work again on that research report your team put out back in May. I don't envy you. The market was a shitstorm."

"Ugh, don't remind me. But, hey," Marcus glanced at Jimmy, who'd released him and moved to complete their little circle, "I didn't realize you were settled."

"I'm not." "It's not official," Jimmy and I said at once. Jimmy shot me a sharp look before wrapping an arm around my shoulders. Suddenly, I was painfully aware of just how hard this was going to be. There would be people here who actually knew me and had interacted with me. A surprise serious boyfriend was definitely gonna raise some eyebrows.

Jimmy squeezed me tighter. "We've been together for ages. Known each other since diapers, if you can believe it. Though things really only got serious that last couple years." Jimmy plastered a kiss on my temple and I was relieved I didn't react this time.

Marcus laughed. "You don't say. Wells, where have you been hiding this guy?"

I opened my mouth not entirely sure what answer was going to come out when Jimmy overrode me.

"He likes to save me for special occasions. Plus, I don't need to tell *you* that this guy is all work and no play."

"Your man has a point," Marcus said, pointing a finger at me. "You may be one of the finest analysts on the East Coast, but I feel like I know next to nothing about you. Relax, live a little. With a mind like yours, you'll never be wanting for opportunity."

I offered a weak smile, not sure which part of that was more unsettling—Marcus calling Jimmy my man or that apparently Jimmy wasn't the only one who thought I was a little uptight.

Jimmy's hand shifted from my shoulder to brush lightly in my hair. "While I agree that Dill works himself too hard, I also admire and respect his dedication. Our whole lives, if there was something that needed doing, Dill found a way to get it done."

I glanced at my best friend, surprised at the sentiment, and was promptly knocked off my axis by the look of sheer affection he was giving me. Okay, maybe I *was* the absolute worst at being in a relationship. I'd certainly never had a *real* boyfriend look at me like that. My cheeks heated as I stared into Jimmy's brown eyes at a loss.

"Good. Looks like the concierge has everything sorted. I'll see you two at this evening's meet and greet?" Marcus asked.

"We'll be there," Jimmy said, giving the hair at the back of my neck a sharp tug.

I shook myself free of my stupor. "Yep," I parroted. "Can't wait."

"You two take some time to get settled in your room. There should be an itinerary of the week's events already there." A member of the resort staff presented Marcus with a collection of room keys. Marcus then passed me a set with my last name written on it. "I'm really glad to see you here, Wells. I look forward to getting to know you and your partner much better."

I smiled and echoed some kind of agreement, because what the fuck else was I supposed to do? In all of my plans for this week, the fact that people would expect to get to know Jimmy as my *partner* hadn't really factored into it. I was the top market analyst in Charlotte. How the hell hadn't I factored that in?

"I'll save you two a seat at our table," Marcus said, shaking my hand, then Jimmy's.

"Pleasure to meet you, sir," Jimmy said with a smile, then ruffled my hair. "Come on, babe, let's get freshened up and figure out what this week has in store."

I kept my peace on the ride up by virtue of the fact that other people were in the elevator with us. Though it didn't stop Jimmy from giving me concerned looks. When I opened the door to our room, our luggage was indeed already there, along with a luxurious king-sized bed. But the one bed didn't faze me. We'd shared a bed plenty of times before, and I was positive we would again. No, what irked me was how grossly out of my depth I felt. The door clicked shut, plunging the room into shadow. I flicked the nearest light switch, turning on the can lights over the bed, and realized that at some point I'd started breathing heavy.

"Dill? You alright, man?" Jimmy's tentative question finally tipped me over the edge.

"No, I'm not alright. Why the hell couldn't we have been a platonic couple? And why did you ask if I knew Marcus? You know, I know Marcus. Why didn't we come up with a backstory? People are gonna want to know when we started dating, for how long, how serious things are. I don't have answers for that." I dropped onto the edge of the bed and hung my head in my hands. "Why did I ever think I could pull this off?"

He let out a sigh, and the bed sank as he joined me. "First off, even if we had tried to pull off being a platonic couple, no one would have believed it. Our dynamic already makes people question if we're involved, and to be frank, I couldn't have done it."

I tilted my head to peer at him, more than a little surprised by the confession.

"Second," he continued, "of course I know *you* know Marcus, but it was a great way to get you two talking face-to-face. And now we're sitting at his table. As for the backstory, we started casually dating after your last breakup because you were tired of guys playing games and why the hell not. After dating for a year, things are definitely more serious, but we're also comfortable with where we're at, considering how important both of our careers are to us right now."

I blinked at the cool, confident person before me, who couldn't remember not to put Styrofoam in the microwave even after getting violently ill—twice—but had somehow come up with an entire back story that was easy enough to follow without things getting too twisted. "Who are you, and what have you done with my best friend?"

"I'm the guy who's gonna get you through this. When it comes to anything work-related, you're an ace, Dill, but when you have to just be a person, you tend to flounder."

I narrowed my eyes at him, "Are you therapizing me?"

"That's not a real word, and no. I know you, Dill. We've known each other our whole lives, and *that's* how *we* are gonna pull this off." He rubbed my back.

I let out a heavy sigh. "You're right. Sorry. Thanks for talking me through it."

"Anytime, bud."

That reminded me. "Do you have to call me babe?"

He frowned as if he truly didn't understand what I meant. "Would you prefer I call you something else? I was pretty sure 'love' would freak you out more, and neither of us has ever done the cutesy pet names in our other relationships, but if you'd rather—"

"No!" I said a little too loudly. "No, babe is…babe is fine."

Jimmy leaned back on his arms and kicked his legs against the bed like he was thirteen instead of thirty. "So, what do you call your boyfriends?"

I gave him an incredulous look. "Why do you want to know?"

"Curiosity," he said with a shrug. "Plus, you never talk about any of your boyfriends."

"Sure I do."

"Uh, no, you don't. I still have no idea what all went down with you and Kennedy after college."

I blanched. Kennedy. I'd been absolutely head over heels for the guy, so much so that we'd been on the verge of moving in together before it had all fallen apart. He'd also been the only guy I'd ever dated who looked even remotely like Jimmy. Kennedy had even had the same sunny disposition. But the more I'd fallen for Kennedy, the more my friendship with Jimmy had suffered. When I'd tried to fix it, Kennedy had given me an ultimatum—I could either have Kennedy or I could have Jimmy, not both.

It took a minute for me to pull myself back together. If Jimmy knew the truth about what had gone down with Kennedy, he'd probably tell me I needed therapy, especially since I clearly wasn't as over it as I thought I was. "I didn't think you'd want to hear about my interactions with men."

He scoffed. "And you wanted to hear about all of my sexcapades with women?"

"Okay, fair point."

"Seriously, we tell each other everything, or at least I tell *you* everything. But I don't know shit about who you are with your partners."

"I tell you some things," I countered. Jimmy just pursed his lips and frowned. Out of nowhere, I remembered the way those same lips had opened for me when we'd kissed for the first time two months ago. I quickly dispelled the memory. "I didn't realize it bothered you so much. What do you want to know?"

He smirked. "Well, you could start by answering my first question about pet names."

"Seriously?" I asked.

"Am I gonna have to remind you after every question that you've already agreed to answer them?" he asked with an arched brow.

"No," I grumbled, then mumbled my response to the original question, my face burning.

"Sorry, didn't quite catch that."

"Baby. When I'm really into a guy, I'll call him baby," I said in a rush, positive my face would be cooler if it was literally on fire. "Satisfied?"

"Yep." He bounced off the bed. "Now come here. We need to work on you being more believable. Don't think I didn't notice your little statue rendition downstairs."

So much for hoping *that* had gone unnoticed. But at least he hadn't asked about the breakup with Kennedy. I pushed off the bed and walked to where Jimmy had summoned, making sure to act as put-upon as possible. "What did you have in mind?"

"Call me babe."

I snickered. "Okay, babe."

Jimmy scowled. "Maybe next time try to do it without so much sarcasm. But we'll deal with that later. Are there any touches you're not comfortable with?"

I frowned. We touched each other all the time. It had never been a big deal before, and I didn't understand why it was now.

"Ugh, you're hopeless," Jimmy bemoaned, then palmed my ass.

I nearly came out of my slacks at the blatant grope with absolutely zero warning. The only thing that kept me from jumping was the challenge written clearly on Jimmy's face.

"Are you going to be able to not freak if I touch your ass? Will you be able to touch mine? Men in a relationship aren't exactly shy about feeling each other up." Jimmy's brows snapped together with concern. "Right? Gay men touch each other's asses all the time?"

I rolled my eyes. "I don't know about *all* the time, but no, we're not shy about it either. And I don't have a problem touching your ass." To prove my point, I mirrored Jimmy's grope. We stood like that for a while until it felt like we were waiting for the other to back down. "Are we really standing here fondling each other's asses?" I asked.

"You're damn right we are. Now kiss me."

The way Jimmy had sunk into the kiss so naturally before, despite not being gay, flashed through my mind. "Why?" I asked, mortified at how raw my voice sounded. I didn't actually *want* to kiss Jimmy. Did I?

He shifted his hand to rest on my hip and gave me a sad, understanding look. "Because I think if you're the one initiating contact and affection, you'll feel more comfortable, more in control."

"You're doing it again," I grumbled.

"Fine, I am therapizing you, but only a little. I want to help you succeed, Dill, but you're gonna have to work with me. Given how tense you've gotten about this, I'm thinking a little practice in a safe space is warranted. And kisses are part of that."

I thought about how Jimmy had disparaged my kissing abilities, and my competitiveness took over. Without a second thought, I used my grip on Jimmy's ass to pull him forward and slammed our mouths together. He released a muffled sound of surprise that spurred me on. Like before, his lips parted almost immediately, and I swept my tongue inside. Our tongues danced together for a few seconds, then I shifted my focus to suck and nip at his bottom lip. Jimmy shuddered and pressed tighter against me, meeting the wild exploration with one of his own.

When I finally pulled away, both our lips were puffy, and Jimmy was thoroughly flushed. He cleared his throat after a moment and dropped his hand from the side of my neck, though I wasn't entirely sure when it had gotten there. "I really just meant a peck on the cheek, but that works too."

Chapter 4

Jimmy

I WAS STILL IN a bit of a daze as we made our way down to the formal welcome dinner. I knew Dill was a stickler for being the best at whatever he was doing, but damn, I didn't know it was possible for him to kiss *better* than he had the first time I'd challenged him. I could definitely get used to this whole practicing thing. When I used to daydream about kissing Dylan, I'd no idea just how *good* it could be.

We drew closer to the main event hall where a not-so-modest banner read "Oak Leaf Spa & Resort welcomes Infinity Financial". I reached out to grab Dylan's hand, then stopped myself. Dill needed to feel like he was in control of the situation, which meant I'd have to wait and see if he would actually follow through. I was on the verge of throwing in the towel and initiating contact anyway when his hand settled on my lower back.

Still high on the earlier kiss, the warmth seeped through me to ignite the crush I'd been fighting for as long as I'd known Dill was gay. I prayed that he didn't notice how I'd basically melted at the simple contact. Thankfully, I didn't have to worry long. Marcus Abernathy caught sight of us entering the hall and waved us over.

"How's the room?" Marcus asked as he gestured for us to join him by the table where he'd been chatting with a small cluster of people.

I scrambled to remember anything about our room. I had a vague impression of deep purple or maybe emerald? With my brain currently short-circuited, all that readily sprang to mind was the feel of Dylan squeezing my ass and dominating my mouth like he owned it. And the bed. I definitely recalled a big-ass bed that looked like it could swallow a person in comfort. I'd be sleeping in that bed with Dylan later. Whatever was left of my brain went up in smoke.

"The room is great. Generous space and a bed to die for," Dylan said when I failed to fill the void.

Marcus let out a loud burst of laughter. "I'm telling you, the beds here *sold* Nancy on the place when she was scouting for this year's location."

"You don't say," I said, finally finding my voice, though it sounded too strained to actually belong to me.

Dylan flashed me a concerned look that was replaced with an easy grin before Marcus could take note. "I can definitely see why, and I only sat on it for a few minutes. Might have to set two alarms in the morning," he added, prompting us all to laugh.

Okay, I could do this. I wasn't about to let one, two—oh, God, please let there be more—kisses distract me from my mission to hype the fuck out of Dylan. Out of the corner of my eye, I noted the nameplates on the table and how ours were conspicuously different colored.

"So whose seats did we steal?" I asked, leaning into Dylan, who thankfully took the hint and wrapped an arm around me. The goal was casual and comfortable, the trademark of any long-term committed relationship.

Marcus dismissed the query with a wave of his hand. "Don't worry about it. I doubt they'll be complaining." Considering everyone who'd been invited was here to hobnob with IF's elite, the statement made sense. And the fact that a district manager had clearly taken an interest in Dylan was a fantastic start to the week.

"What's a person got to do to get a drink in this place?" a newcomer asked of our group, though Marcus was the only one with a drink in his hand.

"Rafe! Have you met Dylan Wells?" Marcus gestured to Dylan. "And this is his partner, James Wallace."

"Jimmy, please," I said, shaking Rafe's extended hand before Rafe moved on to Dylan.

"Not in the flesh, but I'm very familiar with your work. I'm still kicking myself for waiting to read your analysis of the new tech company until *after* the stock had already started tanking." Rafe shook Dylan's hand heartily, and I couldn't help but be proud of my best friend.

"Dylan, this is Rafael Inez, the—"

"No introduction necessary, sir. Much like yourself, I'm very familiar with the head of global operations," Dylan said, and my respect for Dill's impressive corporate skills shot through the stratosphere. Was *everyone* at Infinity Financial familiar with Dylan's work?

Rafe shook his head. "I guess having your name plastered on all the internal memos will do that. Anyway, I'll have to catch up with you later. The spouse is thirsty, and I promised not to 'get lost' on my way."

"In that case, the bar is at the back of the room. There's an impressive assortment of cocktails and mocktails. You know what? I'll join you." Marcus turned to me and Dylan. "Can I get either of you anything?"

"Amber ale," we replied in unison.

"If they have one. If not, any lager will do," I added with a smile.

Marcus chuckled. "You two really have known each other forever. Wish the missus and I could be that in sync. Consider it done."

When Marcus and Rafe had melded with the small bustle of people, Dylan let out a sigh as if he'd been holding his breath and removed his arm from around me. "Really hope they have a decent beer," he said as he took a seat.

I joined him, staring at him with open awe until he took notice. "What?"

"I knew you were good at your job, but you're like a really big fucking deal."

He shrugged. "I'm not all that. The company just prides itself on being familiar with the plebeians."

"Dill," I said with the serious expression this deserved, "the director of the entire east coast *and* the head of global operations just commended your work. That's a big deal."

He ducked his head, and I realized he was trying to stifle a laugh. "It is, isn't it? I knew this event was special, but it's already blowing my mind. This week really could make my whole career."

Someone scoffed behind us. "Make it? Play your cards right and it could catapult it into a new dimension."

I looked at Dylan askance, not entirely sure who'd just graced us with their presence. But judging by Dylan's expression, his brain had turned to pudding. I nudged him under the table, and he blinked.

"Mr. Wu, hi, hello. We're not in your seats, are we?"

"Not at all, but I was looking for where you'd gotten off to. Now I see Abernathy is up to his tricks again."

Dylan flicked a glance at me. "How so?"

"You were supposed to be at *my* table this evening. Not to worry, though. I'll let Abernathy have his way... for now. But tomorrow, you're mine." Mr. Wu gave Dylan a stern look until Dill went pale, then broke into a bright smile. "Relax, we're all here to have a good time and get to know each other. Speaking of which, how rude of me. I'm Qian Wu, but please call me Chase. You must be Dylan's partner."

"James Wallace, Jimmy," I said, accepting the man's hand.

Chase was mid shaking Dylan's hand when Marcus returned with two glasses of amber beer. "I see I've been found out," he said playfully as he set the frosty glasses down.

"Never forget, Abernathy, I see all."

Dylan and I froze while Marcus and Chase had a veritable standoff over our heads. Then the two burst out laughing. Dylan sagged in his chair, only to straighten again when Chase clapped him on the shoulder.

"Like I was telling Wells, you can have your way tonight, but I'll be stealing him back tomorrow." Chase shifted his focus to the two of us. "How are you guys at shuffleboard?"

We shared a look. Last time either of us had played shuffleboard had been on our senior trip in high school... and we were bad. "Uh..." we said together, clearly on the same thought trail.

Marcus shook his head. "You guys really are too much. Don't worry, it's easy enough to pick up, and still fun when you're terrible. But, hey, Chase, while I've got you, I had a quick thing I wanted to run by you regarding the IT merger."

"Step into my office. Or better yet, fill me in on the way to the bar. I want one of those." Chase pointed at the beers Marcus had brought. The two fell in step and ventured back in the direction Marcus had just returned from.

I watched them go, turning over the weird vibe I'd gotten from Chase in my head. "Who's Chase in the company?" I asked when the men had moved far enough away.

Dylan turned wide eyes on me. "Qian Wu is the chief executive of operations for Infinity Financial. He's *the* boss."

"I know what a CEO is, Dill." I squinted at him and decided now was as good a time as any for my next question. "Do you have a sixth sense or something to tell when other guys are gay?"

"What? You want to ask one of your questions *now*?" he hissed.

I rolled my eyes and gazed after where Chase and Marcus had wandered off. "I was just wondering if maybe Chase was gay given the way he looked at you."

Dylan spun around in his seat as if he was gonna launch after Chase. "How did he look at me?"

The first words that came to mind were that Dylan looked like a prize he planned to win, but I wasn't about to say that. I didn't need my experience as a therapist to recognize I was likely projecting. "Nah-ah, my question first."

"No, we don't have a sixth sense or any other innate knowledge beyond paying attention. Now, how was Mr. Wu looking at me?" he insisted.

I held up a finger, and he stared at me like I'd sprouted a second head. "First off, he asked us to call him Chase. If you truly want to succeed here, then you should maybe refer to people the way they ask you to. And second, it wasn't any big thing. He just seemed... I don't know, interested."

Dylan shrugged, much to my annoyance, and reached for his beer. "I doubt it's anything romantic. Far as I know, Mr—Chase," he corrected himself, "is happily committed to his wife, and it's not an open marriage. Besides, this trip *is* about underlings getting to rub elbows with the higher-ups." He took a sip and let out an appreciative sigh. "Dude, you've got to try this."

I grabbed the beer he pushed toward me, internally at-odds with anyone "rubbing elbows" with Dylan. When the smokiness coating the sweet malt hit my tongue, though, I forgot about the unexpectedly jealous thought and echoed Dylan's hum of enjoyment. "Oh, that's good."

"Mmhmm. And if I read the notes on the itinerary right, all the food and drinks are locally sourced. There's a good chance this came from the nearby town, Oak Haven."

I turned to him after swallowing my latest sip. "When did you read the itinerary?"

"While you were standing gob-smacked in the middle of the room," he replied, doing a shit-ass job of hiding a smirk with his cup.

Chapter 5

Dylan

MY MIND WAS A blur of names and faces by the time Jimmy and I made it back up to our room. "I knew the event had an exclusive guest list, but Jimmy, bro, the sheer amount of talent here is messing with me. And that's not even counting any of the directors," I said as I peeled off my polo and stripped down to my boxers. "How am I supposed to compete with the likes of Susan Mitchell? She predicted the market downturn *months* before anyone else."

"Easy. You don't," he said as he repeated the same motions on the other side of the bed.

I paused in the middle of pulling back the covers. "Excuse me?"

He huffed and ripped the covers back, then flopped onto the bed with a sigh of relief. "Don't look at it as a competition. You can stop giving me that face. I know competition is like your lifeblood, but it's not everything."

I fluffed the covers, shooting a stream of cold air at him, then joined him under the sheets. "I'm blaming it on the beers, but I'm not following. How the hell is it *not* a competition?"

Jimmy made the aggrieved sound that I'd become intimately familiar with over the years. "All these people have potential and are amazing at what they do. *All* of them. The head honchos already know that, or they wouldn't have invited them in the first place. The *point* of this retreat is to get to know *people*, not their work. And though I'm sure you'll argue, you can't compete with someone at being a person. So, be yourself. Show them why your team likes to work with *you*."

He was right. I already had an argument on the tip of my tongue... but he also had a point. I'd earned my way here, all of us had. "For the record, I kind of hate it when you're right."

"One of us has to be."

I pushed him on the shoulder. "Ass."

"Ooh, that reminds me, I've got a stockpile of questions we should start digging into."

Now it was my turn to let out an aggrieved sigh. "Right now? Aren't you tired?"

"Hey, I kept all of this stuff to myself for *years*. And I didn't pepper you with any on the flight, drive, or at dinner. You owe me at least a few."

"Fine," I agreed. Honestly, how bad could they be? Couldn't possibly be worse than what *strangers* had the audacity to ask me. "But only a few tonight."

"Deal. Are you a top, bottom, or verse?"

I choked on my tongue and sat up to stare at the shadowy outline of my supposed friend.

"I may not be able to see your face, but you can stop looking at me like that. You don't tell me *anything* about your sex life. Considering how much I've shared with *you* over the years, I think some details are overdue. And before you decide to get all sassy, I'm fully versed in the terminology."

I was kind of grateful he couldn't see my face, because I was sure it was flaming red. Grumbling to myself, I settled back on the bed. "Top," I clipped out.

"You ever bottom?"

I swallowed thickly. Seemed Jimmy was coming out swinging. "Once. It wasn't a bad experience or anything, just not for me."

"Guess that makes sense. Zara had me try a cock ring a couple of times, and I was not a fan."

I didn't have the words to explain to him that the two were not even remotely comparable. "Anything else?" I asked, grateful that my voice was steady.

"Who was the best fuck you ever had?"

I flashed to Kennedy's smile, which really had been eerily similar to Jimmy's. But we'd never really "fucked", had sex, made love, but I wouldn't say we'd ever just fucked. "Um…"

"No passes!"

"Fine, Eric in college."

Jimmy shifted beside me. "Really? I thought you hated that guy."

"Probably why the sex was so good."

He chuckled. "Fair point. Okay, one more."

I braced myself. Clearly, I'd underestimated my best friend's curiosity. If this was night one of questions, what the fuck were the others going to be?

"Is it true that all gay men keep a condom and some lube in their wallets?"

I dared to relax. "Not sure, but I've personally never met one that didn't."

"Does that mean you do?"

"Technically, that's an extra question, but I'll give it to you. Yes, I do. Now can we please go to sleep?"

"Spoilsport." He huffed and wiggled around until his foot was touching my calf.

I waited for some more arguments or shuffling. When none came, I sighed into the pillows. Right on cue, Jimmy shifted closer, and the innocuous foot touch turned into a full-on leg drape. I stifled a laugh. Some things never changed.

When the alarm went off in the morning, I was surprised to find Jimmy standing in a cloud of fog—naked. I sat up and rubbed the sleep from my eyes, not entirely sure if I'd actually woken up and if I hadn't, why the fuck was I dreaming about my best friend naked?

He stretched his absurdly long arms above his head, highlighting his equally long frame. While Jimmy didn't believe in gyms, the way I did, he did believe in eating healthy.

Do not check out your best friend. Do not check out your best friend.

Too late. My gaze roved over the expanse of Jimmy's wide shoulders, down his trim back to the dimples above his tight ass, then down his strong legs. Jimmy had never really grown out of his tall, lanky stage, but somehow he made it work. A towel showed up out of nowhere and hid the beautiful globes of his pert ass. I quickly ripped my gaze upward as he turned around.

"Oh, hey, you're up. Promise I didn't use all the hot water." He winked, and it was only then that I realized his hair was wet... and that I was sporting a boner that could *not* be blamed on morning wood.

I quickly pulled my legs up to mask the erection. "Did you set an alarm I didn't hear?"

"Nah, just woke up thirsty as hell. It was close enough to when you said you wanted to get up anyway, so I figured I'd go ahead and shower. Can't have you running behind on your big day schmoozing with the CEO." He gave me one of those broad smiles and hiked a thumb at the fog that had mostly dissipated. "Anyway, bathroom is all yours."

I waited for him to turn around and made a beeline for the room, barely remembering to grab a fresh pair of underwear on the way. Safely behind a closed—locked—door, I stared at myself in the humidity-clouded mirror. What the hell was wrong with me? I kiss Jimmy a few times and suddenly I'm hot for him? No way. We were crossing lines for sure, but I could and *would* keep a handle on this. Growing up, I'd refused to *ever* think of Jimmy as a possible romantic, sexual, or anything else partner. The last thing I wanted was to be that stereotypical gay guy pining for his straight best friend.

A freakishly cold shower and light breakfast later, we found ourselves wandering onto a lush green space already dotted with many of the faces we'd encountered the night before. We waved to several as we made our way to the epicenter, where I spied Chase speaking with a few department heads.

"Ready to talk me up?" I asked, placing a hand on Jimmy's lower back to guide him like I had the evening before and stoutly ignoring the way my hand tingled like it knew exactly what was beneath Jimmy's tight polo.

"Nope."

I did a double take and dropped my hand. "What? Why the hell are you here then? I answered your insufferable questions," I added in a low hiss while trying not to look like we were arguing. We weren't. Not yet anyway.

"For the record, you only answered a few. As for the other, my coming in with all the hype won't mean much without a foundation. I'll just look like your biased partner."

I smiled as genuinely as I could at Rafe as he passed, then turned to Jimmy with a fierce glower. "How is it that every time we come up with a plan, you go and change it without telling me?"

"You're being dramatic."

I glared at him. "The fourth-grade talent show, the freshman science fair, *rushing* Tri-Delta... I can go on."

He held up his hands in surrender. "Okay, okay. All I'm saying is that I think I'll be more useful *after* they get a chance to see how awesome you are for themselves. Then, when I come in and play up things they already know, one, it'll really stand out in their minds, and two, they'll get to see how passionate you are about your work. Now quit being so dramatic and go get 'em, tiger." He punctuated the statement with a sharp slap to my ass.

"I'm totally smothering you in your sleep tonight."

"Sure thing, babe," he said with a wink as he raised his hand in greeting to someone I couldn't see. "Sierra! Wait up! If you'll excuse me, I'm going to go mingle with the significant partners to see what kind of intel I can dig up."

I was tempted to tell Jimmy he was a freaking genius, but his ego was big enough as it was, and I was still mad at him for altering the plan... again. "Fine, give me a kiss, then go sleuth."

His eyebrow arched up, though I couldn't imagine why. The whole point was to make this believable, and this was the narrative that he'd started. Finally, he leaned forward and pressed our lips together in a chaste kiss. Then he was off to play detective.

Logically, I knew the kiss had been nothing, barely more than a brush of mouths, but that was also where my brain and the rest of my body disagreed. It had been sweet and reassuring, a promise that he would return and that I wasn't on my own in this. I shook my head and wondered if I shook it hard enough, if it would loosen all these romantic notions about Jimmy that seemed to be sprouting faster than I could kill them. Whatever was going on, it was a problem for another day. Right now, I had a CEO to charm.

When I joined Chase, many of the department heads were still there, including Marcus. I stepped into the circle as if I'd been there the whole time and devoted my focus to understanding the current conversation.

"But is it essential to have the main office in New York?" Mai Nguyen, the head of public relations, asked. "What does it really gain us beyond supposed prestige? Plenty of financial centers are moving their base of operations to more practical, cost-effective locations."

"Even if we don't move it, we're still underutilizing other locations like the Memphis and Charlotte offices," Marcus added.

Chase rubbed his chin as he seemed to weigh their words. "You make valid points. What do you think, Wells?"

I managed to suppress my surprise; I hadn't realized anyone had noticed me join. "I can vouch that the 121 West Tower definitely has the potential to expand. The location is prime real estate in uptown, and it turns out another business in the building is relocating its offices to a more centralized location for their industry. Plus, the taxes are better than New York rates, though maybe not Memphis," I added with a smirk.

"Told you this guy had a good head on his shoulders," Marcus said enthusiastically. The others nodded in smiling agreement, and Chase gave me what I assumed was the same considering look Jimmy said he'd given me the night before.

"Any of you catch the consumer report after market close yesterday?" I asked, officially in my element. There was a chorus of groans, but before I could finish seizing the opening, Jimmy materialized at my side.

"Hey, would any of you mind if I steal this handsome man for a minute?" He asked with an over-wide smile that probably only looked fake to me because I knew him so well.

I shot him a look, which he blatantly ignored.

"Fine with us," Marcus said.

"Just be sure to bring him back," Chase echoed.

"Of course," Jimmy responded, his voice sounding mildly strained. Then he proceeded to drag me away without waiting to hear what *I* had to say. If he had, he'd have known I was a special kind of pissed. Fucker had thrown me into the deep end to tread water on my own, and just when I was succeeding, he pulled me away? What the fuck?

With each step he took us away from the crowd, though, my planned tirade eroded. Was something wrong? Where was he taking me? Why was he taking me? But by the time we were approaching what looked like a maintenance building, my concern had taken a hard left into fantasy. Would he drag me in there and press our mouths together? Would he arc into me as I pressed his lithe body against the wall? Would he cup my head like he had before?

Jimmy tugged us through the propped door into a gloom punctuated with spears of light. "Okay, I know you're probably mad as hell that I pulled you away from your little financial love fest, but you needed to hear this."

I struggled to focus on what he was saying, but it was hard to make out his words over the hammering of my heart. "What's so important? Are you okay?"

"Yeah, I'm fine. It's just I was talking with Sierra, Tim, and Colleen, and it turns out—shit," he hissed.

Suddenly, I was jerked forward, and my fantasy came to life as he pressed our lips together. Without pause, I grabbed his hips and turned us so Jimmy was against the wall. I slid a hand around to cup his ass and forced him closer, devouring his mouth with needy abandon. He gave a higher-pitched moan, and I realized he'd cupped his hands around my face just like I'd imagined. Whatever reason I might have still possessed sprouted wings and flew right out the open door.

Someone clearing their throat forced me to cease my hungry exploration of Jimmy's fantastic mouth. "Sorry to interrupt. Jimmy seemed a little upset, just wanted to make sure everything was alright."

While mortification turned me into a statue and burned my ears, Jimmy shifted to offer Marcus a shy smile over my shoulder. "You'll have to forgive us. The honeymoon phase never really wore off," Jimmy said, draping his arms around my neck and relaxing against me.

Marcus chuckled, and my embarrassment tripled. "Glad to hear everyone's okay. I'll see you two back out there in a bit."

I felt Marcus's presence go and worked on getting my chaotic thoughts in order. What the fuck was I doing? This was a fake relationship, not a real one. Jimmy and I weren't *actually* involved. This right here was why I'd worked so hard to avoid ever thinking about him as a potential partner. I *knew* it'd be all too easy to fall into him.

"Way to sell it," Jimmy whispered, his voice noticeably husky.

I stepped back, leaning on my irritation to squash the remaining desire to go back to what we'd been doing before we'd been interrupted. "What's all this about? You did *not* drag me here to make-out."

Hurt flashed across his face almost too fast to catch. "Sorry about that. I saw someone coming, and it seemed like a more probable excuse than why I really brought you here."

I crossed my arms and scowled. "Which was?"

"Right." He brushed his hair back from his head. "So, we were chatting, and it turns out Chase is tired of these retreats always being about business. He wants to connect with people, not machines. And, well..." He held his hands out.

I let out a heavy sigh and leaned against the wall beside him. "How the fuck am I supposed to show them how much I deserve a promotion if I can't talk about work accomplishments?"

He nudged my shoulder. "We'll just have to show them how awesome you are outside of work." Coming from anyone else, I wouldn't have believed it was possible, but Jimmy had always had a way of making me believe the impossible.

Chapter 6

Jimmy

I BRACED MYSELF FOR another day of resisting temptation. As I spat out my toothpaste, a sleepy, half-dressed Dylan joined me in the bathroom.

"'Ornin'," he mumbled, hip-checking me so he could get to the sink. He splashed water on his face, but it did little, if anything, to improve his state of alertness.

As he brushed his teeth, I couldn't stop my gaze from wandering across his torso. The neat, trimmed down of Dylan's chest hair drew my focus. Just like all the other times I followed the golden trail down, I had to resist the urge to reach out and thread my fingers through it. Would the hair be coarse against my hands or soft like the limited chest hair I had? Did he like his partners essentially stroking his fur, or did it weird him out?

"You okay?" he asked, toothbrush hanging out.

I jumped slightly. "Yeah, just lost in thought about how today is gonna go. Especially now that we need to take an alternative approach." I spun around to rest my ass against the counter and gripped the edge to keep my hands from going anywhere they most definitely should not.

His gaze flicked down to take in the action, but thankfully he didn't call me out for acting weird. Instead, he leaned down to rinse and spit, wiping his mouth with a towel when he was done.

Then he grabbed his trimmer and set to taming his beard into cultivated carelessness. "What did you have in mind?" he asked over the whirring.

I mentally shook myself and dragged my attention away from the way his fingers felt along his cheek for inconsistencies. Since when was watching Dylan groom hot? Had our kisses somehow fanned the flames of my repressed crush? Despite the rhetorical question, I knew the answer—an unequivocal yes.

"You still awake over there?"

"Huh? Yeah. Sorry, spaced," I said.

"Hadn't noticed," he teased with a smile that crinkled the corners of his eyes.

My stomach did a swoop, and I prayed he didn't notice my eyes widening in mild panic. We officially had a problem. I blamed Dylan with those unexpectedly intense kisses and innocent hand placements. I scurried out of the bathroom, attempting to look like I wasn't fleeing and failing miserably, then busied myself with pulling out things to wear on our lakeside excursion today. Now I was really grateful I'd thought to pack so many casual clothes.

"Are you sure you're okay?" he asked, placing a hand on my shoulder and instantly stilling my flurry of movement. The friendly familiarity put me at ease in a way that I'd always appreciated.

I let out a breath. "Yeah, I'm good. Overthinking per usual. Now what are you gonna..." I turned to face Dill, who had actually gotten dressed at some point, and finished with an awkward, "Wear?" I took in his tried-and-true polo, neatly pressed, gripping his biceps like an invitation, and staple khaki pants. "Absolutely not. I refuse to let you out of the room dressed like that."

"What the hell is wrong with it?"

"Duude… What did we literally just talk about? New plan of attack. Remember? You look like you're going to a board meeting."

Dylan snorted. "We generally wear suits to those. Not everyone gets to do business casual *all* the time."

I really didn't need the reminder of how good he looked in a suit; I got to see it every time he picked me up from the clinic for lunch. "That's exactly the problem. This is *business* casual. We need casual-casual."

"But I didn't pack anything casual-casual."

"Way ahead of you." I pulled free the outfit I'd been fishing for. "Tada!"

He frowned. "I'm not wearing that."

I looked at the loose-fitting jacket and denim. "Why not?"

"It's orange."

"I think you look good in orange. Besides, you're not gonna zip it up. You pair it with a white undershirt. It'll look great. You know, for a gay man, you have zero sense of fashion. Now take off that ridiculous clown collar."

He took a step back. "No, and that is a hurtful stereotype. Not all gay men are fashionistas."

"Clearly," I countered, following him as if he were a mouse that needed to be caught. Eventually, I cornered him and dragged the polo over his head to his very loud protest. It took some finagling, but I finally got the fabric free of Dill's flailing arms and was once again confronted with a shirtless Dylan in all his glory. Except this time we were chest to chest. My hands seem to have a mind of their own as they settled on his pecs. Chest hair tickled my palms as I stared into his stormy eyes, and my heart raced.

"Happy now?" he grumbled, though his voice seemed off.

"Yeah…" I hadn't meant for that to come out as a sigh. Soft, the hair was soft. I quickly stepped back and cleared my throat. "You have a white undershirt, right?"

He snorted again, grumbling his indignation as he stomped over to the chest of drawers provided with the room. Because, of course, he was the kind of person who unpacked on vacation instead of living out of a suitcase. He yanked out a plain white tee with an exaggerated flourish and popped it over his head. Then added the orange jacket. "Satisfied?" he asked, holding his arms out by his sides.

"Not quite." I couldn't help but smirk at the aggrieved expression on his face as I held out the jeans.

Colleen fell in step beside me, and I pulled my gaze away from the glittering blue surface of Lake Erie. I'd read up about our destination and was pleased to see how well the initiative to clean up the lake was going.

"Beautiful, isn't it?" Colleen asked, echoing my thoughts. A couple of paces ahead, Dill was laughing at some joke Marcus told.

"Sure is. Gotta say, though, I still can't believe our good luck with the weather. What are the chances that *all* the days we're here would be a perfect seventy-two with hardly a cloud in the sky?"

She chuckled. "Around here? Pretty good."

Up ahead, one of IF's bigwigs joined Dylan as Marcus drifted away to chat with another cohort. I recognized her asymmetrical bob and fair complexion, but couldn't place her name. I'd have to check with Dill later. She reached out to pluck lightly at Dylan's jacket. "This is really nice and a *great* color. Wish I'd had the foresight to pack such a versatile jacket. I wasn't anticipating the breeze off the lake to be so cool, what with it being the middle of summer."

Dylan returned her smile and glanced over his shoulder at me. "I can't take all the credit." A warm glow spread across my chest. Luckily, Dill had stopped being so salty about the "garish" jacket around the third compliment. "Jimmy is the one who insisted I wear it today," he added, his gaze briefly sharpening. Okay, *mostly* not salty.

Rather than give in to the temptation to crow, "I told you so," I gave him my biggest grin. The one he'd said made me look like a runaway clown when we were kids.

As I expected, he laughed and shook his head. "You're such a ham."

"Please, you love it. Just like you love that I double-checked the weather," I said with a smirk.

"You mean the double-check *I* asked you to do?" he fired back.

I winked. "That's the one."

"You two are awesome. Why haven't you brought Jimmy to more corporate events?" Miss-dark-bob asked Dylan.

He hiked a shoulder, and I increased my pace before he could flounder on a believable reason. Before I could say anything, though, he beat me to it.

"Our schedules don't always line up. Jimmy's been pretty busy helping to establish a new counseling clinic. You know how new offices can be, Mai."

I gave an inward sigh of relief that not only had he smoothly delivered the excuse, but had also subtly included his companion's name.

Mai nodded her head knowingly. "That I do. The stress and hours can really strain a relationship."

Taking that as my cue, I looped an arm around Dylan's shoulders. "Which is why my man makes a point of having lunch together at least once a week, if not a couple."

Mai let out a sad sigh. "If only Lucy could be that close. But most of the offices I help set up are in locations across the country."

I tapped thoughtfully on my lower lip. "Time zones can be tricky. You could always look into setting up tele-lunches. Granted, it may be a breakfast-lunch lunch-dinner kind of situation. But the important part is that you treat the time as sacred. Plan around the scheduled time, instead of the other way around. It's about prioritizing your partner."

"Oh, he's good," Mai said, looking from me to Dill.

He shrugged. "He keeps me in line."

I fought the urge to do a double take and instead squeezed his shoulders tighter.

"Tell me, Jimmy, what are you looking forward to most during the retreat?" Mai asked.

More kisses.

The thought came so fast and unbidden that I barked out an awkward laugh and ducked my head to hide the sudden burn on my cheeks. "You mean besides getting to meet everyone Dill is always talking about?" Feeling like I had myself—and my wayward thoughts—back under control, I shifted, simultaneously releasing Dill. Maybe a little *less* contact was in order. "Actually, I'm really looking forward to checking out the nearby town, especially the bar that provided the craft beers."

"Did someone mention the Twisted Pine?" Marcus asked, re-joining our group with whom I was pretty sure was Tina, the Pacific Region coordinator.

"Is it really as amazing as all that? I confess, from the itinerary images, it doesn't look like much," Tina said as she slipped her hands into the pockets of her stylish emerald green, wide leg trousers.

Dylan shot me a look over her shoulder, no doubt at how professionally posh Tina looked.

Rather than give him the satisfaction of admitting I *might* have misjudged, I focused on Tina. "The beers, at least, we can vouch for. Had some of their amber ale at the opening event, and it was incredible. Love your pants, by the way."

"Thanks. They have pockets!" She emphasized her tucked hands, and we laughed with her. "To be honest, though, they're way more formal than I was expecting." She shrugged her slim shoulders, emphasizing her bright auburn curls. "Oh well, at least they're comfy."

Definitely not above "I told you so," I gave Dylan a smug look. He rolled his eyes. Hopefully, that signaled the end of any protests I'd be getting from him about what was *appropriate* to wear in casual settings.

"You both seemed to know exactly what you were looking for when I asked if I could get you anything. Don't suppose either of you is a cicerone?" Marcus asked.

Dill released a hearty laugh that brought a smile to my lips. Relaxed Dylan was always my favorite. "Hardly. We like to explore and try new things. We did the usual gamut of testing out various drinks in college, but there was never anything that really stood out. It was actually pure happenstance that we stumbled across a six-pack of craft beers. You remember that?" he asked, turning to me, his eyes bright with memory.

"Like I could forget. We were rushing Tri-Delta, on the verge of actually pledging, when we got invited to one of their legendary parties. Only, turns out, us and a bunch of other hopefuls were there to get the place set up so the upperclassmen wouldn't have to."

"Ah, fraternity days..." Marcus mused. "Don't miss those."

I nodded as I laughed along. "They tried to make it 'worth our while'," I said with air quotes. "But they kept the good stuff for themselves and left us with the worst of the worst."

"We're talking that next level I-think-I-died-last-night worst of the worst," Dylan cut in.

At some point, our small group had grown into a larger one with faces I recognized and had names for, and some I didn't. Nearly all of them winced in commiserating sympathy. We'd all been there.

I glanced at Dylan, who was already smiling in anticipation. He always said he hated this next part, but I thought he secretly loved it. "So this one," I gestured at Dylan who scoffed and rolled his eyes on cue, "had just spit out what had to be the *cheapest* beer the campus had to offer and vowed to never have another beer for as long as he lived when I pull out this six-pack. Someone had squirreled it away in the backup-backup fridge. Unlike the other beers available, these actually looked interesting."

Dill shook his head. "Still don't know how you convinced me to try those. My stomach was already pretty convinced we'd both be dead by morning."

"Always so dramatic. And you tried them because I have great ideas." The look he gave me very clearly said that the jury was still out on that. "Come on, it had this awesome description on the label about what it was supposed to taste like. I wanted to see if it was true. *Anyway...* Not interested in hanging around for the cops to break up the party—" I turned to Tina like I was divulging information of the utmost secrecy, "Which they always did, we hightail it outta there and spend the rest of the night laying in the outfield and starring at the stars."

"How was the beer?" someone whose name I definitely didn't know asked.

"I can't say it's the best beer we ever had, but it was a far cry better than the swill they tried to fob off on us like an untradeable penny stock."

The group laughed, though I could only surmise the essence of the joke. Mostly, I was taken with how at ease Dylan was. Even with the early afternoon sun glinting off his sandy hair, I could still see the way the stars had shone, sparkling in a sky that seemed to wrap around us like a cloak.

"That was one of the best nights of my life." It wasn't until Dylan gave me a double take that I realized I'd said that aloud... aaand that everyone was now staring at me like I was the cutest thing in the world. I cleared my throat and forced a laugh. "Don't get me wrong, finishing the case after all we'd drunk was a terrible idea, and we paid dearly for it in the morning. But worth it."

"Totally," Dylan chimed, giving me a small smile I couldn't quite decipher. "Thus began our crusade of exploring craft beers, though I still have a soft spot for malty brews."

I shook off the weird energy that seemed to have appeared out of nowhere. "And as for Dill not being a beer sommelier, don't be fooled by his humble words. Man could break down the flavors and influences of any beer in three sips or less."

"That's quite a skill," Chase said, clapping a hand on Dylan's shoulder. Judging by the expression on Dylan's face, he also had no idea where the CEO had come from. "A man of many talents. I think I speak for all of us when I say I look forward to seeing you in action."

Dylan rubbed the back of his neck, lifting the hem of his shirt just enough to reveal the smallest stretch of furry abdomen. There was no stopping my gaze from latching onto the delicious tease of skin, especially after this morning. But no amount of distraction would cause me to miss the slight plea in Dylan's eyes. I smothered a sigh. He'd been doing so well when we were wandering down memory lane. Now he was right back to forgetting how to human.

Chapter 7

Dylan

I KEPT REPLAYING JIMMY'S story about how we'd come to discover our mutual love of craft beer as I waited for the alarm to go off. The tale had gone much like it normally did, but I couldn't quite shake his modified ending—*It was the best night of my life.*

True, it was a great night, but there was something about the way he'd said it. Something in his eye, the tone of his voice. If only I could put my finger on it.

Frustrated with my circuitous thoughts, I rolled over to face the middle of the bed and nearly jerked off the back. "Jesus fucking Christ!"

"Morning," Jimmy responded, chipper as ever and remarkably alert for someone who notoriously slept in. His clown-like smile stretched across his face.

I rolled my eyes. "Since when are you awake so early?" I reached for my phone to glance at the time. "Alarm's not due for another thirty."

He shrugged awkwardly on his side and scooted closer, causing the duvet to bunch and reveal his bare chest. "You make it sound like I'm incapable of waking up early."

I swallowed hard, suddenly painfully aware that both of us were only wearing underwear. It wasn't as if I'd never seen him in his boxers or that we'd never shared a bed before. So, what was the deal? Undoubtedly, it had something to do with the "practice" groping and the fact that I'd blatantly checked out his ass the other day. In retrospect, I probably should have sought out a hookup or two before the retreat.

"Besides, when else am I supposed to ask all my questions?"

My gaze snapped to Jimmy's. "What else could you possibly want to know?" We'd only had a few bouts of Q and A and I already felt stripped bare.

"You ever consider getting your dick pierced?"

"What?"

"You know, like a Prince Albert or a King's Crown or maybe a Hafada?"

"Why the hell would you ask that?" It was quickly becoming apparent that Jimmy's "questions" were not good for my health.

"I don't know. It's not something we've ever talked about. Like, I know you're stoutly against ever getting your ears pierced, but that doesn't mean you're against getting *anything* pierced. I mean, I've considered it. Figured you might have some insight."

I cleared my throat and prayed my face wasn't as red as I feared it was. I did *not* need to be picturing Jimmy with a dick piercing. "Can't say that it's ever seriously crossed my mind."

He made a considering face. "Have any of your partners?"

"Umm... I hooked up with a guy once who had a magic cross. He was really into it, but I honestly didn't see the big deal. Could be because he was verse and I'm not. There have been several with tongue piercings. Now *those* I'm all for," I added with a laugh that almost wasn't strained.

"I'm very familiar with the awesomeness that is the tongue piercing." He waggled his eyebrows, and I couldn't help but bark out a laugh. "What about nipple piercings?"

"Eh, I could take 'em or leave 'em. Not interested in getting any myself."

"Okay, more deep dives—no pun intended."

I shoved him, and he rolled away only to return somehow closer. "Like hell it's not." Maybe these questions weren't so bad. Nosy, yeah, but we'd had super personal conversations in the past. In the grand scheme of our friendship, this wasn't all that different. And maybe he was right. I hadn't really been all that open about my relationships. Certainly not as open as he was.

He stuck out his tongue. "As I was saying. What about rimming? What's your stance on that? I've always been curious to try it, but I've been too self-conscious."

I'd never been more grateful for Jimmy's insistence on sleeping in pure darkness, because it meant the thick curtains were still pulled tightly shut and keeping the room dim. Hopefully, dim enough to hide the furious blush burning across my cheeks and down my neck. Bad enough he'd asked. Worse that he'd expressed an interest. There was literally no way to scrub the image of Jimmy on his knees, chest pressed to the mattress, ass in the air, his pretty pink hole on display from my mind.

"Hello. Earth to Dylan. You gonna answer the question?"

I pushed aside all the disturbing thoughts about Jimmy's hole—pretty or otherwise—and focused on keeping my voice neutral. "I've tried it. I'm not opposed." Even in the gloom, I could make out his scowl. Clearly, that wasn't the answer he wanted. "What else?" I asked before he could push for details.

He made a disgruntled sound, but I should have known better than to think I'd put him off questions determined to get me hard. "How about this? What's your favorite sexual act that's *not* intercourse?"

"Umm..." I stalled, because, honestly, rimming was definitely up there, like top-three-up-there. No way was I about to say that, though.

"Come on. You already know about my life-altering discovery of erogenous zones. Spill."

Right. Erogenous zones. Because Jimmy had discovered he had one on his neck and prematurely blown his load freshman year of college with Becky Summers. "I..." Words failed me. I just couldn't shake the knee-buckling image of Jimmy's ass waiting like a buffet to be devoured.

He shimmied close enough to make me fear for the hard-on straining my briefs. "No passes, Dill."

"Frotting. Big fan of frotting," I blurted with absolutely zero finesse.

He tilted his head, opening up the smallest amount of breathing room between us. "Rubbing against each other? Like with clothes and everything?"

"No. I mean, yes, but not like you're thinking. More like two dicks-one hand."

"Oh," he drew out. "How does that feel?"

And just like that, all the air I'd found was stolen by a new image. Why the hell hadn't I thought to get laid before coming on this trip with Jimmy? And why were *all* of his questions about sex? "It's um... well..." I paused to clear my throat and prayed he wouldn't read it as nerves. "It's nice."

"Nice," he deadpanned.

"Okay, better than nice. There's a good amount of friction with just enough give."

His face scrunched. "Doesn't sound all that special. How does it compare with a masturbation toy?"

"It doesn't," I responded a little too quickly. At this rate, I was going to be leaking through my briefs in no time. I took a deep breath and tried to subtly shift my straining dick away from Jimmy. "There's the texture, and pressure, and... fluids."

"Yeah, not really following."

I pinched the bridge of my nose and mentally worked to kill my boner. Images of kittens, and yarn, and knitting old ladies paraded across my mind as I said, "I'm not doing a very good job of explaining it. It's just one of those things you have to experience."

"Okay."

I was still trying to make sense of his upbeat response when his fingers tugged at the waistband of my briefs. I snapped my hand down to encircle Jimmy's wrist. "What are you doing?"

"You said I'd have to experience it to know. So... experience." He shrugged as if it were the most obvious thing in the world while my brain straight up broke.

"W-what?"

"Think of it as an extension of the question—or, more appropriately, your way of answering. Besides, what better way for me to find out than with someone I completely trust?" Jimmy blinked at me, his long lashes fanning across his cheeks in some mockery of innocence.

My mouth hung open, waiting for a rebuttal that didn't come. It was kind of hard to argue with that logic. Wait. Was I seriously considering fooling around with Jimmy? Judging by my loosening grip on his determined hand, the answer was a very disturbing "yes". *Definitely* should have gotten laid before boarding that plane.

"Don't even pretend that you're not totally up for a good jerk right now. Best way to start the day, really." He tugged at my briefs once again, this time with significantly less resistance until my dick popped free. Because, honestly, what else was it going to do after he'd bombarded my half-awake brain with sexy image after sexy image? "Wow," he said once he finished ridding me of my briefs and came back to eye level.

My poor brain was still struggling to make sense of the unlikely situation. Was that an impressed "wow"? Was Jimmy remarking on the size of my dick? Had he forgotten I was uncut? Or was he passing some kind of judgment that I was already hard and worse, leaking like a fucking faucet. Why *the fuck* hadn't I thought to release some steam before climbing into bed with my best friend?

"I..." I what? Wasn't a thousand percent into this? My dick clearly said otherwise. I'd already crossed so many lines with Jimmy throughout our lives, and especially this week. What was one more?

He twisted around, kicking off the covers and yanking his boxers down to reveal an equally erect cock.

I let out a slow breath. Okay. This would be fine. I clearly wasn't the only one turned on by our weird ass game of twenty questions this morning. We could do this. It would just turn into yet another one of our weird ass funny stories. We had plenty of those. What was one more?

He spun back around, fully liberated, and wiggled closer. "There, that's better. Any tips?" He chuckled at the poor pun.

I struggled not to roll my eyes. Leave it to Jimmy to crack jokes at a time like this. Then my gaze caught on the small bottle in his hand. "You brought lube?"

His brow furrowed. "Didn't you?"

"Why would you bring lube?" I asked, ignoring the assumption that I would or *should* have brought some as well.

The lid snapped open, and he shrugged as he poured an ample amount into his hand. "Didn't know how often or for how long I'd be relegated to the room while you did your business schmoozing. Seemed like a good idea at the time." He shifted his hips closer so our cocks lined up. Then, before I could summon any kind of last-ditch protest to this unexpected turn of events, he wrapped a hand around both of us.

Whatever delusions I had about not being interested in this died a quick death. I smothered a moan as Jimmy's long fingers liberally spread the lubrication and gave a light stroke.

"Like this?" he asked, bordering on breathless.

I was about to tell him his hold was a little loose when he tightened his grip and gave a decisive drag. I reflexively bucked into the tight hold, barely stopping myself from rolling him onto his back so I could take control, rutting against his long, lean body until we'd spent ourselves and were panting for air.

"Oh," he gasped, his firm hand gliding over us. "I get it," he added, along with a couple of his own shallow thrusts.

My restraint took a heavy blow. I reached for his hip, digging my fingers into the flexing muscle in a vain attempt to ground myself while his noises of pleasure and the lewd sound of wet skin continued to rattle me. A deep groan climbed its way free of my throat. I was one stroke away from telling Jimmy exactly how I liked it, how good a job he was doing, how hot he sounded as he moaned and gasped. Or worst of all, how I wanted to taste that sweet ass before fucking him senseless. To keep the words at bay, I surged forward to claim his mouth in a sloppy kiss.

His strokes faltered as his lips parted to invite me deeper, where our tongues tangled. When he found his rhythm again, there was an edge of urgency to the fast passes of his fist. We were so close that his subsequent moan could just as easily have been mine.

I broke the kiss and pressed my forehead against Jimmy's while I fought to keep my imminent orgasm at bay a little longer. My grip tightened on Jimmy's hip and there was literally nothing I could do to stop myself from fucking into his hand, reveling in the glide of our dicks against each other.

"Close," he groaned while his wrist twisted to add another sensation, rubbing our swollen heads together before stroking back down to the base where he squeezed.

I wasn't far off either. Then his passes turned frantic, and he was bucking haphazardly into the tight hold.

"Fuuuuck..." Jimmy groaned as he milked his release, hold never loosening. His spend mixed with the lube, increasing the intoxicating slide.

The heady combination of Jimmy's dick pulsing against mine, along with his sexy as fuck groan as he came, had me climaxing so hard I forgot to breathe. My come shot between us in thick ribbons to mix with his and coat the sheets.

The aftershocks of my orgasm faded, and my hips finally stopped their half-hearted thrusting. We lay there in a weird bubble of suspended reality, panting while our dicks softened in Jimmy's loose hold. Despite the endorphins still lazily drifting through me, the more my heart rate steadied, the louder my mind got. What the hell had just happened?

I felt like I should say something—*do* something. I was usually so much better at taking care of my sexual partners, but my brain clearly wasn't operating on all cylinders. I'd just had sex with Jimmy. *Jimmy.* My best friend. My ride or die. My—

The alarm split through the air with a shrill cry of birds and wind chimes. Normally, I found the melody a soothing way to wake up, but with the backdrop of my freak out, it was nothing more than a cacophony. I released my death grip on Jimmy's hip and spun to stop the abrasive chirping.

"You can take a shower first. I'll take care of the bed."

I sat up and stared at him, though my rebellious gaze kept trying to slide to the mixed streams of come that had landed on his chest. "You sure?" Part of me wondered if I should invite him to join me. Or would that make it weird? Weirder?

"Yeah. Imma... Imma need a minute," he mumbled. "You're right, words don't do it justice."

I blinked at him, then rolled out of bed. "Right. I'll be quick. Don't want to be late for breakfast. Might miss the bus."

"That's right! Today we're taking that field trip into Oak Haven." He gave me a broad grin, clearly not fazed in the least about what we'd just done. "Well, hurry up, slowpoke! What are you waiting for?"

This time, I did roll my eyes. If he could be cavalier about this, then so could I. Besides, it wasn't like I'd never had a casual hookup before or a friend with benefits. I reached for my clothes, not even thinking about the fact that I was still buck ass naked.

"Don't forget—"

I held up the outfit he'd set out last night to head him off.

"No need to be scowly about it. Not *my* fault you don't have a fashionable bone in your body," he countered.

Shaking my head, I finished grabbing the essentials and stepped into the bathroom. Last thing I wanted was *another* lecture from him about how business-casual was not the same thing as life-casual.

Chapter 8

Jimmy

THE "BUS" TAKING US to town turned out to be a small collection of SUVs. Much to my surprise, not everyone enjoying the retreat wanted to explore the neighboring town. Consequently, we only needed a couple of vehicles to transport the handful of people interested, with more joining later for Happy Hour at the Twisted Pine.

By the time we settled into our designated ride, Dylan was already deep into a conversation with a couple of people I didn't recognize, but that he clearly knew well enough to have inside jokes with. I was content to let them chat while I watched the scenery slip past, lost in my thoughts.

When I'd baited Dill this morning, I hadn't actually expected him to roll with it. Push back—probably. Tease him—definitely. But cave with hardly an argument? Maybe after all these years, I should have known better. But, yeah, this morning had been a surprise. How long had I been wanting to truly get hands on Dylan like that? And, whoa, had I gotten a handful. My hand drifted to my hip for probably the hundredth time since Dill had gotten up to take a shower. I fingered the bruises, reliving just how tight he'd held me, the way our cocks had felt squeezed together, the hot glide of Dylan thrusting in my hand, the almost pained look of pleasure on his face.

I blinked and glanced at the trio, still deep in conversation about stock splits and mergers, or at least, that's what I thought they were talking about. I shook my head and removed my hand before I could truly work myself up. Beyond the window, the country landscape evolved into quaint brick buildings. Some looked like they should be classified as historic, while others were clearly much newer.

"I think we're here," I said.

Dylan immediately broke off mid-laugh to look out the window. "Wow, this place is straight out of a postcard."

His breath caressed my neck, and I struggled to control a shiver. I'd known after finally kissing Dylan that once would never be enough. And now... now I wasn't sure if anything short of everything would be enough.

The SUV pulled to a stop in front of a colorful coffee shop, and the driver spun around. They gestured to the general area beyond the glass. "This is Main Street, where you'll find some popular attractions and fun places to eat. Did everyone get a map?"

Dill and the other two held up brochures. I groaned to myself, realizing I'd been so distracted by my epic morning with Dylan that I'd totally missed it.

Dylan leaned close to whisper in my ear. "Don't worry, I got yours." Then he squeezed my thigh, and all I could do was stare at him, almost missing the driver continue.

"The town maps clearly mark The Twisted Pine along with some other hot spots, like the gem beside us. Happy Hour is slated for six, but if you want to head back sooner, call the resort and a driver will be sent. Enjoy exploring!"

The four of us spilled onto the sidewalk and in a few brief minutes, the driver headed back to the resort. We collectively turned to see the "gem" they'd pointed out.

"This place looks cool. What do you say we treat ourselves to some fancy coffee this morning?" Dylan nudged me in the ribs and gave me what I secretly dubbed his boardroom smile. The one I was sure he used when he gave presentations and could win over an entire room without even trying.

"Sounds good," I replied, never able to say no to that smile, and certainly not after this morning.

"Hey, isn't that Margo and the Gulf Coast regional manager?" one of the guys asked. "I can never remember their name."

Dill's attention shifted, and I immediately felt the loss. "Kim Joon?" He peeked through the window. "Yep, that's him. And pretty sure that's Kamal from the San Antonio office."

"Always wanted to meet him," the other guy said. "His work in projections is inspired."

"Well, what are we waiting for?" the first said, grabbing the door.

Dill walked through, then darted a look between me and the table of execs.

"Go ahead. I'll get the coffees." When he continued to waffle, I gave him a gentle shove and a reassuring smile. "Go schmooze." His resulting grin made my heart skip a little, and I couldn't help but give him a goofy one of my own.

I watched Dill walk with the others to the table, somehow feeling relaxed and tight at the same time. It was unusual I couldn't nail down my feelings, but then, this entire trip had been unusual. I'd have to figure them out later. Right now I was getting coffee and supporting my bestie.

With a sigh, I wandered to the counter and stared up at the menu, where I immediately became overwhelmed. "Oh." Considering all the colorful, quirky art on the wall and a name like Kaleidoscope, I shouldn't have been surprised that the board was an explosion of color and had drink names I'd never heard of.

"Welcome to Kaleidoscope Coffee."

I shifted my focus to the barista. They were cute, maybe in their early twenties, with bright teal hair just dark enough not to wash out their fair skin and a welcoming smile. A glance at their tag provided both his name and his pronouns. "Hi, Jace. I'd ask what's good, but..."

The guy chuckled and twisted to look at the impressive board. "Yeah, it's a lot, but that's what I'm here for. Why don't we start with your partner?"

"My..." I trailed off.

"The blond guy you came in with," Jace said, gesturing toward the table Dill and the others had settled at.

"Oh. We're not—" I cut myself off so fast I almost bit my tongue. This was a wrinkle I hadn't expected. I was so used to correcting people—people who were usually fishing to see if Dylan was available—that I hadn't thought twice. Except we were "together".

"Shit. I'm sorry. I shouldn't have assumed." Jace winced, though I wasn't sure if it was at the presumption or the inadvertent profanity.

"No, you... assumed right." Wow, could I be any more awkward? I tried to hide the heat staining my cheeks with a cough, but was pretty sure the guy wasn't buying it, especially when he gave me a sad, understanding smile.

"In case you hadn't heard, Oak Haven is one of the queerest cities in the US. No one is going to judge you here."

I didn't think it was possible, but my cheeks flamed hotter. "It's... It's not that. It's um, just... new. I mean, we've known each other for pretty much forever, but the 'together-together' part is... recent," I finished awkwardly, not sure why I was giving this guy my life story.

"I get that. So, tell me about your man. Coffee-wise," Jace added with a smirk that had me cracking a grin and relaxing.

"Bold as hell with a side of works-too-much."

Jace chuckled. "I've got just the thing. And you?"

After explaining I liked my coffee on the milkier, sweeter side and paying, Jace set to work. A few minutes later, he set down two to-go cups that boasted being made of fully recycled materials.

"So, what did we get?" I asked, turning the cups to find some kind of hint.

Jace pointed to one with a star on it. "This is a Dark Desire with an extra shot of espresso. That'll be for your man. And this one is a Sweet Surrender."

I snorted a laugh as I plucked up my designated drink. "Those names are... unique."

The barista echoed my humor. "That they are. You're lucky the manager is on a supply run, or you'd be getting the complete theory about how the names reveal something about the patron."

I lifted an eyebrow and inspected the cups. "Is that so?" I could certainly see how that might be the case. "Thanks for the drinks. And the insight," I added with a wink. At the table of Infinity Financial execs, I waited for a lull in the conversation before sliding into an empty seat beside Dylan.

"Hey," Dill said. "What did you get?"

"Got you a Dark Desire."

Dylan accepted the drink with a smirk. "That's... a name." His eyes drifted shut as he cautiously sipped the hot beverage, then let out an appreciative hum that went straight to my dick. "Wow, that's..." He took another sip.

My heart rate kicked up a notch as I watched his tongue run along his upper lip to capture the foam.

"Decadent," he finally said in a husky voice.

I rushed to take a sip, barely checking myself in time to prevent scalding my tongue. Flavor exploded in my mouth, rich and creamy with an undercurrent of sweetness that took me a moment to place. Honey. I smiled at my cup and made a mental note to leave an extra tip in the jar when we left. Jace knew his stuff.

"What did you get?" Dylan asked, his eyebrows lifted in a comical display of childish curiosity.

I passed him the cup without having to be asked. "Sweet Surrender."

His gaze flicked to mine. A whole host of things passed behind his stormy blue eyes that I didn't have a prayer of nailing down, but had me holding my breath, nonetheless. At last, he blinked and lifted the cup to his lips. Vaguely, I realized that there were other people at the table, an animated conversation swirling around them, but my universe had narrowed down to watching his lips curve around the rim and his Adam's apple bob as he swallowed.

"That's really good," Dill said as he returned the cup to my numb fingers. Then he leaned forward and pressed a kiss to my cheek. "Thank you."

The soft brush of his beard on my face instantly transported me back to this morning when he'd fucking *owned* my mouth. I wanted that again. Wanted that *now*. Wanted to feel his weight on top of me, his fingers digging into my sides, while his panting breaths addled my senses.

"We'll see you all at Happy Hour. We've got a farm to explore," the woman I assumed must be Margo said as she stood to be joined by the other execs.

One of the men extended a hand to his companions. "It was nice catching up."

I offered a wave as they made their way out with more promises to continue chatting later. No sooner had they exited than the two guys we'd arrived with stood.

"Guess we should get going, too. I want to hit up the town hall before catching an early matinee at the renovated theater. You sure we can't tempt you, Wells? I'm sure there are still a couple of tickets left."

Dylan shook his head with a smile. "Appreciate the offer, but we're out on period dramas."

I repressed a shudder. I *hated* period dramas. They always ended up being way darker than advertised, with a lot of screwed-up history to boot. No, thank you. A light squeeze on my thigh made me jolt. I glanced down to find Dylan's hand. "Thanks anyway," I piped up per Dill's blatant cue. Once they had left, I turned to him. "Now what?" We'd been so caught up in planning for the Happy Hour, it hadn't occurred to me to take advantage of any touristy things in town.

"Now? We explore."

I followed Dylan's lead, glad I'd opted for to-go cups. We were lucky that it was a beautiful, cloudless day. Not so much, though, that it didn't take long for it to heat up. By the time we'd wandered the length and breadth of Main Street, any appeal of venturing further had vanished. Neither of us was much for shopping, so while we'd appreciated the quaint vibe of the boutiques and sampled a fair number of treats along the way, we'd spent more time in the sun than not.

"What time is it?" I asked when we stopped at the corner just beyond the coffee shop where we'd started. From what I could tell, the place was still hopping. "Do you think it would be ridiculous if we headed to the Twisted Pine now?" When no response came, I turned to Dill to find him staring off into the distance. "Did you hear me?"

"Huh? Yeah. Weird or not, I could use a drink. Preferably ice-cold and sitting down."

"Sold." I reached for the map tucked in his back pocket, since "mine" had never manifested. And maybe I enjoyed the slide of my hand along his ass before tugging it free.

He frowned at me. "Really, Jimmy?"

"We talked about this," I teased as I unfolded the map and found the marker for the bar.

"Yeah, but it's not exactly like there's an audience to impress."

I snickered to myself. Apparently, my casual ass-grabs were impressive. I'd take that. "Oh good, looks like it's not too far. Think we can manage some more walking?"

"As long as there's beer at the end, I'll manage. But you're evading," he said as he fell in step.

"Who's therapizing now?" I lifted an eyebrow, obstinately continuing to evade, as he put it.

"Yeah, yeah. Seriously though. I get the practice before, but I think I've gotten better and there's no one around now. So, what gives?"

I gave him a serious once-over, noticing the tightness in his shoulders and the weird stiffness to his gait. This wasn't about the ass grab—or not *just* about it. "First off, yes, you are doing much better at not flinching every time I pull a boyfriend-move, and you're even initiating. Props, by the way."

He nodded at the acknowledgment of his efforts, but his tension didn't fade.

I let out a huff. "And second, you don't actually know that no one is watching. Plus, I... I maybe slipped up a little at the coffee shop."

"What?" He turned to face me so fast I was worried he'd get whiplash. "What happened?"

"I may have told the barista we weren't together."

He groaned and wiped his hands over his face. "Seriously, Jimmy?"

"What? It's weird not being your wingman. Okay? Normally, when cute twinks come at me, they're trying to find out if one or both of us is available. I reacted out of habit."

He sighed. "I know what you mean. It's not like I expected this to be easy, but—"

"You kind of expected this to be easy."

"Yeah." He ducked his head, and we turned onto the next street. To our right, a modestly large building with almost as much moss as aged stone sat on an oak-studded lot with a sign that read "Public Library".

I referred to the map again. "We should be getting close."

"Thank fuck. And, uh, while we're still sort of on the subject, what was the deal this morning?"

"What about it?" It was solely thanks to years of practice keeping a straight face with patients that I did so now. Seemed my efforts to not make a big deal about the epic jerk-off this morning had not dissuaded Dill from digging.

"That wasn't exactly practice."

"No, it was answering questions. Which, I'm sure you remember, is part of the deal for this little excursion." I watched his mouth open and close a few times as he floundered in the face of my evasion. "Speaking of which, how are you doing? I know leaning on your people skills rather than your work skills is not exactly what you had in mind." Unable to resist, I reached out and squeezed his shoulder as I'd probably done a million times before.

He sagged. "I have to admit that though your approach is… unorthodox, it seems to be working."

I gave him another squeeze before releasing his shoulder. "Just remember that's all it is. An approach. I'm nothing more than backup. You're the one doing all the real work. How's the elbow-rubbing going, anyway? I can't believe I'm saying this, but I have no idea who the guys we rode over with are."

He chuckled. "Truth? Me neither. Never met them before today, but they seemed to think we knew each other, so I went with it."

I threw an arm around his shoulders and tugged him into a tight side hug, made that much more awkward because we were still walking and Dylan nearly fell over. "See! You're doing great. You should have more faith in your peopling."

"I know my peopling is fine. It's when that peopling hinges on talking about myself that I struggle."

"Interesting," I mused aloud.

"What?" he asked, still in what bordered on a headlock.

"You never seem to have any trouble talking about yourself to me. You're constantly telling me how much of a badass you are in the boardroom. Honestly, it's like you never *stop* talking about yourself."

"Shut up." He shoved me, nearly taking us both down.

After a desperate attempt to keep us from crashing into the ground, I spied the sign for our destination and realized we'd wandered right into a stabilized aggregate parking lot. Seemed everything about this town focused on sustainable design. That was certainly something I could respect.

"This should be it," I said, pulling us up short. I took in the long strips of burnt wood that made up the exterior. I'd seen pictures of fire-finished buildings before, but nothing of this scale, and honestly, pictures didn't do the design justice.

"Uh, Jimmy."

I tore my attention away from the unique way the siding had been laid and wondering whether it had been scorched before or after being attached. "Yeah?"

Dylan looked at me. "Where's the door?"

Chapter 9

Dylan

AN EMBARRASSING TEN MINUTES later, we found the door. Luckily, the inside wasn't nearly as enigmatic. High-tops ranging from four-seaters to eight took up the floor between the bar and the far walls, which were lined with some very comfy-looking booths. I explored the decor on the walls while Jimmy went to the bar to inquire about a table and whether the place served lunch. Snacking only got you so far, and it was early enough in the afternoon that there wasn't a host stationed up front.

I stopped at an expansive display composed of several framed images of trees, some of which were legitimately on fire. By the time I finished reading all the descriptors, I finally understood that the burnt exterior of the bar was intentional—all the trees were twisted pines, just like the bar's namesake.

"That's pretty cool," I mused aloud.

"What is?" Jimmy asked as he walked up behind me.

I pointed out the story of the trees and their life cycle; how they needed fire to thrive. "This place really went all out." I turned to Jimmy, who was now peering intently at the images. "What'd they say about food? We snacked a good amount, but I'd rather have something more substantial going into my stomach if we're going to be drinking."

"I hear you, and we're in luck. They absolutely serve lunch. But... because of the corporate event later, we're working with an abbreviated menu." He held up a letter sized, laminated page. "Upside, it's got all our faves."

"What about seating?"

He shook his head and gave me a serious expression. "Barkeep said we'd have to fight for one."

I shoved him and he laughed as expected. "Ass. You could have just said it's open-seating."

"Where's the fun in that?"

No sooner did we slide into our seats at the nearest high top than a server came over. She was on the shorter side with wide hips, freckles, a bright smile, and wavy brown hair. And most importantly, a thousand percent Jimmy's type. I sat back, already knowing exactly how this would go.

"Hello, my name is Cassie. What can I start you two off with? Joe mentioned you'd be interested in some bites as well." She capped off her introduction with a sweet smile. That Jimmy totally ignored.

He smiled briefly at Cassie and returned his focus to the menu. "Joe would be right. We'll start off with some barbecue wings and loaded fries. He said, y'all did flights?"

I sat up a little straighter. Was he really not going to flirt? Not even a little? He hadn't even twitched at the "bites" comment, practically begging to be an innuendo.

"We do. There are some by beer type, like IPAs or hefeweizens, but I'd recommend the curated flight. It's a little pricier, but Joe puts together his favorites, including any specialty recent additions."

"That one," we said in unison.

"Excellent. I'll get that order put in and be right out with some waters." She turned on her heel, but didn't get far.

"Oh, hey, Cassie?" Jimmy called, pulling her up short. Aha! I knew he wouldn't be able to resist. "Can we get a Cobb salad as well?"

I looked at him with open disbelief. What the hell was happening right now?

"Absolutely. Will that be one salad or two?"

"Just one. We'll be sharing. And could we get the house dressing on the side?" He gave me a stern look, and judging by the quick way Cassie hid her face, I was scowling.

I waited until she'd gone behind the bar to let loose on my "friend". "Seriously, Jimmy? We're gonna share a salad?"

He shrugged and took a swallow of water. "What? I wanted some greens after all the grease and sweets, and we both know I won't eat it all. Besides, you could stand to have a few more greens in your diet."

I harrumphed back in my seat, crossing my arms. "You're the worst. Even on vacation, you have opinions about my diet."

"I think you mean the best. And considering I'm supposed to be your boyfriend, I'd hope I had opinions about your diet. Gotta keep my man fit." He wiggled his eyebrows, and I couldn't help but laugh. Was it even possible to stay mad, let alone disgruntled, with him?

It didn't take long for the flights or the food to come out, likely because of the shortage of patrons. Then again, it was also an early afternoon in the middle of the week at a bar. The sample of beers was phenomenal, and we quickly had new favorites to add to our ever-growing list. Much to my surprise, the wings were extra saucy and *extra* tasty. Even the salad was pretty good.

Jimmy wiped his mouth with a napkin and took a sip of an oaky amber. "Time for a few more questions."

I nearly choked on a sour IPA. "What? Here?" I glanced around as if at any minute someone was going to pop out of the walls to record us.

"No need to be so dramatic. I can behave."

Considering how long I'd known him. I seriously doubted it.

He leaned forward, resting his forearms on the table, his expression suddenly serious. "What did you really think of Carrie?"

"Carrie who?" I asked behind my glass. It was a bogus counter. There was only one Carrie.

He raised an eyebrow and obstinately didn't take the bait.

"I don't know what you mean. Carrie was fine," I hedged. Carrie was, in fact, twenty gallons of crazy in a ten-gallon hat, but I hadn't admitted that then and I wasn't planning to now.

"Uh-huh. I figured it went without saying, but you also aren't allowed to lie."

I grimaced. This was *so* not going to be pretty. He'd been so enamored with Carrie, he'd almost proposed.

"Out with it, Dill. You were always weird around her. I think it's time you came clean why."

"Because she was a total psychopath! I didn't understand how you couldn't see it. She was completely two-faced and treated you like a commodity, *not* a partner. There, are you happy now?" I deflated into my seat, not meaning to have shouted, but remembering Carrie's catty nature and the way she'd always had a simpering smile for me while she possessively hung off Jimmy made my skin itch.

He stared at me, shock written plain as day in his wide eyes and open mouth. "Well." He cleared his throat and reached for a beer. "Okay."

I groaned. "Look, I'm sorry. I wanted to like her. I really did, but she just pushed my buttons in all the wrong ways." She'd even propositioned me to have a threesome with her and Jimmy. It had been tempting to take her up on it, if only to call her bluff, but I wouldn't do that to my best friend, even if the cow deserved it.

His gaze stayed focused on his now empty glass as he slowly shook his head. "Why didn't you say anything?"

"Because you were happy. I didn't want to let my bias ruin that for you." I mirrored him and grabbed a fry. After a few moments of silence, I added tentatively, "It was *really* hard not to throw a party when y'all finally broke up... for good." That comment earned me a frown.

"Rude. We weren't that bad."

"Considering you've been the poster child of committed re-lationships for as long as I've known you? That you even had one off-and-on-again spell, let alone *five*... Yeah, you were." I snagged another fry, feeling lighter now that he finally knew the truth—most of the truth—about his horrid ex. There was really no need to dredge up the horrible things Carrie had said about his mom's cooking or our friendship.

"Alright, Mr. Truth-Sayer, Simon Candesky."

"What about him?" I asked warily, my ease gone as quickly as it had come.

"At least you're not pretending you don't know who I'm talking about this time. That's something." He pointed a fry at me, and I watched a glob of cheese with bacon bits in it plop onto the plate. "You two fooled around on the DL for almost a year, then out of the blue, you have a black eye and Candesky is tanking the football team's chance at the state championship. When I asked about it then, you were hella vague. I think it's past time I got the full story, don't you?"

I shifted in my chair, more than a little uncomfortable that my best friend seemed to have been keeping tabs on all my sketchy behavior over the last thirty years. "What does it matter now? That was *fifteen* years ago. And why the history questions? You were all about the sex questions before."

His mouth twisted to the side. "This is hardly the place, Dill. But if you'd rather tell me all about your experiences with docking—yes, I know what that is—than tell me what really happened with Candesky, go for it."

"Jimmy!" I hissed to zero effect.

"What'll it be?"

I scrambled for a way out of this, but he'd pulled out his counselor-face, the one that said he had the patience of an immortal who could and would wait you out until the end of time or you died, whichever came first. "It's gonna sound really bad."

He snorted. "I figured as much since you glossed the hell over it in high school and basically pretended that you didn't even know him for the rest of school."

"I broke up with him, but I didn't handle it very well. I was kind of... a complete asshole about it."

His features softened. "Dill, you were a teenager with more hormones than sense. Don't be so hard on yourself."

"You might change your mind about that when you hear the truth."

"Doubtful, but we'll see."

I shook my head, at a loss. He was a great counselor and, sure, he could have these infinite wells of acceptance for his patients, but they were different. After stalling for another minute, I let out a harsh breath. "So, I went to the game against Edgemont, knowing full well I planned on ending things with Simon. The thrill of sneaking around had worn off, and I was ready to have a proper boyfriend."

"Please tell me you did *not* break up with Candesky right before our school's biggest rivalry game."

I reached for the last of my flight. "I didn't *plan* to. Even I know that's cruel. It just sort of happened that way. The original plan had been to cheer him on one last time, then end things the following day."

He flagged Cassie and ordered two of the beers we'd had at the IF welcome dinner. "What happened?"

My face heated something fierce. "We, uh, ended up in the lockers and I ended things, anyway." I paused, hating myself all over again for what I was about to admit to doing, then added, "*After* he blew me... and told me he loved me."

"Shit, Dill. That's... That's fucking *cold*. What the hell?" The look on his face was exactly why I'd refused to open up about it then. It was a beyond garbage thing to do.

"Look, I'm not proud of it. When I called him out for not being gay, or bi, or pan, or anything other than straight, he said he was gay for *me*." I curled my lip. "He didn't even deny being straight, didn't offer to be together publicly or drop his cheerleader girlfriend." Simon had told me to my face that I was a great side piece and had argued about not ruining a good thing. The bastard had genuinely expected me to go along simply because he was the star quarterback and clearly I was desperate. "I lost my shit."

Jimmy looked at me long enough that I squirmed. Like somehow he could hear all the parts I hadn't told him. "Dude, that's really fucked up. Kinda feels like karma that Jessica dumped his ass after he threw that game."

I chanced another look at him. It shouldn't have surprised me he was giving me that understanding smile that had supported me throughout our lives. But it did. I'd been so ashamed of how I'd handled that, I'd vowed going forward to be the kind of guy who always took care of my partners. Except for this morning, I'd held to that promise. Gradually, the tension in my shoulders lessened, and I reached for the fresh beer.

"Damn, you've been carrying that around all this time? You should have told me, man."

I traced the ring of condensation left by the glass and shrugged. That sounded fine and dandy over ten years later, but I could barely believe it myself at the time. And I'd just been so—

He placed a hand over mine. "It's okay to be angry. No one deserves to be treated like that. And sure, you didn't have the best tact, but you were also seventeen. Probably for the best you didn't tell me the whole truth back then. I'd have had to kick his ass."

I barked out a laugh. "If by 'kick his ass' you mean getting *your* ass handed to you and *both* of us ending up in the principal's office, then yeah, probably."

"Eh. Tomato, tamahto."

"You're ridiculous."

"You know you love it."

I smiled into my drink. Yeah, I kind of did. Jimmy kept me grounded in the strangest ways, and I wouldn't trade anything in the world for our friendship.

"But don't think I've forgotten about that docking question. We'll circle back to that later."

My groan was cut short by the entrance of several members of Infinity Financial. Looked like we wouldn't be killing so much time on our own after all.

Chapter 10

Jimmy

OUR ROOM WAS SUSPICIOUSLY empty when I returned from fetching ice. I scanned the space for any clues where Dylan had vanished off to, but all I found was a dresser drawer half open. More concerning, his shoes were by the sitting chair.

"Dill! Where the hell did you go? I wasn't even gone two minutes. You better not have bounced," I added with a growl. Forget that I had a surprise. We were supposed to be in a relationship—a good one. My running around asking people if they'd seen my partner would definitely suggest otherwise. Irritated, I reached for the bathroom door, which opened before I could grab the handle.

"Stop shouting. I'm right here." He rolled his eyes and stepped into the main room, wearing possibly the shortest board shorts I'd ever seen. The dark palm leaf pattern with flares of bright color caught the eye and looked more like something I would have packed than Dylan.

I swallowed thickly as my treacherous gaze slid further down to his hair-coated legs. And I definitely did *not* notice the perfectly packaged bulge on the way down. The rogue impulse to palm him had my hand moving with a mind of its own. I subverted the wayward appendage by crossing my arms, tucking my hands into my pits like I was five, for good measure. Then I forcefully dragged my mind out of the gutter it was currently attempting to build a house in.

"What are you doing?" I asked as he pushed the drawer closed and plopped on the edge of the bed, forcing his shorts higher. I couldn't help but wonder how high they could get before this turned into a peep show.

He leaned forward to snag a pair of sandals I hadn't noticed from the chair. "Going swimming. What's it look like?"

"Uh, no, you're not."

"Uh, *yeah,* I am. The next scheduled event isn't until tonight. Plenty of time to swim and catch some sun. Besides, have you *seen* the pool here?" He leaned back on his arms and looked at me. "Better question is why aren't *you* in swim trunks?"

By sheer force of will and the fact that Dill was watching me, I kept my focus on his face and far away from his gloriously hairy chest and enticing abs. "Because I signed us up for a couple's massage class."

"You what?" He sat forward, eliminating my opportunity to sneak an appreciative peek.

I huffed, definitely at his attitude and not at my denied ogle. "You heard me."

"Yeah, I did. But why?"

"Because Sierra was telling me about it, and it sounded like a good time." I held up my hand to stall the argument already brewing on his face. "*And* Rafe and Tina chimed in that they were checking it out as well. So, in the interest of rubbing elbows and helping you socialize, I snagged us the last spot." I neglected to add that I thought it would be good for him, considering how awful he was at relationships. Giving my partner an intimate massage had never failed to bring us closer, cool tempers, or end in sex.

Really, if you thought about it, I was doing him a solid. Except he didn't look convinced. "Look, it's only a couple of hours. We'll each learn how to give the ultimate massage, then end by getting one ourselves. See? Win-win. And if you want to swim afterwards, you still can. But you need to hurry and change, or we'll be late."

He tossed his sandals back on the chair and glared when one had the audacity to bounce off, landing on the floor with a thump. "I *will* check out that pool before we leave," he grumbled as he disappeared back into the bathroom, presumably where the clothes he'd worn to brunch were. He emerged a few minutes later, and we wound our way to the spa side of the resort in tense silence. His scowl deepened when he saw the giant poster for "The Intimate Art of the Couple's Massage".

After a quick look around to make sure no one was watching, I yanked him aside. "For fuck's sake," I hissed beneath my breath. "It's a massage, not a knitting class. Are you gonna be a grump the whole time, or are you going to lighten the fuck up?" I met his scowl with a glare and hoped anyone that might happen by mistook our standoff for a lover's tiff and not me having to reprimand my best friend because he was acting like a two-year-old threatening a tantrum.

Finally, he relaxed. "Fine, you're right. We can swim later."

I gave his shoulder a sympathetic squeeze. "Hey, I get it. Last-minute plan changes mess you up. I should have texted you or something to give you a heads up. Forgive me?" I gave him a light shake and a tentative smile.

He let out a deep sigh and squeezed the hand I still had on his shoulder, causing my heart to give a little thrill. "No forgiveness necessary. We both know I'd try to spend the whole retreat impersonating a wallflower if you weren't here."

"Please, you're too handsome to be a decent wallflower," I scoffed. His eyes widened with obvious surprise, but I didn't give him a chance to respond. "Now come on before they shut the doors. And try to look happy about being here. Never know, you might learn something useful." I pushed him toward the entrance that really was in danger of shutting us out, so of course he obstinately dug his heels in. If he hadn't already agreed to play along—and wasn't snickering at my struggle—I'd think he was genuinely trying to sabotage our surprise adventure. "You. Are. The. Worst," I grumbled under my breath... right before he stopped fighting me and I nearly fell face-first through the propped doors.

"You okay there, babe?" he asked, a wicked twinkle in his eye that betrayed his concerned tone.

"Doing just great, *babe*." I wove between occupied floor cushions toward a pair of empty ones.

"Hey! You made it!" Tina shout-whispered.

I gave her a double-thumbs up as we took our places on the oversized pillows. "Wouldn't have missed it."

Dill waved in greeting at Tina, then at several others who echoed her enthusiasm at seeing us. By the looks of it, at least a third of the IF big-wigs were here.

"Stop it," he whispered as the room quieted.

"I'm not doing anything," I whispered back.

"You're smirking." He glanced at me. "Yeah, that's the one."

That he didn't even need to look to know the grin I was sporting was testament to how many times we'd had similar conversations. One of these days, he'd get with the program and *start* with assuming I was right, instead of being such a grump-a-saurus every time I suggested something outside his comfort zone.

The lights dimmed, and twitters of anticipation filled the gloom. Then two women emerged at the front of the class, where a spotlight illuminated a dry-erase board on an easel.

"Welcome everyone. It is such a joy to have you with us today for the Intimate Art of the Couple's Massage. My name is Miranda, and this is my partner—in life and in business," she added with a wink, "Sienna. Together, we will walk you through several techniques to provide the ultimate relaxation for your partner. Once we've completed the lesson, you'll each test them out for yourselves." Miranda winked, and giggles filled the room.

Dylan glanced at me and I shrugged, not anymore enlightened than he about what was so funny. We didn't get the chance to dwell, though as Miranda launched into an abbreviated history and evolution of massage. In short order, Miranda and Sienna took turns demonstrating techniques on a rubber mannequin I hadn't noticed before, while the other explained the intent of the movement using the dry-erase board. To my surprise, I even picked up a few tips and best practices, like using the heels of my palms rather than my fingers for pressure to avoid fatigue. Before we knew it, the two instructors were thanking us for our time, and anticipation buzzed in the air.

"Thank all of you for your time and attention. It has been a pleasure to share our knowledge with you. Now let's see how well you were paying attention." Once again, giggles filled the room at Miranda's statement.

Sienna clapped her hands together, and the lights brightened subtly. "To prevent any discord around who will enjoy their massage first, would the people sitting on the red cushions please stand and follow me? I'll be escorting each of you to *semi*-private rooms." She gave the room a stern look that did nothing to discourage another round of giggles.

I was still trying to discern what the hell was supposed to be so funny or why the rooms weren't fully private when Dylan let out a triumphant whoop. Of course, he was on the red pillow of our duo. "Yeah, yeah. It's not like we don't both get a turn," I said, twisting my lips at his over-the-top enthusiasm.

"But *you* have to wait." He stuck out his tongue as he stood, and I stuck mine out right back.

I shared an excited smile with the others waiting while Sienna led the first group away. A shockingly short few minutes later, she motioned for the rest of us to come forward. Confused, but not about to complain, I got in line.

Miranda met me with a welcoming smile when I reached the front of the line. She asked my name, then had Sienna lead me to a door. With a wink, Sienna left me.

Practically bouncing on my toes with excitement, I pushed aside the curtain strung between two portable wall panels. When was the last time I'd received a massage instead of giving one?

My gaze fell on an undeniably familiar body, lying face down on a massage table as the curtain fell closed behind me with the barest whisk of fabric. I quickly darted out of the room and searched the narrow corridor formed by the other wheeled-panels. When I spotted Miranda, I frantically waved her over.

"Is something wrong?" she asked, standing close so she wouldn't need to speak loudly.

"There's already someone in my room," I whispered back.

Her forehead wrinkled in a frown. She glanced from the pinned number nine on the curtain back to her clipboard. "James Wallace, right?"

"Yes."

Her frown deepened with concern. "Is Dylan Wells not your partner?"

I bit back the reflex to explain we were just friends. "He is. But where's his massage specialist?"

"Today, that's you." My surprise must have shown on my face, because she tucked her clipboard beneath her arm and gently turned me back to the curtain. "It is the *Intimate* Art of the Couple's Massage. Just don't get too carried away," she added with a stern look before giving me a final push through the curtain.

I swallowed hard as she loosely secured it behind me. Well, wasn't this the clusterfuck of the century? Leave it to me to neglect reading the not-so-fine print and get us into this mess. I took another moment to fortify myself and walked to his side. Dill had already stripped down to his briefs, judging by the band poking out from the sheet covering him from the waist down. I'd promised him he'd be getting a relaxing massage today, and damn it, he would. Upside, I was pretty fucking great at giving massages.

Before I could psych myself out, I reached for the conveniently supplied lotions, grabbing the one labeled eucalyptus. I squirted a healthy amount onto my hands and my evil brain flashed back to our epic morning getting off together. Once the lotion was appropriately warm, I smoothed it across Dylan's shoulders and down his back.

He released an appreciative hum that instantly transported me to that special place in my mind I went to when giving my partners massages. I dug the heels of my palms into the slick skin between his shoulders in a smooth rolling motion that had his hum turning into a groan. Thanks to the defined muscles he was sporting, I didn't have any fear of hurting him.

I gradually worked my way, kneading and rolling along his upper back and down to where it dipped. It was difficult to tell if my palms were tingling from the lotion or the sheer exhilaration of getting to touch him like this, exploring his body in a way I'd only ever dreamed about. His increasingly loud moans didn't hurt either. My blood was practically singing by the time I shifted the sheet to massage his legs.

"Don't worry about any no-touch spaces. I'm good," he mumbled into the face pillow, startling me and prompting a stream of potential scenarios that could rival even the best porn.

The traces of lotion on my hands ran out midway through his left calf. Reticent to stop touching him, I kept one hand on his leg and stretched to reach the bottle, causing the erection I'd been sporting since his first groan to brush against his thigh.

Dylan lurched up, nearly sending me crashing to the ground with the bottle I'd secured. "What the fuck?" he hissed, not so quietly. Then his indignant gaze landed on me. "Jimmy? What the hell are you doing here? Where's the professional?" The undercurrent of accusation in his voice had me shrinking inward with guilt, like the time I'd signed us up for the charity car wash, not realizing it was a *bikini* car wash.

"So, it, uh, appears that I didn't read... *all* of the class description," I began sheepishly.

He narrowed his eyes, and I could practically see the anger arcing off his previously relaxed body.

"Turns out the couples learn how to give a decent massage and then get to practice... on each other."

"For fuck's sake. What is it with you and not reading directions? *All* of them," he added before I could interject. "And what gives with the boner?"

"Why are you moaning like a porn star?" I countered with a huff.

"Because, unlike some people, I *enjoy* getting massages."

"Yeah, well—"

The curtain whisked back to reveal an irritated Sienna. "Gentlemen, you'd do well to remember that others can hear you."

My face heated, and I noticed that Dill's had also turned a rosy color. "Sorry," we said in unison.

Once she'd left, I worked to school my compounded embarrassment. Okay, I hadn't read the class description beyond the first couple of lines before signing us up. I shouldn't have taken my irritation out on Dylan, and I wasn't really sure I could touch him at all now without getting at least a semi.

"Jimmy," he said, significantly quieter.

I lifted my gaze from the edge of the table to meet his, fully prepared to abandon whatever was left of my dignity. "It wasn't on purpose."

To my surprise, his gaze softened. "I know, and maybe I should have been a little more respectful of our surroundings before moaning like a—what was it?—a porn star." He gave me a lopsided grin, and I shoved his shoulder.

"Shut up."

"In my defense, you are *damn* good at giving a massage."

I couldn't help but brighten. "Yeah?"

He rolled his eyes. "Please. Don't even pretend like you didn't already know that. I didn't realize you'd gotten so many massages before. You clearly know what you're doing."

"I haven't. Gotten any massages, that is."

"Then how..." He trailed off, his face clouding with confusion.

I shrugged. "A *lot* of internet tutorials."

"Why am I not surprised?" he asked with a small laugh. His blue gaze met mine, an ocean of calm I'd happily float away on. "I ever tell you that you're one of the most selfless people I've ever met?"

Words failed me as I got lost in the gentle curve of his lips. More than anything, I wanted to close the meager distance separating us and press my lips against his. Not for appearances or for practice, but for me. Because *I* wanted to kiss him.

A faint bell chimed, cutting through the soft music, and Miranda's voice came quiet but clear. "That marks our halfway point. You may now trade places."

My gaze flicked back to Dill, sitting almost naked on the table. "You don't have to. This isn't really what you signed up for."

He scoffed as he slid off the table. "Nope. Fair is fair. Strip down and get on the table." He added a ridiculous eyebrow wiggle that had me stifling a laugh.

"You're ridiculous," I said as I pulled my shirt over my head and kicked my shorts aside. I'd barely finished settling when he draped the sheet over my legs to keep them warm. Then he leaned down until his breath tickled my ear.

"And I think it's about time you got to experience what all the fuss is about."

The purr of his voice, coupled with his choice of words, went straight to my dick. It took every ounce of willpower I had not to squirm on the table.

"Especially after you've been so good." The sharp scent of citrus filled the air, and his fingers dug into the base of my scalp, massaging their way into my hair, and all bets were off.

A groan that rivaled his earlier ones rolled out of me, and I melted into the touch. Dylan had definitely been paying attention to the class, turning first one muscle, then another into pliant goo. Maybe I hadn't made such a horrible mistake after all.

Chapter 11

Jimmy

I SCURRIED DOWN THE hall, trying not to look epically suspicious, mentally crossing my fingers that Dylan had forgone his "nap" and headed to the pool. If I were lucky, he'd still be there and I could slip into our room with my purchase and he'd be none the wiser. At our door, I took a calming breath and offered a friendly wave to one of the IF people walking by whose name I was totally spacing on. *Nothing to see here. Just keep walking.* Once they'd vanished around a corner without detouring to chat, I let out a relieved breath and fished out the key card. All I had to do was get inside and I'd be home free.

The second the door opened, Dylan spun to face me. His hair wasn't wet, and there wasn't so much as a trace of fresh sun on him, not to mention the stark absence of a pool towel and swimwear. So much for my luck.

"Where have you been?" he asked, sounding irritated. Because of course he'd be upset. I'd vanished the second we'd finished the massage class and had been gone all day without so much as a text to check in.

"Just wandering around." I moved the thankfully nondescript bag behind my back.

He frowned. "What's that?"

"Nothing." I scooted closer to the bathroom. "Did a little shopping while I was out. Nothing major. Ended up bumping into Tina while I was exploring, and she talked me into going with her into Oak Haven for lunch." Five more feet and I could put a barrier between us.

Hurt flashed across his face. "You went into town without me?"

Guilt stabbed into me hard enough that I winced. Normally I would have reached out, but I'd needed a little breathing room after having his hands all over my body, which had led to my arguably overly optimistic purchase.

"She kind of caught me off guard. I didn't have a chance to see if you'd be free to join. But you're right, I should have texted. Just didn't think we'd be out so long."

"Yeah, I suppose." The lukewarm sentiment only made me feel more guilty.

"I know the dinner event is early tonight, and we need to get going soon. Pull me out something while I take a quick shower?" Rather than wait for a reply, I left Dylan and his pole-axed expression and zipped into the bathroom, locking it for good measure.

I twisted on the water, casting an anxious look at the shut door, before untying the unremarkable plastic bag. Chewing on the inside of my cheek, I took out the two boxed enema kits—one to be used in the shower and the other a little more versatile. I knew how they worked in theory, but I'd never actually used one before. Hopefully, it wouldn't take me too long to figure it out. Dylan liked to be prompt to events, especially corporate ones, and I'd promised him a *quick* shower. I read through the instructions as fast as I dared and hopped beneath the scalding spray.

By the time I stepped out of the steam-filled room, I felt disturbingly clean and oddly self-conscious. I didn't even know if or how I'd convince Dylan to have sex with me, but on the off chance he went for it, I wanted to be prepared, because damn if I didn't want that experience with every cell in my body.

Dill glanced up from where he was sitting on the edge of the bed, playing on his phone. Did his gaze linger on my naked torso, or was that wishful thinking? "What happened to quick?" he asked, setting his phone aside. He looked as delicious as ever in skinny gray slacks that might have actually been denim and an equally fitted cobalt blue polo.

I forced my gaze away from the way the fine fabric clung to his biceps. Last thing I needed was another fucking boner, least of all while I was only wearing a towel. "What are you talking about? That was quick." I hiked a shoulder and wandered over to the clothes laid out beside him.

He snorted. "Dude, I've seen you take a shower in under two minutes."

"I had to give you enough time to pick out something decent to wear." I crossed my arms and gave him my smuggest smirk. "Be honest. How long did it take?" It was difficult to tell if he was blushing, but there was no missing his eye roll.

"I'm fully capable of dressing myself, and you, for that matter. Now hurry up, slowpoke." He stood as I reached for the slate-green polo he'd set out. It was one of the few solids I'd packed. It was also a trimmer fit than I typically wore.

"Why this one?"

He shrugged. "Because as much as you love your patterns, you look good in solids, and it's soft." He fiddled with pocketing his phone and wallet, still not having met my curious gaze. "I was a little surprised you packed it. You hardly ever wear it despite how awesome it looks on you. Anyway, are you going to get dressed, or were you planning on going in the towel?" He finally lifted his head and cracked a smile.

It was hard not to feel like I was on display when we walked into the ballroom. Besides my little secret, Dill had grabbed my dark wash jeans—that also hugged me like a second skin—to go along with my tight shirt. Then he put his hand on my waist. The move simultaneously grounded me and damn near sent me into the rafters. I released a shaky breath and tugged at my shirt hem.

"Stop fidgeting. You look great," he whispered into my ear, sending a wave of goosebumps prickling up the back of my neck.

"Thanks," I squeaked out. His gaze narrowed with suspicion. Or was it concern? Concern made more sense. I was just being paranoid. He didn't know what I had planned. I glimpsed the drinks table and made a beeline for it.

"Oh, hey, they have that IPA we liked so much at Twisted Pine," Dill said at the same time I knocked back one of the featured mixed drinks.

I gave him an anxious smile as I turned to where he was holding two pints of the aforementioned beer. "Maybe *I* should have taken a nap if I didn't see these," I added with a laugh that sounded strained even to my ears.

His frown returned as I took the offered beer. He waited until I'd taken a sip, then gently grabbed my elbow and led me off to the side. "Is everything alright? You seem... off."

The instinct to blurt out the whole truth—that I was bi, that I'd been into him practically our whole friendship, that this retreat was showing me just how good we could be together—warred with the logic that this was neither the time nor the place for such a confession. So I settled for a version of the truth.

"This morning threw me for a bigger loop than I was expecting."

"Come on. I know I'm not exactly a massage savant like you, but it wasn't that bad. Was it?"

I laughed and shook my head. "No, it wasn't that bad." Somehow hearing that he was also self-conscious, if about something different, eased my anxiety.

"Phew." He dramatically wiped the nonexistent sweat from his brow. "I was a lot worried when *you* didn't make any porn star noises."

I choked on my beer and scowled at him, then shrugged. "I guess I'll just have to give you pointers later."

"I guess you will." The teasing twinkle of challenge in his eye instantly had me smiling.

"Right, now that we've got me being an awkward goose out of the way, I say we mingle."

He wrapped his arm briefly around my waist and pressed a firm kiss to the side of my head. "You'll always be an awkward goose. But I agree. Let's chat up some people."

I trailed after him, slowly sipping my beer. My cheeks were stubbornly still warm after the modest gesture of affection when I caught up with him where he was already embedded in a conversation with a group I mostly recognized. Why he thought he wasn't capable of being social was beyond me. Sure, he had his weird moments, but not any more than the rest of us. Mentally shaking my head, I joined the crowd.

"There you are!" Colleen exclaimed, yanking me across the informal circle.

Steven—or was it Stephan?—squeezed in on my other side. "We tried to find you for lunch, but both of you were MIA."

I caught the glimmer of mirth in Dylan's eyes before he reached across and gently tugged me back to his side. His hand made a pulse-skipping return to my lower back. He tilted his head toward me, giving the impression that he was about to whisper in my ear again, but instead, he directed his words to the gathering. "I've tried explaining that after the amazing massage my boyfriend gave me this morning, I passed out like a total loser. And Tina commandeered you to go into town." His hand coasted up my back and lightly squeezed my neck. "Sorry about that."

"About falling asleep like an old man or leaving me to fend for myself with the wolves?" I fired back, doing my best to quell the sudden flutters in my stomach that his touch had evoked.

Everyone, including Dill, laughed. He was about to say something when a space opened up at the center of the room with Chase at its heart.

"Much as I'd love to do a mic check joke, I fear that none of our three Michaels present go by Mike." Light laughter rippled through the room. Chase waved a hand. "No, don't laugh. That was awful. But tonight's event is far from it. Who's ready to get this party started?"

Whoops filled the room. The rather club-y outfits Dill had us in suddenly made sense as I recalled the night's event theme: The Nightlife of our Youth. Eager anticipation filled the room as Chase gestured toward a set of double doors. It hadn't occurred to me that the ballroom we were in was acting as a sort of antechamber. Two sharply dressed staff stepped forward to grab the handles.

"Then what are we waiting for? Just remember to take it easy on the candy." He winked, and the doors were pulled apart. The confused murmurs turned to whistles of excitement, as not a dance floor was revealed, but an arcade. Infinity Financial really knew how to pull out all the stops. They'd transformed the adjoining room with black lights, neon signs, every game I'd ever loved as a kid, and then some.

"Holy shit!" Dylan exclaimed beside me.

"Last one to the s'mores table is a rotten egg!" Colleen shouted as she joined the surge of people making their way inside.

Stephan—pretty sure it was Stephan—glanced back at us. "You two coming or what?"

"No way am I fighting Colleen and Larry over snacks," Dylan responded with a laugh while he hooked a finger in the belt loop at the small of my back.

"What about you, Jimmy? I think we can take 'em."

The slight tug on my jeans tempered my eagerness to agree. "You go ahead. We'll catch up."

Looking more than a little put out, Stephan scoffed. "Don't come crying to me when it turns out Colleen has hoarded all the marshmallows." Once he'd gone a good ten paces away, Dylan turned to laugh into my shoulder.

"How is it that you charm everyone you meet?"

I frowned, still at a loss for why he'd held me back like he didn't also fucking love s'mores. "What do you mean?"

He chuckled and stepped back far enough to give me a solid once-over that had my skin heating. Was it possible that he found me as attractive as I found him? Had he specifically chosen this outfit because *he* liked the way it looked on me? Shaking his head, he stepped in close once more and dropped his voice so it wouldn't carry. "If I wasn't one hundred percent positive that

Stephan wasn't attracted to men, I'd be convinced he was trying to steal you away from me."

I couldn't help but snort at the ludicrous thought.

"I'm serious. Did you see his face when I said you'd been commandeered by Tina? Like he hadn't realized abduction was on the table. At the rate everyone is taking to you, *you're* going to have a job offer by the end of the week."

I waved him off. "Nah. They all know you're the real financial superstar. And if they don't, I'll just have to tell them some more," I added with a smirk and started making my way toward the entrance to the surprise twist event. Was that pinball? *Two* foosball tables? And be still, my beating heart. A massive screen equipped with top-of-the-line gaming consoles and a veritable tower of games?

"I'm completely serious about Stephan. Maybe I should adjust my hundred to ninety-seven percent positive," Dylan said as he fell in step.

I quirked an eyebrow. "Yeah? A whole three percent chance I might get kidnapped?"

"Never say never."

"Wouldn't dream of it. More importantly, what are *you* going to do to dissuade him?" I shoulder-bumped him, but he didn't stagger. Instead, he caught me and pulled me toward him until only a few inches separated our faces.

"I guess I'm just going to have to keep you close," he said, his voice dropping to a sultry purr of promise.

I swallowed thickly, caught by the unexpected heat in his blue eyes. Suddenly, I had absolutely no desire to check out the kick-ass arcade set up. I wanted to be in our room, behind closed doors, preferably naked.

"Oi! Lovebirds!" Marcus called, popping the intense moment. "You've got the rest of your lives to do that. Right now, one of you is about to get your ass handed to you in Rogue's Revenge."

I threw an arm around Dylan's shoulders. "Wouldn't count on it. My man is a freaking legend." I'd referred to Dill as my man a hundred times over, but what if he really could be?

"We'll see about that, Wells," Marcus said to Dylan as the three of us walked in together.

Joyful laughter surrounded us as we made our way across the room. My initial impression that Infinity Financial had gone all out renting arcade games was reinforced as I spied some retro classics and the clusters of eager people waiting to play them. I glanced at Dylan to see what he thought of the blast back to childhood, only to find him watching me and sporting a smile. "What?"

"You." He shook his head, but the twinkle of mirth in his blue eyes didn't fade.

I snorted. "What about me?"

"You're grinning from ear to ear."

"And you're not?" I countered.

He chuckled, but before he could respond, Marcus called us over to an impressive gaming setup that supported games easily a few decades old, as well as more recent releases. Marcus gestured to one of the beanbag chairs—because, of *course*, there were beanbag chairs—for Dill to take a seat while he popped in the comparatively newer "Rogue's Revenge".

"You ready to get schooled?" Marcus asked as he fell with a crunch of Styrofoam into the beanbag next to Dill.

Dylan scoffed and accepted the controller Marcus held out. "I think you mean, are *you* ready to get schooled?"

I laughed under my breath. Dill was atrocious at smack talk. A quick glance around revealed a stack of multicolored beanbags ready to be commandeered. Tickled at all the nostalgia, I moved to claim one.

"What are you doing?" Dill asked as I maneuvered a neon green one closer so I could watch him hand it to Marcus.

"What do you mean? I'm getting comfy."

His expression of curiosity transitioned into an exaggerated pout. "Without giving me a kiss for luck first?"

I could have sworn the entire room froze, but that was probably my imagination. "Right," I said with a voice that didn't sound like it came from me. The light in his eyes brightened as I took a step closer and leaned down. Our lips brushed over each other, and I was hard-pressed to decide if I was kissing pure electricity or the softest silk.

"That's more like it," he said, heat once more simmering in his gaze.

"What about mine?" Marcus asked, jerking both of our gazes toward him. I was pretty sure my expression was still stuck on stunned, but Dylan's must have been something else entirely, because Marcus instantly threw up his hands in surrender. "Whoa! I was kidding. No harm intended. Promise, no one is going anywhere near your man without an explicit invitation."

Finally shaken out of my stupor and not entirely sure what the hell was going on, I placed a hand on the back of Dill's neck. "Hey." When he didn't immediately relax, I ran my thumb along the side, much like I had that morning. "You know I'm all yours." I doubted he would ever understand the full extent of how true that statement was, but his shoulders unclenched. On a whim, I brushed my lips against his temple and gave his neck a firmer squeeze. "Now show Marcus why we got banned from the gaming group in college."

He gave me a wry smirk, and Marcus officially looked scared.

I scooted the beanbag close enough so that our knees were brushing and his cologne filled my senses. My ass had barely sunk into the chair when Dill reached out to squeeze my knee. I didn't bother hiding my grin. His focus was on the loading screen anyway. While I had no idea what had just happened, my hope that he'd go along with my plan for tonight strengthened.

Chapter 12

Dylan

JIMMY AND I STUMBLED into the wall by our room, laughing and waving at Barb and Kennan further down the hall.

"Tie!" Barb shouted at the same time Kennan shouted, "Jimmy by a mile!"

Jimmy crowed with triumph beside me. I shook my head and waved them off as I turned to key the door open. What was it with all the guys at this place being "Team Jimmy"? While I was used to fielding inquiries from women when we were out, Jimmy turning into a total dude magnet for every guy in a five-mile radius was disorienting. Which wouldn't have bothered me at all—Jimmy was a good-looking guy, especially in that t-shirt and those painted-on pants—except he was supposed to be in a relationship... with *me*. Oh, and he was straight.

"Dibs!" He squeezed past me the moment the door beeped. Before I had a chance to even process what was happening, he'd vanished into the bathroom, much like he had earlier this afternoon. Strange to think that not twelve hours ago, he'd been giving me one of the best massages of my life. Which, considering how frequently I got them, was really saying something. The way his fingers had played across my skin had been downright sensual. It wouldn't surprise me in the least if all of his massages ended in him getting laid. Hell, I'd been one "porn-star" moan away from coming undone myself.

I leaned against the chair and took out my phone to distract myself from thinking about how damn good his hands had felt... or how much I wanted them again. But no amount of scrolling or playing games could hold my attention. I tossed my cell behind me to bounce on the cushion and clasped my hands. When my knee began bouncing, I lurched to my feet. What the hell was he doing in there? Not that I needed the restroom, but I damn sure didn't want to be a wired disaster by myself. As it was, the only reason we'd left early had been at his suggestion. That and other couples had been breaking off to return to their rooms, no doubt for a different kind of nightcap.

A disturbingly *not* small part of me couldn't help but wonder if Jimmy would be up for fooling around. Wasn't like we hadn't already crossed a few lines. I shook my head to clear the ridiculous desire. That we'd crossed so many lines already was exactly why I *shouldn't* suggest crossing a few more.

The bathroom door opened at last, and an entirely too chipper Jimmy emerged. "Damn, tonight was fun."

"Yeah, total blast." My traitorous gaze slid down his torso. He really looked amazing in that outfit. If I'd realized the evening wouldn't involve some kind of club atmosphere, I might have chosen something a tad more relaxed for him and significantly less distracting for me. I mentally groaned at the scene I'd caused in front of Marcus. What the hell was wrong with me? Even if Marcus *had* been serious about Jimmy laying one on him, I knew Jimmy wasn't interested. My reaction was entirely unwarranted, but be it the impressive kisses, that mind-blowing massage, or something in the water, this place was activating my primitive brain. Honestly, I was shocked Jimmy hadn't teased me about it yet.

Oblivious to my borderline existential crisis, he spun to rest against the wall, wearing his characteristically broad smile and a gleam in his eyes that suggested he'd caught me checking him out. Which was bad. Right? Did I want him to catch me looking? I'd blame my tumultuous thoughts on booze, except I'd intentionally moderated my alcohol intake. Last thing I needed was to be inebriated around him in my current headspace.

"Still can't believe Infinity got their hands on an *original* Pac-Man console. And *you*, I can't believe you let Marcus beat you! I feel so betrayed." He laughed as I scoffed.

"He only won once. Cut me some slack. It's been a while," I countered. It wasn't my fault that Jimmy's good-luck kiss had turned me into a caveman, or that his leg pressed against mine the whole game kept me distracted with thoughts of touching him without pants... again.

He rolled his eyes and popped me in the arm, drawing my attention to how close we'd gotten, or more accurately, how close I'd gotten. *He* was still against the wall. It reminded me of something I'd learned in school about how all things, no matter their size, exerted a gravitational pull. This felt a lot like that, but then Jimmy and I had always come together over the years. Maybe this was just a twisted extension.

He popped me again. "Look at you, always so serious. You work too much. You gotta make more time for fun, games, *life*."

"Hey, I'm plenty of fun." I also hadn't meant for that to sound so damn suggestive. If I couldn't even control the things coming out of my mouth, then he was going to need to do more of the talking. "Speaking of games, I noticed you haven't asked any of your questions today. Run out?"

"Figured you could use a break. But if you're missing them that much..." Try as he might, Jimmy had never managed what I would call a "wicked smile", and the one he was giving me now was no exception, mischievous maybe, but not wicked.

"I didn't say I missed them."

"In that case, instead of a question, a proposition."

Apprehension and a peculiar sense of excitement merged into an unsettling tilt in my stomach that made me wish I'd brought a beer or six back from the event. "And what would this proposition be?"

"I think you should fuck me," he said without batting an eye.

"I'm sorry. What?"

"You heard me. But if you need me to repeat it for your old man ears, I said you should fuck me."

"We're the same age." Really? *That's* the best I could come up with? How about, "No, that's a terrible idea," or, "What the hell have you been smoking and why the fuck didn't you share?"

He raised an eyebrow. "Then you *don't* need me to repeat it." His cavalier attitude was really wreaking havoc on my perception of reality. Was this actually happening? Maybe I'd dozed off in the chair while he spent a small eternity in the bathroom. If that was the case, then why was I dreaming about *this*? I didn't actually want to fuck him. Did I?

"Why?" I blurted out instead of the dozens of actual arguments against this ludicrous idea. Holy shit, I really *was* tempted.

He shrugged and gave me a smirk. "Honestly? Because I'm horny as fuck and... I want to know."

If there were a more Jimmy response, I couldn't think of one. But his explanation didn't change the fact that none of this was a good idea. Except voicing that was damn near impossible now that my libido was getting involved. I *really* should have hooked up before coming here. If I could just get my thoughts together. "Okay."

"Good. Glad you agree."

I'd actually meant it more as a thinking out loud "okay," but before I could say that, he twisted his fingers in my shirt and tugged me forward. Our lips crashed together, briefly short-circuiting my brain and letting my libido override the logic I was desperately clinging to. I raked my fingers along his sides, then slipped my fingers beneath his shirt, giving into the craving for skin on skin that had been haunting me every minute since the massage this morning. His tongue dove past my lips, and I imagined he tasted the same lingering flavor of hops that I did on his. My hum of appreciation might have been more of a moan, but he certainly wasn't protesting. Which meant it was up to me.

I broke the kiss, though I couldn't seem to bring myself to pull away more than the space it took to speak. "Are you sure? This isn't... Isn't exactly practice."

"I'm sure. Besides, we wouldn't be the first ever friends to hook up." He shrank the distance between us, so the words ghosted over my face in a teasing promise of possibility.

He had me there. Friends with benefits was absolutely a thing, and one I'd taken advantage of in the past. And those friends hadn't been nearly as close as Jimmy was, didn't share the history we did. Our friendship had survived three decades and more misadventures than I cared to count. It could survive this, too. With that conclusion, the last of my reticence evaporated. My driving focus now was getting his taste back on my tongue and getting his clothes *off.*

His insanely wide mouth captured mine with equally hungry fervor, and I had to admit, he wasn't the only one horny as fuck, especially when I had images of that same mouth stretched around my cock running rampant through my brain. I nipped and pulled at his lips until they were gorgeously swollen and we were struggling for air. Then I abandoned his decadent mouth to brush my increasingly sensitive lips over his evening scruff while moving my hands to grip his ass like I'd wanted to since our first morning here. Real shame his pants were in the way. My exploration ventured to the curve of his neck.

He jerked against the wall as if he'd been electrocuted, then moaned loudly, which addled whatever was left of my senses. Curious, I kissed the side of his neck more aggressively, teasing the tender flesh with light nips of my teeth. He gasped, his fingers digging into my biceps, and I swear his dick jumped on my thigh.

"Well, well. Not an exaggeration, after all," I purred.

"No, it's fucking not, and if your dick is going to get anywhere near my ass, then you need to stop."

"Oh, this is going to be fun." He may not be able to do a wicked smile, but I sure as hell could. His groan could have been at the threat of tortured pleasure, or it could have been in anticipation of it. Whichever it was, he was right about one thing—we needed to slow down.

I took a steadying breath while my brain floundered for reason. Maybe inserting the necessity of practical preparation would restore both of our senses. "Do you need a minute to... you know, flush?" Supereloquent, Dill. Great job.

His goofy grin was as unsettling as ever. "What do you think took me so long earlier?" He tilted his head. "Well, both earliers."

Fucker had premeditated this shit. And I... officially couldn't care less. He may not know everything about what he'd so non-chalantly proposed, but he'd at the very least thought about it in enough detail to be prepared. "You're something else."

"So you keep telling me," he said before stealing another kiss.

I tugged him away from the wall, and we stumbled our way to the bed, laughing as we tripped over our discarded shoes. Then he was on the bed, still clothed. Why the fuck was he still wearing clothes? Hoping he'd get the hint, I leaned back and pulled my shirt over my head. He mirrored the movement and moved his hands to his fly, but I beat him there. With the skill that comes with a lot of practice, I had the button undone, fly down, and his long ass legs well on their way to being free despite how insanely tight his pants were.

I'd scarcely tossed them aside when he hooked a hand around the back of my neck and tugged me down for another bruising kiss. I palmed his erection through his boxers, and he moaned. He was so hard, hard for me. I squeezed the outline of his shaft just shy of too hard and attacked the side of his neck again. He bucked under me and clawed at my bare shoulders.

"Mmm. So good. That feels so fucking good," he panted.

I was point-three seconds away from flipping him over and plowing him into the mattress when my brain finally intervened. "Wait, wait."

"What?" he groaned with exasperation instead of ecstasy.

"How drunk are you?"

He gave an indignant snort. "I'm not. Stopped drinking a while ago. How drunk are *you*?"

I shook my head. "I'm not. Stuck mostly to lemonade."

"There you have it." He reached for me again, and I pulled back. "Passphrase."

He pushed up to his elbows to give me an incredulous look. "Are you fucking serious?"

"Dead. Secret passphrase, or this stops right here." The passphrase, one of our more ingenious ideas from our youth. If you weren't in a sober enough state to say your unique passphrase, then you weren't sober enough to consent.

His glare could have drawn blood. Then he let out a huff and flopped back onto the pillow. "French fried frogs are freaky fast."

"See, not so bad," I said, though I was conflicted whether I was glad or disappointed that he recalled his phrase with such alacrity. I'd examine that later. Right now, I had a mostly naked, very willing, and, most importantly, consenting body beneath me begging to be fucked. I leaned down to recapture his mouth when his hand on my chest stopped me.

"Now you."

It took me a hot second to realize how succinctly he'd turned the tables. "What?"

"You heard me. Pass phrase. I don't want you pulling some weird shit on me later because you were tipsier than you thought." He gestured impatiently for me to get on with it.

I scowled at him. "Red Rover, red Rover, send Roger right over." Feeling more than a little smug, I leaned down once more.

"It was Robert."

I pulled up short. "Excuse me?"

"It was Robert, not Roger," Jimmy insisted.

"We were *fourteen*. Roger is close enough," I argued, finally realizing how much I *wanted* this. I wanted to be buried balls deep in Jimmy's tight ass. Wanted to see his face twist with unexpected pleasure.

"I'm just fucking with you, Dill. Hell, if I know what the original name was."

I growled and captured his mouth. "I'll show you who's fucking with who."

His small gasps and moans chased me as I worked my way down his chest, pausing at each hint of definition to trace it with my tongue. Inches from his straining cock, I pulled away and worked on removing my jeans, going ahead and taking my boxer briefs with them. By the time I kicked them away and returned to Jimmy, he had the bottle of lube held out for me. Smothering a laugh, I worked his boxers off his legs, then took the bottle.

He hissed as I stroked his length and tilted his head back to expose the column of his throat. Unable to resist the temptation before me, I stretched across his body to suck on his neck. His resulting moan vibrated through my chest and had his cock pulsing in my hand. I continued lavishing his hyper-sensitive skin while I lined up our cocks and rolled my hips. We moaned in unison as I ground against him.

"For the record, *this* is what I meant when I said I enjoyed frotting," I said, emphasizing the statement with a nip on his neck.

He made a strangled sound that simultaneously bolstered my ego and tested my restraint. I tortured him a bit longer, growing heady with his needy moans, then shimmied further down. As much as I wanted to feast on him, that hadn't been part of the proposition, and I doubted I'd get far before I completely came undone. Yet even with as keyed up as I was, even with the secret phrases, I paused, lubed fingers so close to his clenching hole I could feel his heat. When I continued not to move, he released a small whine and sat up on his arms.

"What's the holdup?"

"Are you sure?" I didn't even realize how worried I was until the words were out.

"Very."

I swallowed hard, still hesitating.

He sighed. "Dill, look at me." He waited until I met his steady gaze before continuing. "I know what I'm asking and I know what all it entails. And while I may not have personal experience with anal sex, I'm no stranger to ass play."

That was a revelation. My fingers seemed to move with a mind of their own, first circling his quivering rim, then sliding in with shallow thrusts and remarkably minimal resistance. Would Jimmy ever cease to amaze me? I kept my gaze fixed on his face, fascinated by the play of expressions I found there. Once I was deep enough, I curled my fingers, applying just enough pressure. His head dug into the pillow while he squeezed around me, then his head popped back up, revealing dilated eyes.

"That's more like it. Now I want the full Dylan Wells experience. Show me what you've got." He squeezed my fingers again, as if to emphasize his point.

"Fuck," I hissed. "You want it, you've got it."

He flashed me a self-satisfied grin that dissolved into a moan of pure pleasure as I stroked his prostate again with more conviction. I stretched him until I was sure he could take me, then reached for my wallet, which was unfortunately still in my pants... on the floor. By the time I retrieved it, he was back to giving me that look of narrow-eyed irritation. Then I pulled out the condom I kept there.

"Holy shit, you really do keep a condom in your wallet."

I snickered. "Told you I did." Before he could decide to ask for more details about whatever came to mind, I sheathed my aching cock and lined it up with his clenching hole. Then, with agonizingly slow thrusts, I worked my way deeper. I hadn't even gone my full length when Jimmy bowed off the bed.

"Fuck fuck fuck," he panted with his whole body.

"Like how that feels?" I asked, bordering on breathless myself.

"Yes," he moaned so deep I felt it in my soul.

I stroked slow and deep, fascinated by the way his face contorted with pleasure. "Jerk yourself."

For possibly the first time in his life, he obeyed without a quip or so much as a raised eyebrow. He fisted his swollen cock with deliberate motion.

"That's it. Just like that. You're doing so good," I encouraged him as I continued my slow passes, increasingly frustrated at my lack of foresight to place a pillow beneath Jimmy's hips. Desperate for that perfect angle, I looped my arms under his thighs and lifted him. Everything lined up and I *finally* bottomed out, my balls slapping against his ass with lewd perfection. I steadied myself with a few deep breaths and looked down at his face, which was stuck somewhere between awe and completely blissed out.

"Think you can keep up?" I asked in a more even tone than I would have thought possible.

"Try me," he snapped back, his fist already tightening around his cock.

Challenge accepted. I pistoned my hips, driving in and out of his gloriously tight ass at a pace that had my abs and thighs burning. But not even the burn in my arms from holding his ass at just the right angle could temper my intensity. Jimmy could think whatever he wanted. This shit right here was why I made a point of regularly working out. And fuck, he felt good. So so good. Taking my cock like he was made for it. Squeezing and squeezing until I thought I might pass out from the overwhelming ecstasy of it.

Sweat rolled down my forehead and chest. The base of my spine tingled, and my balls pulled up with the promise of imminent release. Jimmy's fist faltered as he struggled to keep up with the punishing rhythm. His abs clenched tighter and tighter until I could see the outline of each one, along with the cords of his neck, straining against the onslaught of pleasure. Suddenly, his thighs flexed against my arms, lifting him to a new angle, and his hand sped up without a discernible pace.

"Dill!" he shouted, his ass clenching as he fell over the edge, cum decorating his chest in beautiful ribbons.

I managed a few more strokes before I was falling with him, the combined pulse of his heart and mine an erratic rhythm massaging my draining dick. It was absolutely perfect, milking every ounce I had to give and made me long for the days when my recovery time was almost nil.

I retained just enough sense not to drop him onto the mattress, instead slowly lowering him and gently pulling free. He released a small sound of distress. Not surprising, considering the pounding he'd just taken. His ass would be tender for a while yet. While he lay there trying to recapture his breath, I slipped off the bed, disposed of the condom, and dipped into the bathroom. Once I'd finished my business, I returned to him with a warm, wet towel and began cleaning him up with as much, if not more, care as I would show any other hookup that had taken those punishing thrusts like a champ.

His eyelids fluttered when I introduced the towel to his sensitive hole. "Mmm," he moaned half-heartedly.

I chuckled under my breath and tossed the towel aside before lying next to him in his wonderfully overcooked noodle state. "How you doing?"

"Why the hell didn't you tell me you were so good at sex?" He rolled his head to look at me, his expression an interesting mix of disbelief and betrayal.

I snorted a laugh. Then his words registered, and I levered myself to look down at him. "Did you think I was bad at it?"

"Well..." He shrugged as well as he could lying down and gave me a sheepish grin.

"For real?"

"Don't be like that. In my defense, there had to be *some* reason you can't keep a boyfriend."

I flopped back down. "You're an ass."

"I mean, I *have* an ass, which you just pounded the fuck out of, by the way." He raised a fist, and I mirrored him, meeting his bump halfway.

"I certainly did."

Chapter 13

Jimmy

DYLAN WELLS WAS OUTRAGEOUSLY good at sex. It was unfair really. I felt like I should be taking pointers or something. A *mostly* full night's sleep and a hot shower where I optimistically got myself squeaky clean later and I still couldn't process it. Which was exactly why I was lying buck ass naked on the bed, still feeling like an overcooked noodle while Dill took his morning shower. If I'd known it would be like that, I'd have pursued my little crush a hell of a lot sooner.

"What happened to getting dressed?"

I grumbled incoherently and resisted the urge to turn around at the sound of a towel coming free. Not that I'd complain about getting an eye full of Dill naked and wet. But I doubted that I'd be able to keep any modicum of cool, which I suspected would be sorely needed. As it was, I'd spent most of my shower bracing myself for him being weird about hooking up. I closed my eyes and mentally followed him as he moved around the room, getting ready. The shuffle of fabric as he dug through the drawers. The quiet curse when he bumped into the chair. The zip of velcro. Velcro?

Before I could investigate, a sharp sting hit my ass. I squawked and spun around to glare at my so-called friend. "That hurt!"

"Don't look at me like that. You had plenty of time to get ready." He smirked and swirled the towel for another attack. "What are you gonna do about it?"

"Don't you dare."

An evil grin that I was all too familiar with spread across his face. "You sure about that?"

With the grace of a newborn giraffe, I scrambled to get off the bed. A sharp pop too close for comfort had me scurrying even faster and silently cursing my decision to face plant on the bed soaking wet. "Asshole!" I yelled as I hit the ground with an undignified thump.

"Me? I'm not the one wasting away the morning."

I pushed off the ground, ducking behind the chair a second before the towel snapped against it. "Would you cut it out? I'm up!"

"I don't know. I'm kind of enjoying myself." He had the towel mid-twist when I tackled him. He let out an "Oof" when we hit the ground in a tangle of limbs.

We wrestled across the carpet in a tumbling, laughing mess. I was positive I had the upper hand right until he flipped me around and I ended up on my knees, chest pressed against the carpet. He smacked me on the ass in the same spot the towel had struck earlier and chuckled.

"Rude!" I squirmed to get free, but Dill's days at the gym ensured my efforts were in vain.

"What's the rush? I've got you right where I want you."

I lifted my chest off the ground, surprised at the sudden lack of resistance, and glanced over my shoulder just in time to see Dill move his hands to grip my ass, one cheek in each palm. He flicked me possibly the naughtiest look I'd ever seen from him, then spread them. My brain was still trying to catch up when a breath of hot, moist air ghosted over my exposed hole, promptly followed by a firm stroke of tongue. I made a strangled sound and collapsed back to the ground.

"That's right, just relax and enjoy it," he crooned. "You're doing so good."

I wasn't sure if it was the unexpected praise or the firm thrust of his tongue. Whatever it was, I was rock hard and moaning hard enough to vibrate the floor. He traced my rim with the tip of his tongue, teasing and titillating, then pushed it through the sensitive muscle. I clawed at the carpet and shamelessly pushed back against his face. Judging by his subsequent groan, that was a good thing.

He pulled away enough to nip lightly at my ass cheek. Then his tongue was back, tracing, torturing, thrusting. Even the scrape of his beard was incredible. I squirmed beneath the onslaught of sensation, though I wasn't all that interested in getting away. I knew I enjoyed ass play, but this... this was a whole other level. As it was, I was absolutely leaking all over the carpet, and my dick had yet to be touched.

The stiff pad of Dylan's finger joined his persistent tongue, and I gasped. He mercilessly rubbed my prostate while he continued to feast on my ass until my moans blended with my desperate pants for air. A telltale tingle formed at the base of my spine, and I squeezed my eyes shut against the pending release. I didn't want this to end, not ever. But it was out of my hands. I flailed blindly around, feeling along the floor for any scrap of fabric I could get my hands on. No way was I going to explain to housekeeping why there was jizz all over the floor.

I gulped down air. "I'm... I'm..." I meant to say "close", but the words never stood a chance. My fingers caught on loose fabric and I jerked it beneath me. "Fuck!"

He pressed his lips in a firm line along my crease and decorated the inside of each cheek with a kiss while I shuddered through my release. He placed a hand over where he'd smacked me with the towel earlier, caressing the cheek. "Still hurt?" he asked softly, with a hint of humor.

"Mngh," I mumbled incoherently, my face pressed against the floor like I was trying to tattoo the carpet onto it.

He chuckled and placed a kiss at the base of my spine. "I might have fibbed before. Rimming definitely tops frotting." He tapped my ass, which was still propped up and at his complete mercy. Clearly, he had none. "I'm going to brush my teeth and trim. I suggest *you* get dressed. I took the liberty of pulling out your swimsuit."

Swimsuit. Right. That explained the Velcro.

Just when I thought he'd gone, I sensed him leaning over me. A feeling that was reinforced by the tender press of lips on my shoulder. "Oh, and you owe me a new shirt."

Breakfast consisted of snagging what we could before the staff finished packing everything up. Apparently, between my dawdling and our... adventure, we'd missed the big spread. Not that Dylan seemed to mind. He had one singular focus: to spend as much time in the sun today as humanly possible. I certainly couldn't fault him for that.

The day was beyond gorgeous, and he was right about the resort's impressive pool. Actually, pools, as in three. One of which was reserved exclusively for the Infinity Financial retreat guests for the day's surprise event: Tiki Bar Pool Party. But it was hard to appreciate the beauty of the day or the impressive themed decorations when my brain was a bowl of self-conscious pudding. Could people tell what we'd been up to this morning? Did I still have carpet weave imprinted on my face? Was that lady staring?

"What do we have here?"

I squeaked in surprise at the gravelly voice and ripped my wandering gaze away from a cute family splashing in a nearby pool to the man who had addressed us. He wore the typical Oak Leaf Resort shirt, but looked like a damn bouncer. "Huh?"

Dill gave me a strange look and hiked his pool towel higher over his shoulder. "We're with Infinity."

"You're here early. Event's not for another couple of hours." Mr. Bouncer glanced between us. "But I don't see any harm in letting you enjoy the amenities now. They're for your organization, after all." He reached behind a podium I hadn't even noticed and pulled out a tablet. "Name?"

"Dylan Wells, and this is my partner, James Wallace."

Mr. Bouncer checked the info against his list. "I've got you. Enjoy your day."

I followed Dylan around the massive pool to a set of colorful deck chairs. He plopped down his towel and reached for the sunscreen he'd had the foresight to pack. To my dismay, it was of the spray variety, which meant I would *not* be getting my hands on his golden skin. Still, it didn't stop my gaze from lingering wherever the spray glistened.

"Heads up."

I got my hands up in time to catch the spray bottle. He rubbed sunscreen into his face with his fingers while I made quick work of spraying myself down. "Ta-da. Basted and ready for the oven," I said with a cheeky grin when I was finished.

He scoffed. "Give me that." I plopped the canister into his outstretched hand, and he twirled his fingers. "Now turn around."

"I got that," I grumbled as he sprayed down my backside far more liberally than I had.

"You say that every time, and you always end up looking like a lobster."

"Do not," I mumbled under my breath.

"Sure you don't." He tossed the can onto the folded towels.

I turned toward the pool, fully prepared to cannonball into the cool liquid, but he pulled me up short. "What? No one's even here."

"You actually have to let the sunscreen set. Otherwise, it just washes off. No wonder you always get burned." He shook his head and worked on spreading the towels out on the chairs and organizing his things. Hating how he was right—again—I mirrored him. I was nearly done when he gave me a sidelong look. "Why haven't you been asking questions recently?"

"Ha! I knew it. You *do* like them."

He rolled his eyes and strolled toward the pool steps. "I did not say that."

I caught up to him and bumped his shoulder. "But you do."

"No, I just think it's weird, given how... persistent you've been."

I smirked at him as he led the way into the crystal-clear water that was the perfect cool contrast to the swiftly warming day. He totally missed them. We waded out until the water was chest-high.

I bided my time for him to get comfortable against the pool wall, then struck.

"You're right, seeing as how we have the whole place to ourselves for a bit, now's the perfect time to *dive* back into some questions."

He groaned and dropped his head back.

"Come on, just admit you like them." I splashed water at him, careful to stay out of reach, because he would absolutely dunk my ass given the opportunity.

"Fine, fine. They're not so bad," he said as he wiped his face. "Some of them are... interesting. Just, can we keep them to the silly ones? The day is so perfect, I'd hate to spoil it by traipsing down a shadowy memory lane."

Grinning wider than a Cheshire cat, I floated closer. "I'll do my best. But *you* have to try not to be so uptight about them. They're *fun.*"

"Yeah, yeah." He sent a half-hearted splash my way.

I rubbed my hands together gleefully. "Where to start? Ooh! I've been dying to ask this one for ages. You ever get hard over one of our teachers?"

"Jimmy!" he hissed, swiveling around to see if anyone was close enough to overhear. They weren't. Not by a mile.

"What? You can't honestly say you haven't. Mr. Metcalf was a silver fox, if I've ever seen one."

His mouth opened and closed a few times, while what was definitely not sunburn reddened his face. "He wasn't so bad. But mister," he mumbled over the name, "was a problem."

"Sorry, didn't quite catch that."

"Sharma. Mister Sharma," he huffed.

I raised both eyebrows. "Our fifth-grade teacher?"

He glared at me. "Look, we both know that it doesn't take much when you're that age."

I held up my hands. "No judgment from me. Just surprised. I suppose he did have a nice look to him. Is he how you knew you were gay?"

"What? No. I knew before that." He crossed his arms and har-rumphed.

"How *did* you know? I never asked when you came out. Didn't really seem like the thing to do." But I'd be lying if I didn't harbor at least a small hope that I was part of that revelation. Kind of like how he'd been part of mine.

He took a deep breath and dropped his defensive posture. "No, it wouldn't have been the thing. So, thanks for that. I don't know, I just did. Same way you knew you liked girls."

I doubted I'd ever get a better opportunity to come clean about my feelings for him or for men in general. Except his suddenly gloomy expression suggested we'd wandered a little away from silly. "Do you keep your socks on when you have sex?"

"Shouldn't you already know the answer to that?" He sent a wave of water crashing over my head.

I shook my hair out, spraying him with droplets and spluttering. "What can I say? I was a little distracted."

He snickered, clearly pleased with himself. "Not generally. Unless it's really fucking cold. Or I'm in a hurry." His playful gaze turned wicked, causing the hairs at the nape of my neck to stand on end.

I swallowed thickly and asked the first question that came to mind. "You ever have a crush on one of our mutual friends?"

"Uh, no." He pushed away from the wall to drift toward the center of the pool. "You?" he asked over his shoulder.

"Pretty sure you asking *me* questions wasn't part of the deal," I said, stalling for time as I followed in his wake, the ripples tickling my chest and arms. The universe was clearly trying to tell me something. But was I brave enough to listen? We'd gone this long. Sure, the sex was mind-blowing, and I was now officially at a loss for why he couldn't maintain a relationship longer than it took for paint to dry, but confessing the truth after all these years... Our friendship would change forever.

He spun in the water to face me. "Well? You going to answer or what? Ever have a thing for one of your friends?"

My thoughts tumbled over each other faster than I could grab them. Scenarios of what would happen if I came clean, if I didn't. I opened my mouth to respond, not entirely sure what would come out.

"Geronimo!" Mai shouted a moment before she hit the surface, sending water everywhere.

We didn't have a chance to recover from the impromptu cascade before Rafe followed, hot on her heels. "Woo!"

Mai's head popped up near us, sporting a shit-eating grin. "Glad to see we're not the only ones who can't resist a pool party."

"You've got that right. Check it out!" Rafe shook his hair free of water and pointed back toward Mr. Bouncer.

At some point during my questions, half, if not most, of the IF crew had shown up. People waved and chatted excitedly as they congregated around the pool and virtually mobbed the tiki bar, which was now staffed. An inflatable ball plunked down between us and Dill laughed as he sent it sailing. While he was distracted, I swam closer, channeling the stealth of a tiger shark. Once I was in range, I sank down, prepared to launch. I'd scarcely shifted my weight when Dylan spun around and forced me under the water.

I spluttered as I came back up and wiped my face. "Damn it. I thought I had you."

He drifted closer, and I braced for another assault. "Would have thought you'd learned your lesson this morning," he whispered, his eyes shining with malicious glee, before he dove under the water.

My face instantly heated with what was definitely *not* sunburn.

"You coming or what?" he shouted back.

I turned to find him bouncing a volleyball that had come out of nowhere and setting up with a group of others for a game of water volleyball. What in the holy hell was going on? With me? With him? I'd been completely prepared to handle his being weird. But nothing could have prepared me for *playful* Dylan. I glanced at him as I took up my position by the net.

He winked and tossed the ball straight up. "Serve!"

Chapter 14

Dylan

I PLACED A HAND at the small of Jimmy's back and leaned closer to be heard over the current conversation. It still boggled my mind how easy it was to go from getting his attention by touching his arm to using a more intimate gesture. But then we'd never really had any qualms about physical affection, public or otherwise.

He turned to look at me with that clownish grin of his, humor dancing in his eyes. "What's up?"

"I'm going to grab another drink. You want one?"

His eyes brightened even more, though I wasn't sure how that was possible. "Yes, please. One of those mango cocktail things if they still have them."

I pointed at Tricia, who'd been the one to bring the fruity con-coction to his attention and cost me my beer buddy. "This is all your fault," I said as I pushed away from the table.

"Thanks, babe," Jimmy crooned with a cheesy smile.

I rolled my eyes and leaned back down to press a kiss to his temple. "Yeah, yeah. Just no embarrassing stories while I'm gone."

"No promises." He smirked, and it was all I could do not to shake my head.

"You two are hashtag relationship goals," Susan said.

"You're making the rest of us look bad," Rafe added, squeezing his wife and making her giggle.

Damn right we were. See, I could totally do the fake relationship thing. Like it was hard. Feeling rather smug, I made my way to the tiki bar, grateful to be wearing shorts. Over the last couple of hours, many people had wandered off to their rooms and changed clothes before returning to enjoy the rest of the night. And while I wouldn't admit it to his face, I was glad Jimmy had talked me into doing the same. My swim shorts might have been relatively comfortable, but not sit and talk for hours comfortable.

The bar was every bit as popular now as it was when it opened, though at least it didn't look like it was being mobbed now. They also appeared sufficiently stocked with the "mango thing". I waited patiently for the line to thin, then took my place at the counter. The bartender tilted her chin in my direction to acknowledge me, then returned to finishing up with the couple before her. A hand landed solidly on my left shoulder, and I turned to see who it was. To my surprise, Chase stepped up beside me.

"Wells, how are you doing? Enjoying the retreat?" he asked, releasing his firm grip.

I shifted to rest against the counter and face him. "Doing great, sir. I've heard people talk about what an amazing opportunity being invited is, but this is far beyond anything I could have imagined. IF really goes all out."

"Glad to hear it. What about James? Is he enjoying himself as well?" His brow furrowed with concern. "Not feeling left out?"

I snorted. "Jimmy? He's having a blast. Doesn't hurt that he's never met a stranger." I nodded toward the table where I'd left him holding several of my colleagues and their partners enthralled. "Can't take him anywhere."

Chase laughed good-naturedly, then his face took on a slightly more serious expression. "I was wondering if I could steal you away for a few minutes. There were a couple of things I wanted to run past you."

"Um, sure. I mean, of course. Jimmy will be fine without a drink for a little longer." I nearly swallowed my tongue to get it to stop flapping and betraying my sudden spike of nerves.

Chase smiled encouragingly and clapped me on the shoulder once more. "You're a good man, Wells. Why don't we step to the side for a bit of privacy?" He glanced around, then leaned in conspiratorially. "Can't have the missus knowing we're talking shop."

I chuckled nervously and let him steer me away from the crowd. We continued to wander farther away until we stopped by a small cluster of empty chairs partially obscured by cultivated hedges.

"What did you want to talk to me about, sir? Is everything alright? I confess, I haven't been checking the markets everyday like I normally would. Jimmy's been..." Distracting. "Insistent," I finished instead.

"Relax, Wells. You're not being singled out for anything negative. I make a point to speak one-on-one with all the IF attendees."

"Right. Of course." I let out a breath, though I wasn't sure if his explanation made me feel better or worse. I shoved my hands in my pockets so I wouldn't be tempted to fidget and forced my shoulders to relax. I'd delivered data analyses to board rooms filled with some of the most influential business people in the country. I could talk to the CEO of Infinity Financial without losing my cool.

"What I'm most interested in is learning about your goals—personal and professional. We can start with what you'd like to be doing with Infinity Financial. Or somewhere else," he added with a shrug.

I blanched. "I love my job, truly. Since I started a few years back, it's never even crossed my mind to look for somewhere else."

"Easy there." Chase held up his hands. "I'm not implying that you might be looking to jump ship. It's good to know you enjoy working at IF, but for argument's sake, if you weren't entirely happy, the company has connections and subsidiaries. Supporting talent when we find it is a cornerstone of our business model."

"Oh." My ears heated with chagrin.

"I want you to be honest with me. Tell me about your goals and ambitions. For example, how open are you to relocating?" He pulled one of the pool chairs closer and sat, gesturing for me to do the same.

"If I'm being honest, I enjoy living in Charlotte. I've worked hard to make a life for myself there, even bought a house. It's not much by some standards, but it's mine. Plus, Jimmy started at a new mental health clinic and has only recently got his bearings there." I let out a slow breath. "All that's to say, much as I would relish the opportunity, if any sort of... movement within the company is contingent upon relocating to a different region, I'm content with where I am."

That was a bold statement, and one I hadn't realized I held so strongly until Chase had asked. If Jimmy were here, that would have come out way smoother. Who was I kidding? If he were here, he'd be kicking me for essentially torpedoing what might be the greatest opportunity of my career. Oh, God, I was gonna be sick. I resisted the urge to swallow.

Chase nodded. "I appreciate your frankness. The team at Raleigh speaks very highly of you and the work you've done over the years. It's also refreshing that you include consideration for your partner. Sadly, the financial sector sees so many 'yes-people', it can be difficult to deduce genuine motivation." Given his tone, it wasn't hard to deduce how he felt about that. Maybe I hadn't ruined everything because I didn't want to leave Raleigh.

"As I said before, we want our people to be happy, thriving. I think we can do a little better than 'content'." Chase winked, and I couldn't help but smile. When I joined Infinity Financial as a Retirement Specialist five years ago, I'd known they were a good company, but I never could have fathomed this level of support.

"I suppose we can."

"Excellent." Chase clapped his hands together and leaned forward intently. "Tell me what it is about your current position that you enjoy. Are there parts you wish you could do more of, or any skills that you feel are being underutilized? And don't try being humble. Remember, you're here because we already know how incredible you are. This is your chance to brag about the things *you* find important."

It took me a second to pull my head back together after it exploded. "I... well, I... I wouldn't know where to start."

He clapped a hand on my knee. "Don't be shy, Wells. Or do I need to get Jimmy over here to brag for you?" Chase gave me a knowing look.

I chuckled. "He is pretty good at talking me up to anyone who will listen." And hadn't that been true our whole lives? Sometimes I wondered what I'd ever done to deserve such a stalwart friend. But that was a question for another time. Right now, the CEO of Infinity Financial was waiting for me to toot my own horn. "Whoo, okay. What I enjoy most in my current role is combing through the data, especially historical data, and finding patterns where others only see random points. Uncovering what connects 'isolated incidents' so that we can better anticipate them in the future."

"Yes, I've read some of your reports. Your attention to detail is inspiring, and you have a knack for conveying information without leaning too heavily on industry jargon. It makes the information more accessible to our clients, no matter their level of investing expertise."

"Thank you. That's... Wow. That's high praise."

Chase shook his head. "Just call it like I see it. How about some of your other skills? Regional Director Langdon mentioned how well you handled things when she was unexpectedly out last year."

"Truthfully, I didn't realize how comfortable I'd be leading the team like that, but there wasn't time to doubt myself. We were days away from consolidating a smaller local firm. Trial by fire, if you will." I smiled because I really had enjoyed taking charge like that. More impressively, the rest of the team had run with it, and the merger had gone off without a hitch.

"That's some impressive leadership. Not many would have been willing to step up like that."

I struggled to maintain a modicum of professionalism and not do something as heinous as squirm beneath his penetrating gaze. "I wasn't about to let Margaret and the team down, not after we'd put in so much hard work to prepare."

Chase scowled. "What did I say about being modest? Yes, the Raleigh office is a gifted, competent staff. Could they have managed without you? Probably. But what matters is that they didn't have to discover if they could. You took initiative. That in itself is a valuable skill." He held my gaze until I nodded, and he mirrored the movement. "One more question, and you can fetch those drinks. I'm sure James—Jimmy—is beginning to wonder where you've gotten to."

I chuckled. "I'm mostly sure he won't send out a search party. Mostly."

"You two are a good match. Your foundation as lifelong friends has clearly benefited your romantic relationship. Inspiring, really. Have you two given any consideration to..." Chase smiled conspiratorially and gestured vaguely, "tying the knot?"

The modicum of ease I'd acquired vanished, much like the breeze we'd been enjoying. Marry? Jimmy? The last time I'd "considered" anything remotely close to marriage had been when I'd been with Kennedy. After that epic disaster, I not only avoided anything remotely related to matrimony but also any kind of serious relationship that *might* lead to that kind of talk. I just wasn't the marrying type. That's all there was to it.

"You okay, Wells? I apologize if I put you on the spot."

I needed to pull it together, remain calm. Wasn't like we were completely lying about our relationship status or that marriage between me and my straight friend was literally ever going to happen. I cleared my throat as quietly as I could and straightened. "No, it's fine. You did say you wanted to know about personal goals as well. As for... that, I can honestly say that is not a conversation we've had."

"Understandable. I believe you mentioned earlier in the week that this evolution of your friendship was fairly new."

If Chase had heard that—*remembered* that—what else had he noticed? Did he know it was all fake? Was he waiting for me to admit it? What would Jimmy do? I racked my brain while seconds slugged by. He'd focus on facts. "Evolution is a great way to put it. We're taking things one day at a time and not worrying about tomorrow. As impossible as it sounds, even after all these years, we're still learning things about each other." Like Jimmy could seduce anyone with a massage. Or the maddening whine he'd made when I'd first tasted his ass. And apparently, I kept my dating life locked down in Fort Knox.

"Like I said, an inspiration. Right, I won't dance about it any further." Chase leaned forward, and all the blood that had rushed to my face at the mention of tying the knot raced to my toes. "Where would you like to be within the company?"

For a hot second, my mind was irritatingly blank. I'd come to the retreat for a career-launching promotion, but it was for others, like Chase, to decide what that promotion would be. Jimmy was gonna murder me if he found out I didn't actually have any roles in mind when I talked him into being my hype man. "Are we still being honest?"

"Of course." He gestured for me to go on.

"I hadn't thought about it much. As far as an actual role is concerned," I quickly amended. "There are so many avenues in IF, it'd be difficult to pinpoint just one. If I were to disseminate it down to the day-to-day tasks, that might be of more use. I enjoyed taking the lead and have found a few opportunities since then to organize teams. It felt... natural, and it's a skill I'd like to continue developing. I'm good at understanding people's talents and strengths, then directing them where they'll have the most impact. I don't think I'll ever truly leave trend analysis behind, as it was my first love in the financial world, but I believe I'm ready for a challenge."

Chase rubbed his chin while he gave me a thoughtful look. Mentally, I berated myself. Of all the things Jimmy and I had practiced, why hadn't it occurred to me to do an interview role-play?

He smacked his hands on his bare knees and pushed up. I followed suit and took his hand in a firm shake.

"You've given me quite a bit to think about. I've appreciated your candor, but I don't want to keep you much longer." He released my hand and tilted his head back the way we'd come. "Go get your man a drink. We'll catch up more later."

"Thank you, sir."

He released my hand, and I wandered in a daze of insecurity back to the bar. Had I done all right? Was Chase disappointed in my "candor"? He was likely used to employees fawning over him and having a list of jobs they'd love to secure. But that wasn't me. Never had been. Was he onto our ruse?

"Hey, you. Get lost?" Jimmy asked as he joined me at the counter.

I blinked as I realized I'd just been standing there without placing an order. "Sorry, Chase wanted to have a private word."

A strange darkness flitted across Jimmy's normally jovial face. "Did he make a pass at you?"

"He wanted to talk to me about my goals within the company. Like an informal interview."

"Huh. And he needed to do that out of sight from everyone?"

The argument was on the tip of my tongue when my thoughts flashed to Chase's hand on my shoulder, then on my knee. I hadn't detected any romantic or even sexual vibes from him, but I'd been wrong before. "Why are you so convinced he's interested in me like that?"

Jimmy didn't deign to answer. He flagged the bartender, securing himself another mango cocktail and a beer for me. He passed me my drink and led the way to a now empty table where he took a seat beneath the umbrella. "Well, how did it go?"

I sank into the wicker chair with a heavy sigh. "Not sure. He wanted to know what I liked about my job, skills I wanted to exercise." I glanced at him out of the corner of my eye. "If I'd be up for relocating."

He froze, the straw of his drink millimeters from his lips, his gaze transfixed on me. "What did you say?"

"I told him I was happy with the life I'd built in Raleigh and wasn't all that interested in uprooting it." I tried to give him a reassuring smile, but the weight of the moment seemed to be holding it down. I cleared my throat and used reaching for my beer as an excuse to shift around. "Anyway, I probably screwed it all up. No doubt he intentionally grabs people when they least expect it, so they fumble all over themselves." And ask questions guaranteed to put you off guard, like whether you intend to marry your best friend. My drink turned into chugging half the bottle before I set it back down.

Jimmy placed a hand on my forearm, and I reluctantly looked at him. "Hey, I'm sure you did fine. You're probably right about the ambush tactic, but I think it's more to get unrehearsed responses than to intentionally trip you up."

"You're right. I know you're right. It's just... you *know* how awful I am when it comes to talking about myself or my job or, fuck, a job I want." I groaned and pinched the bridge of my nose. At the harsh scrape of chair legs on concrete, I glanced up from my misery only to get an eyeful of Jimmy right before he plopped himself in my lap. "What are—"

He looped his arms around my neck and leaned in so that his mouth was right beside my ear. "Shh, shh. This is less conspicuous than whispering across the table. You are *amazing*, Dylan Wells. You've never encountered a problem you couldn't fix.

Everyone here knows what a rock star you are. No matter what comes of that interview, every single person here appreciates getting to work with you."

I swallowed hard, then wrapped my arms around Jimmy before burying my head into his shoulder and squeezing him close. The sex had been both unexpected and incredible, but this... I didn't ever want to lose this.

Chapter 15

Jimmy

Everyone held their breath as Mai pulled free the oversized wooden block with agonizing slowness. The tower swayed, and the tension cranked up another notch. I sipped my latest mango cocktail before passing it to Dylan, who drank it without even looking. She chanced a victorious smile as the piece came free. No sooner had she held it up though than the whole construct came tumbling down with a crash.

"Damn it. I totally thought I had that," Mai huffed and tossed her losing piece on the ground to join the others.

Those gathered laughed good-naturedly. Not one of us had actually managed to "win". I blamed the free-flowing alcohol. A glance around revealed several other clusters of IF people playing their own yard games: cornhole, ax throwing (with a plastic ax), giant Connect Four, yard pins. I turned my focus back to Dylan, who unabashedly had commandeered what remained of my drink. His smile shone in his blue eyes and seemed to infect everyone around him. Or maybe that was just me. My face was starting to hurt from smiling so much.

Out of the corner of my eye, I spotted Marcus nod. A quick search discovered that he was nodding at Chase. My grin slipped slightly. Dylan was adamant that Chase hadn't made a pass at him, but he clearly couldn't see how Chase watched him. I placed a hand on Dill's thigh to get his attention, then nodded toward the CEO, who was moving to take center-stage such as it was. One by one, people caught on that something was up and turned to investigate. There were still a few players intent on their respective games when Marcus stepped up beside Chase.

"We're glad to see everyone is having a good time, but it's time to mix up the festivities." Marcus glanced at Chase.

"I know we've made a point to avoid *too much* shop talk." Collective laughter flitted around the pool. "Yeah, yeah, I know. Financial professionals are the *worst* when it comes to work-life balance."

Dylan shifted beside me to lean into my side, and I placed a hand on his hip. As much as I'd tried to comfort him after his "chat" with Chase, I could tell it was still bothering him. On a whim, I planted a kiss on the side of his head, and he seemed to relax.

"We've put together a sort of decathlon to test your industry knowledge," Marcus picked up.

Excited chatter sprang up among the IF employees, and Dylan stepped away. The rest of us "plus ones" shared anxious looks and nervous laughter. Even after *years* of listening to Dill break down financial trends and explain what he did at his job, there was no way I could contribute.

Chase held up his hands. "We've also added general trivia to make it fun for everyone. Now, rules for gameplay. You'll be in teams of four and must complete a task at each tent before moving on. That means no skipping around if you get stuck. Questions and puzzles will be similar for each team, but none will be repeated. So if any of you were thinking of piggybacking off another team's answers, think again." He gave everyone a meaningful look that just as quickly dissolved into a grin. "You'll have two minutes to pick your teams. When the air horn sounds, those to the left of the tiki bar will take the path there, and those to the right, the path behind me."

I looked around to get oriented. A pair of tiki torches highlighted each of the aforementioned paths, along with a resort staff member.

"First team to finish will win bragging rights! Oh, and a goodie bag that includes brand new tablets." The resulting cheers nearly drowned out his next words. "Your two minutes start now!"

Chaos erupted as people scrambled to create their ideal teams. I was trying to make sense of the madness when someone grabbed me around the middle and jerked me backward.

"You'll be on my team, won't you, babe?" Dill crooned in my ear before nibbling at the side of my neck.

Goosebumps pricked my skin, and I squirmed in his grip. "I *never* should have told you about that."

He laughed. "You told me about it when you were seventeen. *Now* I just know it's not an exaggeration."

"You're the worst." I twisted around to give him my best scowl.

He pouted. "Does that mean you won't be on my team?"

I huffed and rolled my eyes. "Why would you want me to be? I'll only hold you back."

"You've never held me back, Jimmy," he said with a sincerity I hadn't expected.

I wanted to say something, look away, *blink* for fuck's sake, but I was very much caught in his intense blue gaze and falling. My heart fluttered with the truth. No, not falling, fallen. I didn't have a crush on my best friend. I was absolutely in love with him. Panic that I prayed didn't show on my face swirled in my chest. This was bad. This was really, really bad. And I *still* couldn't look away.

The spell faltered when his focus flicked to something over my shoulder, then returned. He placed a kiss on the side of my mouth, and I finally blinked. "I'm still waiting for an answer. You with me?"

Obstinately, my brain refused to supply the answer he was looking for, far too preoccupied with the dozens of others filling my head. Topping the tumbling list was when the hell had this happened, closely followed by what the fuck was I going to do. This was a *fake* relationship. We weren't together, not the way my heart believed we were, the way we should be. Shit shit shit shit shit.

"Always," I finally said, though my voice sounded broken. Why the fuck hadn't I told him the truth when I had a chance? Or, even better, years ago, like a real friend would have?

"If y'all are going to be doing that the whole time, I'm finding another team," Tina declared, effectively snatching my attention to the present.

He squeezed me tighter against his chest with a laugh directed at Tina. "We'll do our best to behave."

A few stragglers beyond us were still looking for teams to join. Abruptly, Stephan and Colleen raced for us.

"I win!" Colleen shouted as she skidded into our little cluster. Stephan groaned and spun to find another team.

Dylan leaned past me to high-five Colleen and Tina. "I'd say we've got the best of the best, wouldn't you?" Before anyone could answer, the short blast of a foghorn split the air, and it became a mad scramble as people tried to remember which way to go. I really shouldn't have been surprised that Dylan already had a heading, given how competitive he could be. He grabbed my hand and started dragging me while I flailed to snag the others.

By the time we pulled up in front of a tent, we were laughing and breathing hard from our impromptu sprint, and, most importantly, I'd shoved down my personal crisis of feeling. Two buzzer buttons sat on a long folding table with a resort staff member on the other side. Within seconds, another team stumbled in beside us.

"I'll ask three questions. Best two out of three advances. Loser waits for the next team," the guy said.

We shared looks with the other group. "Bring it!" Tina shouted, pushing to the forefront, her hand poised above the buzzer. Someone from the other team followed suit, and we waited for the first question.

The guy referred to his cards. "What year was Infinity Financial founded?"

Tina smashed the buzzer. "Nineteen seventy-nine!"

"Correct." He flipped to the next card. "What was the first country Infinity Financial expanded to?"

There was a collective pause as both our group and the other shared looks and attempted to confer quietly. We were still stuck between the UK and Dylan's insistence it was France when the other team's buzzer sounded.

"Japan!"

"Correct." Another card flip. "Name the first stock Infinity Financial ever traded."

"I know this one!" Colleen shouted. She lurched forward and smashed the buzzer. "Boston Properties."

The guy paused. "Correct. You advance."

We whooped and raced for the next tent, which turned out to be a memory card game. After getting out-stripped by one team, we got all of our cards matched and moved on. This tent had a banner that read, "Name the ticker" and a whiteboard.

Dylan snagged a marker and hurriedly scribbled answers to the five companies listed on our side.

The poor woman monitoring the tent referenced her answer card and squinted at the mess of letters. "Ugh…"

I stomped forward. "Give me that. How is it that after all these years, your handwriting has gotten *worse*?" I translated his writing into something more legible, ignoring the face Dill was making to look at the woman. She gave a thumbs-up, and we were off.

The next few tents didn't pose much of a challenge for our team. I was basically an expert with movie quotes, Colleen had a secret skill for ring toss, Tina had some of the fastest reflexes I'd ever seen and a disturbing knowledge of corporate mergers, and Dylan knew more about stocks and IF's corporate structure than any one person had any business knowing.

At last, we ran into the final tent, which already had five other teams struggling to complete their picture puzzles. Each team had several tiles and a magnetic board, but upon further inspection, the images were all lines and curves with a faint grid-like background.

Our team huddled around our table. "Is it supposed to be an outline of something?" Colleen asked.

"Maybe it spells something," Tina ventured.

I scratched my chin. "Could be one of those negative-image optical illusions. What do you think?" I glanced at Dill, who was frowning at the pieces and moving them around on the table. "Dylan?"

He looked up, but barely spared me a glance before his gaze slid past me to the other teams and their equal lack of progress.

"We all have different puzzles," I reminded him.

"Oh, fudge," Colleen dismayed, dropping the two tiles she'd been fiddling with to clatter on the table.

Dylan looked back down at the sound, and his brow furrowed. "I know this." He picked up a tile with what I'd come to recognize as a ticker symbol with a "1Y 1D" beside it, then set it at the top left of our magnetic board.

"What?" Tina asked as he reached for one tile, then another.

He placed several on the magnetic board, swiveled a couple and replaced another before smirking. Apparently satisfied with the nonsensical image coming together, he grabbed more tiles, studying each one intently before placing it haphazardly on the board.

"Uh, Dill?" I scooted closer. "Whatchya got, babe?"

He glanced up, his eyes alight with excitement. "It's a graph."

I shared a look with Tina and Colleen, who appeared equally baffled.

"More specifically, it's an Impulse Study," he said matter of fact.

Tina stared at him in amazement. "You can tell that just by looking at it?"

He shrugged and continued placing tiles, each one snapping into place faster than the one before as he found his stride. "Yeah. Look at the colors. You've got bearish, neutral, and bullish. I don't use this particular study very frequently, but it's hard to miss. Now that one," he subtly angled his head at our neighboring team and dropped his voice, "pretty sure that's an Elegant Oscillator. I'd have figured it out sooner if we'd had that one or even an Elliot." In a final definitive move, he snapped in the last tile and stepped back, revealing a graph that made no more sense to me put together than it had apart. "Done."

The other obviously stumped teams glanced over at where Dylan had solved the impossible in a matter of minutes. All of a sudden, their flurry of movement resumed, only to be cut short by another blast from the foghorn.

"We have a winner!" Marcus exclaimed, walking into the tent along with Chase. As they passed, Chase clapped Dylan on the shoulder and winked. My hackles rose, and I instinctively took a step closer to Dill.

"We do?" Tina asked absently from where she was still scrutinizing the colorful graph.

"We do!" Colleen shouted, grabbing Dylan's and my hands and lifting them into the air. Tina spun around, the meaning of the declaration finally sinking in, and threw her arms up with a loud whoop.

I smiled at Dill, basking in the way he shone. That man really did love winning. It wasn't even about the four baskets that got carted out and passed to each of us. While Tina and Colleen dove into their prizes, my focus remained on Dylan as first Marcus, then Chase congratulated him on his swift deduction of the puzzle. My heart gave a painful squeeze. I was so freaking proud of him. He didn't need me to hype him up or even talk to people. He did that all on his own. And I loved that about him. Loved. Because I was one hundred percent in love with him.

He flashed me a smile, and I dug deep to return it. Judging by the hint of concern that darkened his eyes, though, it wasn't as convincing as I needed it to be. He shook Marcus's and Chase's hands one more time, then tucked his prize basket under his arm. "You okay?"

"Pfft, totally." I waved a hand to dismiss his worry as unfounded.

He stepped closer, invading my personal bubble, so he could whisper without being overheard. "Hey, don't do that. If something is bothering you, then it's bothering me. Is this you thinking that you didn't contribute enough? Because that's bullshit."

I ducked my head and barked a laugh. "You got me. I was totally the dead weight on this team. But you," I chucked his arm, "you're a badass."

"Well, yeah, but so are you."

I blinked rapidly to clear the sudden, *very* unwanted moisture in my eyes. My heart really couldn't take this. "Who's therapizing who, now?"

"Shut up." He bumped me with his shoulder, then wrapped an arm around my waist. "If it's alright with the rest of you, I think we're going to explore these back in our room." He angled the prize basket up for emphasis.

I offered an awkward wave that no one really seemed to notice. Half of the teams had returned to adamantly attempting to decipher the tiles of random lines, while the other half had begun to disperse. Dylan led the way back into the resort proper with an urgency I struggled to keep up with. By the time we reached the room and he'd keyed it open, I was at a complete loss. Surely, my sudden bout of "insecurity" hadn't made him leave the party. What kind of shit friend would I be if that were the case?

"Here, give me that." He took my all but forgotten prize basket from me and set it beside his. I was about to ask what was up when he spun around and caught me in a kiss that pressed me into the wall and stole the words. He laughed awkwardly when he pulled away. "Sorry, I just needed an outlet. I can't believe we won. And don't you dare say you didn't help. We couldn't have done it without you. *I* couldn't have done it without you."

I scanned his face. Outlet? I could be an outlet. Before doubt could creep in, I surged forward to recapture his mouth.

He made a muffled sound of surprise, but rather than push me away, he kissed me back, his tongue darting past my lips. "So much mango," he mumbled between nipping and sucking at my lips.

"Stop complaining that I taste good."

He chuckled and slipped a hand past my waistband to grip my ass.

I mentally snickered. And he thought not wearing a belt was a bad idea. I ground against him already half hard and loving that he was as well. I'd worry about what my feelings meant for our friendship later. Right now, he was all in on getting our freak on, and I was right there with him.

"Wait. Wait," he gasped, pulling out of the latest kiss.

Or maybe not. Anxiety crashed over me like a bucket of ice water. Maybe we weren't on the same page. This whole adventure was a horrible mistake. I never should have indulged my crush, and I definitely shouldn't have encouraged him to cross so many lines with me.

"Stop looking at me like I just stole your last candy bar on Halloween. I'm just trying to say I don't have any more condoms. Which, admittedly, really sucks, given how horny I am."

I couldn't help but laugh at the unexpected twist in our predicament. "You really only had *one* condom in your wallet? What the hell kind of bachelor are you?"

He echoed my laugh as he took a step back and ran his hands through his hair. "The kind that wasn't expecting to have sex on this trip. Especially not with..."

Me, I silently filled in for him.

He groaned and scrubbed at his face before reaching down to rearrange himself. "Probably for the best. We've been drinking and... I'll just take a cold shower. A *really* cold shower," he added under his breath, stepping toward the bathroom.

"Hold on." I met him in the middle of the room, careful to ensure his path to the bathroom had to go through me. "We've already established that, booze or no booze, we're fine with this."

There was no missing the wariness in his eyes when he looked back at me. "What are you thinking?"

I leaned forward to taste his lips and dropped my voice. "That there's still plenty we can do to... scratch that itch that doesn't involve a condom."

"I'm listening."

"Good," I said, slipping my hands beneath his shirt and pushing it up. It had scarcely cleared his head when his mouth was back on mine. I hummed my appreciation of his exploration and threaded my fingers through his chest hair. "Question for you."

He laughed. "Of course, you have questions. I'm assuming they're exceptionally inappropriate, or you'd have asked earlier in the pool."

"Maybe." I shrugged and curled my fingers. I couldn't get over how soft the hair was.

"Let's hear them then."

"How do you feel about guys petting your fur?"

He frowned. "My what?"

I raised an eyebrow and ran both my hands up his chest until I could tweak a nipple.

"Ow. Easy with those pincers. It's nice, but I've never been with anyone who was super preoccupied with it. Or called it my fur," he added with a laugh.

I nodded. There was a first time for everything. I was *definitely* preoccupied. "What about you with other guys? You like 'em just as hairy?"

He chuckled, making my fingertips vibrate. "I don't seek out extra hairy guys, if that's what you're asking."

"So... twinks?"

"I'd rather avoid the drama, thank you. It might not be all of them, but in my experience, twinks can be high maintenance and eat drama for breakfast. I'll take my men average."

I snorted, none too quietly. If Dylan attracted "average" men, then I was short. I placed a trail of kisses along his neck, relishing in the way his throat bobbed beneath my tongue. "Another one for you. You ever choke going down on a guy?"

As I'd hoped, Dill choked. I leaned back to give him room to clear his airway. Once he could breathe again, he glared at me. "You did that on purpose. And yes, once or twice, but I have no delusions about my lack of deep-throating skills."

"Not quite your jam?" I teased, leaning heavily into the innuendo.

"What is wrong with you?" he asked, but it was hard to hear any censure in it, considering he was laughing.

"Did you want that alphabetically or by severity?" I re-closed the distance between us. "So... what's it like? Giving head, obviously. I know what getting it is like." From either sex. Not that Dylan knew that. But he didn't need to. Eventually. I owed him that. But not right now. That was tomorrow-Jimmy's problem.

"You're seriously asking?"

"No, I'm messing with you. Of course, I'm seriously asking." I trailed my lips along his neck again, if only to feel him swallow. "Well? Details."

"It's, um... it's different for everyone, I guess. I mean, I know," he quickly corrected. "Some guys are really into it, prefer it over penetration. No shade. To each their own."

I nodded along as he spoke while I traced the veins and muscles in his neck with the tip of my tongue.

His breath hitched, and to my delight, he swallowed hard. "It's just one of those things."

"Good point," I murmured, reaching for his fly and releasing it with an ease he thankfully didn't question.

"What is?" he asked, before tilting my chin to catch me with a searing kiss.

"If I want my question to be answered, I'll have to answer it for myself." I hooked his briefs with my thumbs and pushed them down with his shorts. By some miracle, I didn't ogle how his swollen cock jutted out from its perfect nest of golden curls, but kept my gaze fixed on his face as I wrapped my hand around his length.

His eyelids fluttered, and he let out a low moan. "Jimmy."

I slowly kissed my way down his torso, resisting the urge to rub my face against his chest. "Hmm?"

"You don't... This is... Have you done this before?"

There it was again, another chance to come clean about my sexuality. While I was at it, I could confess that I'd wanted to do this with him for practically ever. But I wasn't willing to sacrifice this perfect moment and risk his fury. Because he *would* be furious. "I'm the one asking the questions, remember?" I gave his length a decisive stroke, and he nodded. "If you're so worried I'll do it wrong, then you should tell me what to do." I lifted one eyebrow in challenge, then closed my mouth over his once more. When

I pulled away, I was pleased to find only lust shining in the blue depths of his eyes.

"You... You're..."

"I'm what?"

"Still standing."

With his hand on my shoulder to encourage me, I sank to my knees. Then waited for him to finish kicking his shorts aside to ensure we were on the same page.

"Are you suuuuuure?" he tried to ask, the final word devolving into a moan as I mouthed his balls.

Rather than answer, I traded my mouth for my hand and greedily licked up his shaft again and again, like I could commit every contour, every vein to memory with my tongue. Then I teased his tip, running my tongue along the slit, before pulling back his foreskin and easing him into my mouth. I moaned around him, already addicted to the way his dick throbbed.

"Jesus," he gasped, dropping his head back while he slipped his fingers through my hair.

As much as I loved feeling a guy harden in my hand or on my tongue, I absolutely loved it when they put their hands in my hair. I made a pleased hum and bobbed my head, causing him to elicit another moan. I gave up my hold on his balls to cup his ass.

"Look at me," he said huskily. Unable to deny him anything, I opened my eyes and groaned at the intense look that awaited me. He brought his free hand to the side of my face and used his thumb to trace my lips. "That mouth of yours looks even prettier stretched around my cock than I imagined."

My eyelids fluttered, but I couldn't bring myself to look away from the sheer adoration beaming down on me. I licked the bottom of his shaft and his fingers tightened in my hair. Just the weight of him on my tongue was making me lightheaded.

"That's it. You're doing so good." He rocked his hips, leisurely fucking into my mouth. "Just relax your jaw. Yeah," he sighed, "exactly like that."

I attempted to meet his thrusts, and he pulled back until he popped free. Worried I'd done something wrong, I glanced up at him again.

"Easy. I'm not a fan of gagging. Understood?"

At a loss for words, all I could do was nod.

"Good, boy. Now open." I did as he said without a second thought, and he guided my head back to his glistening cock. "Fuck," he hissed as he resumed thrusting slowly into my mouth. "You feel so good. So warm and wet." He pressed his lips together and moaned as I twirled my tongue around him with each stroke. "You're doing so damn good. Such a gift."

I'd never considered I might have a praise kink before, but Dylan's words washing over me were sending me higher than I thought possible. As it was, my dick was straining painfully against my cargo shorts. But I couldn't bring myself to do anything about it, because that would mean I'd have to stop touching Dill.

His rhythm picked up, and he gave up tracing my mouth to bury both hands in my hair. "God, you feel good. That's it. You're doing so good taking me." He dropped his head back once more as he continued to use my mouth, and we groaned in tandem. "Fuck, I'm getting close. Fuuuuck. Don't want it to end." Despite his declaration, he didn't stop moving or even slow.

He plunged in and out until my jaw ached and tears spilled from the corners of my eyes. But I was right there with him. I didn't want this to end. Not this moment. Not this week. Not any of it.

"So close." He looked down at me. "Can I come on your face?"

With his cock still stretching my lips, I nodded, lightly squeezing his thigh to underscore the yes.

He pulled out of my mouth and started fisting himself in earnest. But he didn't close his eyes or look away. Not even when he grunted, and I felt the first drop of cum land on my cheek. He continued to milk his cock until every last bit of his release decorated my face. I'd never been harder in my life, and it had nothing to do with how hot that just was, and everything to do with the look of reverence in Dylan's blue eyes.

I felt lost in my body, completely untethered. The weight of my wet lashes was disorienting. The slight sting of my lips from being stretched so long barely registered. Even my aching dick seemed to belong to someone else. There was only Dylan and the way he was looking at me right now. That and the knowledge that I was well and truly gone. There was no way I could go back to the way things were before, not now that I *knew*.

Dylan dropped to his knees before me and cradled my face. "Hey, you still with me?" he asked softly.

Too delirious to form words, and torn between a bottomless abyss of despair and the highest of highs, I blinked.

"It's okay. I'm right here. Let's take your shirt off." He used the soft fabric to gently wipe my face clean, steadily cooing to me the whole while. "Have you ever heard of being cum drunk before? Sucking your first dick can do that to you." He chuckled.

I blinked. I'd heard of it. Maybe seen it, but never experienced it firsthand. But that definitely wasn't my first dick, not even my fifth. But it was Dylan's. And it was Dylan holding me, caring for me in a way I'd been terrified most of my life to admit I wanted. There was no hiding from it anymore.

"Yeah, I think that might be it." He tilted my head up to look at him. "Feeling a little floaty?"

By some miracle, I managed the barest of nods.

"You'll be okay. I'm going to take care of you."

I heard the zipper before I felt the fabric around my waist shift. Then Dylan's hand wrapped around the steel spike my dick had become, and I made a strangled sound at the back of my throat. He brushed his lips along the side of my mouth before leaning back to add some spit for an easier glide. I shuddered in his hold as he slowly stroked me.

"That's it. Just relax and let me take care of you." He closed his mouth over mine and lavished me with kisses, every bit as slow and deliberate as his strokes. His grip tightened at the same time as his fist sped up. Then his mouth was on my neck, nibbling, kissing, licking.

I lurched beneath the onslaught, clawing first into his shoulders, then tangling my hands in his hair. "Dylan," I moaned, no longer in charge of my body, merely at the whim of whatever he wanted to do to it. "Fuck. God. Dill." At some point, I'd started rocking into him. Between the friction and the torture of kisses on my sensitive neck, it felt like every synapse in my brain was misfiring. All I could do was hold on tighter.

He placed a kiss on my throat. "You gonna come for me?"

"Yeah," I replied breathlessly.

"Yeah? You gonna show me how good you feel?"

"Uh-huh," I whined as I fucked into his hand, meeting him stroke for stroke while he sucked on my neck and continued to whisper an endless litany of praise in my ear. I groaned hard, the buildup of sensation close to a precipice.

"That's it. Come for me."

At the quiet command, my whole body tensed, then my release rushed through me with such force that it decorated both our chests and even hit my chin. I was still groaning through it when Dill's mouth captured mine. By the time he released me from the owning kiss, the floaty feeling had returned with a vengeance, and I collapsed against him like the overcooked noodle I'd become.

He peppered my face and shoulders with light brushes of his lips. "You did so good. So proud of you."

There was that praise kink again, surprising me with tingles that felt like being lifted by thousands of fireflies. I tried to say something, but all that came out was an undignified whimper. We officially had a problem. I was head over heels in love with my best friend, and I had no idea what to do about it. In just a couple of days, we'd be back in Charlotte, back to *reality*. Me back to my serial monogamy and him back to his meaningless flings. And... and I couldn't bear it. I held him tighter, trying to say with my body what I couldn't find the words to express.

Dylan ran his hand down my back in a constant, soothing motion. "There you go. What do you say we get ourselves cleaned up?"

"Mm hmm," I mumbled into his neck.

"Okay. Up we go."

In an awkward effort that rivaled the time we accidentally ate an entire bag of edibles and wandered into a ditch, we managed to stand. Of course, what made it awkward and nearly impossible was that I refused to relinquish my hold on him. It wasn't until he pushed me beneath the warm spray that any sort of cognizance returned to me.

"Dill?"

"Shh. It's okay. Let me take care of you." His arms slipped around my torso, and whatever it was I wanted to say flitted away to join the rapidly building steam.

The rest of the impromptu shower was filled with his soft encouragements and continued words of praise. Once he had us both clean, he helped me dry off, then guided us to the bed. I crawled beneath the sheets, every inch of my body feeling as over-sensitized as my raw feelings, and waited for him to do the same.

He fished out our phones and plugged them in to charge. Then he turned off the bathroom and front lights, plunging the room into abrupt darkness. By the time my eyes adjusted, he was slipping beneath the covers. Once he settled, I scooted closer, sliding my leg over his and reaching to place a hand on his chest.

To my surprise, his arm was open and waiting. Once I was near enough, he wrapped it around me, bringing me even closer. I nestled against his side, determined to focus on the perfection of this moment and not about how it was doomed to inevitably end. Despite my best efforts, though, I couldn't ignore the mental clock counting down, each tick increasing the ache in my heart.

Chapter 16

Dylan

THERE WAS NOTHING REMOTELY casual about what had happened last night. Not the way I'd basically attacked Jimmy when we'd gotten to the room, or the way I'd pushed him to his knees, or how I'd taken care of him, and *definitely* not the way he'd looked at me, setting loose an uncomfortable flutter of butterflies in my stomach. Casual was no longer part of the equation. And yet...

"What are you going to wear? Never mind." Jimmy flung a shirt from his suitcase at me, then moved to the dresser where the remainder of the clothes I'd packed were still put away. A pair of my cargo shorts joined the pile of clothes on the bed. He glanced over his shoulder. "Well, come on, pokie-mon."

And yet, Jimmy was still Jimmy. Smiling to myself, I pulled back the covers, heedless of the fact that I was still stark naked after our impromptu shower last night. "I wasn't aware of anything on the itinerary until tonight."

Jimmy paused in his excavation of the drawer to look at me, his gaze dipping down and lingering for half a beat before flicking back to my face. Much to my surprise, I *liked* him looking. "Tina messaged, suggesting a group of us spend some of our last day in Oak Haven." He returned to the drawer and threw a pair of briefs at me. "Don't worry, we'll be back in plenty of time for the shindig tonight." He gave me one of his clownish grins as he sauntered back to his suitcase. "I don't think anyone wants to miss the big send-off."

"Considering how they've handled all the other events, I should think not." I dressed unhurriedly, kind of wishing his gaze would return and wondering how promptly we were expected to turn up for this outing. "So what's with Tina constantly absconding with you?"

"Jealous?" He wiggled his eyebrows and barked a laugh before giving my chest a light push, which only served to remind me how good his hands had felt last night. "At least you're invited this time. And it's a bunch of us."

"Yeah? Like who?" The second I asked, I already knew who one of the people would be.

"Stephan," we both said at the same time.

He chuckled and pulled on an undershirt, obscuring the light fuzz of brown hair on his chest. "I'm not saying you're right about him wanting to abduct me, but I *do* think he might be angling for a bromance."

"You did *not* just say that."

"Pfft. Don't be fooled. Straight dudes have 'em all the time. Though they get a bit dodgy about it when pressed."

An elephant sat on all my unexpected butterflies. *Straight.* Because that's what Jimmy was. Right? He'd have said differently if not. I worried my lip as I pulled on the shirt he'd laid out. It was loose and perfect for a hot day, and definitely not mine. I rubbed the soft fabric between my fingers. Maybe he was experimenting. If he was, how did I feel about that? A glance over showed him slipping into a short - sleeved button-down—his trademark summer outfit. Was I upset that he'd chosen to experiment with me?

I'd closed the distance between us before I'd even processed that I wanted to.

Jimmy started. "Oh, hey, what's-"

I pulled his head down to capture him in a kiss. Like all the other times over the last few days, he went completely slack, melting into me as his lips parted in invitation. I traced his lip with my tongue, then dove in to tangle with his. I teased the hair at the nape of his neck, while his hands slid around my waist, sliding beneath my shirt to caress the skin beneath. As I continued the kiss, I had my answer: No. I didn't mind that he was using me to experiment. Who knew? Maybe the experiment would yield some unexpected results.

A notification pinged on his phone. His nails scratched along my lower back, and as much as I would have liked to see where this ended up, he leaned back and cleared his throat. "I should probably check that."

I reluctantly let him go and resisted the urge to rest my head on his shoulder as he checked the message.

"Oh, snap!" He turned bright eyes on me.

"What's up?"

"Tina talked Marcus into coming along. And it turns out his wife, Bethany, was able to make it down for the last day. She'll be joining us in town as well." His phone pinged again. "Looks like Tina's already calling the front desk to schedule another shuttle bus."

"Damn, how many people has she roped into this excursion?"

He squinted at his phone. "Looks like maybe a third of everybody. Possibly more." He tossed his phone onto the sitting chair and rested his arms on my shoulders.

The squished butterflies in my stomach fluttered at how unbelievably natural it felt to have him in my arms. He was smiling when he leaned down to give me a searing kiss that had me regretting how quickly we'd dressed. When he pulled back, though, the smile had been replaced with something crossed between remorse and... disappointment? "I really hate you," he said with a sigh.

"Why is that?" I asked, angling for another kiss.

"Because you only brought one condom," he whispered when I was millimeters away from his lips. He gave me a quick peck, then stepped away. "Plus, we don't exactly have time for any... questions," he finished with a wicked grin.

I snorted. "The day you don't have time for questions is the day the world ends."

"Touche." He slipped on his sandals and kicked mine over. "In that case, ever been skinny-dipping?"

I finished strapping on the fisherman sandals. "Like you don't know. I went skinny-dipping with you and half our senior class the summer before we graduated."

"I can't believe I forgot about that!"

"Probably because you were preoccupied making out with Amanda Stevens." I gave him a pointed look.

"Amanda-who?" He gave me a cheeky wink, then reached for his phone and pocketed it. "You ready?"

"Just about." I zipped into the bathroom to grab my toiletries bag and pulled out a small thing of sunscreen. When I came back, Jimmy took one look and immediately groaned.

"We're going to town, not the pool."

"And the sun is out," I countered as I finished rubbing the cream into my nose. "Come here."

"Why can't I just use the spray stuff?" he griped, though he did come closer.

"Because *someone* used it all. Hold still. I'm just trying to make sure your face doesn't turn into a hot plate."

He scoffed and gave me a look filled with equal parts mischief and heat. "You just like putting white stuff on my face."

I smeared a thick stripe of sunblock on the bridge of his nose. "What can I say? Wrecked is a good look for you."

He released an indignant squawk, and I made a beeline for the door, barely remembering to snatch up the room key and my phone. "You're gonna pay for that!" he hollered as he chased me down the hall.

I got a good enough lead on his long ass legs that I actually beat him to the foyer and could lie in wait. When he careened around the corner, I caught his arm and yanked him back toward the wall. "And what were you gonna do if you caught me?" I asked, panting for breath and smiling from ear to ear.

"Wouldn't you like to know?" he responded, mirroring my grin.

I would, but there was something else I wanted to know more, especially considering my new plans. I dropped my voice so no one beyond our bubble could hear. "Why didn't you ask to top?"

Confusion clouded his face. "Because you don't bottom."

A veritable kaleidoscope of butterflies swirled in my stomach as I leaned forward.

"If they're going to be that cute the whole time, I'm out." Stephan's voice cut through the unlikely moment.

We chuckled, and I rested my forehead against Jimmy's briefly before turning to face the group that I'd completely missed in my single-minded focus on Jimmy. I looped an arm around his waist because I wasn't quite ready to surrender him to the others. "Hope we haven't kept you waiting."

"Actually, we're still waiting for a few stragglers," Tina said, walking closer in far more sensible Bermuda shorts and a flowy tank top. So that's why she'd commandeered Jimmy to go into town with her the other day. Much as it smarted, he did have solid fashion advice.

"Now I know you're not talking about us. *Especially* after you badgered me into coming along." Marcus and a woman I assumed must be Bethany joined the growing collection of adventurers.

Tina made an exaggerated gesture at herself and mouthed, "Moi?"

Marcus chuckled and turned to the woman. "Beth, I believe you're familiar with most of the faces here, but there are a pair in particular I'd like to introduce you to." He led her across the room and stopped a couple of feet in front of where we stood. "This is Dylan Wells and his partner, James Wallace."

"Pleasure to meet you both." She extended a graceful hand with stunning chestnut overtones, first to Jimmy, then to me. As she shook my hand and I returned the pleasantry, she paused and glanced at Marcus. "Wait. This wouldn't be the Wells you've been telling me so much about, would it?"

Marcus puffed out his chest. "One and the same."

I glanced uncertainly at Jimmy, but he was busy making star-eyes at Beth. "Hopefully it hasn't all been bad," I said, adding an awkward laugh.

"Nothing but the best. I promise."

"So you're really a scientist?" Jimmy blurted over whatever she was going to say next.

She laughed good-naturedly. "A virologist, actually."

I hugged Jimmy a little closer. "You'll have to forgive my partner's enthusiasm. He wanted to be a scientist more than anything when he grew up."

He shrugged. "Turns out I don't have the right temperament."

"Or a grasp of chemistry," I added snidely.

Marcus and Beth laughed while Jimmy smacked me in the arm. "Excuse you, *sir*. Your chem grades weren't any better than mine."

"And that's why I'm in finance," I replied with a smug grin.

Marcus clapped me on the shoulder while Jimmy harrumphed indignantly. "And aren't we all grateful for that?"

"I *suppose* you're really good at what you do." Jimmy rolled his eyes, but there was no malice in his tone, only a touch of pride that had my chest swelling, much as Marcus's had.

"And what do you do?" Beth asked Jimmy.

"I'm in the mental health profession."

I scoffed. "Don't be fooled by his sudden bout of modesty. Jimmy is an incredible counselor and recently helped start a new clinic."

"It's really not that big a deal," he countered. "Not at all like what these guys do." He gestured to encompass the rest of the IF people milling around.

"I happen to think that mental health is a cornerstone of well-being and that the profession is largely undervalued. Wouldn't you say, Marcus?" Beth turned a sharp look on her husband.

He held up his hands in defeat. But before he could respond to the very pointed question, Tina spoke up.

"The shuttles are here!"

Happy voices filled the foyer and spilled out onto the sidewalk as we exited the resort en masse. I kept my hand at the small of Jimmy's back as we plodded along with the others, fully prepared to hook his belt loop if it looked like we were going to get separated.

"Wells, why don't you ride with us?" Marcus called over the heads of people boarding the shuttle his wife was already on.

It only took a quick look to see that there was room for only one more. I glanced at Jimmy.

"Go ahead. Get your schmooze on," he said with a wide smile and a shoulder bump.

I placed a kiss to his temple. "Okay, I'll see you in town."

Right on cue, Stephan looped an arm through Jimmy's. "You can sit by me."

Jimmy rolled his eyes so Stephan couldn't see, then let himself be pulled away.

Shaking my head, I returned to the other shuttle where Marcus, Rafe, Beth, and Colleen were waiting for me. As I settled into my seat, I glanced up to find Jimmy making faces at us in the rear window of the other shuttle. I laughed along with the others. Jimmy was a ham. Always had been. He also wanted to get fucked again. And *that* I could arrange.

"What's got you looking so smirky?" Rafe asked, leaning on his elbows from the back row.

I twisted in my seat by the far window to see not only him, but everyone else. "Just planning."

"No work talk!" Beth admonished, triggering a fresh round of laughter as the shuttle lurched into gear.

"Promise, nothing like that. A hundred percent personal."

Rafe and Marcus shared a knowing smile, and I had to tamp down the urge to roll my eyes like Jimmy had. They were likely thinking grand gestures and proposals. Whereas I was thinking about how best to get my best friend naked and moaning. But this wasn't really the best place for those thoughts.

To help move the conversation in a safer direction, I addressed Marcus. "What sights in town were you wanting Bethany to see?"

"Please call me Beth," his wife said before Marcus could utter so much as a syllable. "I heard there's a cute little coffee shop in town that carries local art and has some of the wildest drink names. Have you been?"

"Yep." I nodded. "I had a Dark Desire and Jimmy got a Sweet Surrender."

"Well," Beth said, fanning herself while the rest of us chuckled, "those are some *names*. Are they all like that?"

"They might switch up the drinks periodically, but from what I could tell, yeah," Rafe supplied.

"From what Jimmy told me, the real fun is letting the barista choose," I added, then turned to Colleen. "Please tell me Tina hasn't planned the *whole* outing."

Colleen shook her head, smiling. "Not from what I heard, but I know the Twisted Pine made the list of musts."

I didn't bother holding back a smile. "Jimmy will be pleased."

"And the two of you will have to educate the rest of us on what you've discovered." Marcus nudged my shoulder and added to Beth, "The two are practically experts on all things beer."

"Expert might be pushing it. Aficionados," I clarified.

The shuttle pulled to a stop, and all focus was diverted to the quaint town beyond.

"Oh look, the coffee shop!" Beth exclaimed as she eagerly exited the vehicle. "You and Jimmy will join us, won't you?" she asked, turning to me.

"Of course," I replied before returning to search for Jimmy. The other shuttle had already spilled most of its occupants onto the sidewalk, but no Jimmy yet. Finally, he stepped out, followed by an equally smiling Stephan. They were still chatting when I pulled up behind Jimmy, wrapping my arms around his middle. "Hey, babe. Beth and Marcus were hoping we'd join them at Kaleidoscope. What do you say?"

He leaned into me. "That sounds great. Maybe I can convince Beth to share some sciencey insight stuff."

"You're hopeless," I chuckled into his neck.

"What? I like learning."

"I thought we were going to hit up the antique shop a couple of blocks over," Stephan interjected.

Jimmy sucked his teeth in what I'd come to recognize over the years as false remorse. "Ooh, sorry, bro. Looks like I'm otherwise engaged. Maybe we can catch up later." The fact that he'd very clearly *not* invited Stephan to join us at Kaleidoscope did not escape my attention.

I waited for Stephan to wander further down the sidewalk before releasing Jimmy. "Antiquing, huh?"

"Shut up. I only agreed because I was *really* hoping you'd be able to bail me out."

"You sure?" I hiked a thumb in the direction Stephan had gone. "It's not too late. Could find a fancy candelabra or maybe build on your Hummel collection."

"It's not a collection! My grandmother gave it to me."

I laughed and steered him through the door. Marcus and Beth waved from where they'd already secured one of the couches with Rafe and Mai. "Okay, fine. If it's not a collection, then why is there more than one?"

He huffed and crossed his arms. "Collection or not, I left them all at Mom's."

"Only 'cause your tiny ass apartment doesn't have room," I teased.

"Ugh, why are you so awful?"

"Welcome to Kaleidoscope. What can I get you? Oh, hey! It's you!" the cute twink behind the counter exclaimed... not to me. "Sweet Surrender," he said, pointing at Jimmy, then he eyed me up and down. "And *you* must be Dark Desire." He glanced back at Jimmy and winked. "*Totally* get it."

I glanced between the two of them. "I feel like I'm missing something."

"Nah. You two want the same or planning to mix it up?" The barista wiggled his eyebrows before tossing his teal hair over his shoulder.

I tugged Jimmy closer. "Let's see, what would recommend for the last day of a kick-ass vacation?" There were a million other things I could have said. Like finding out you probably have feelings for your best friend. Or you might be getting the biggest promotion of your life? Or maybe even that you're absolutely terrified of what will happen when all of this ends and you return to the real world.

The barista seemed to give the question some serious consideration, his gaze darting between the two of us before finally proclaiming, "I've got it. An Epiphany and a Midnight Casanova."

Jimmy and I shared a look, then he asked, "Whose is whose?"

"Guess you two will just have to figure it out." He winked and queued up the payment terminal before turning to begin the drinks.

Chapter 17

Jimmy

I LIKED BETH. SHE was charismatic, outrageously smart without rubbing your nose in it, and had a smile that made you want to smile with her. What I didn't like was Marcus's single-minded focus on Dylan. Further, they were talking business. *Business.* Which we all knew by this point was a major no-no. I sipped on my Epiphany and tried not to scowl while mentally debating how to best break up all the shop talk.

"Who'd have ever thought something called a Triple Play could taste this good? I kind of want another, but I'm also inclined to try something new. Any suggestions?" Beth set down her cup and looked at me.

I mirrored her and refused to think about how she was probably used to Marcus always talking about work or markets or financial-what-have-you. Would that be what it was like to *be* with Dylan? All work, all the time? "Not sure about suggestions. I can say that all four of the ones that we've had have been stellar." I glanced over my shoulder to see if the same barista was still at the counter. A shock of teal hair confirmed it. "If you're willing to take a chance, I'd ask Jace to pick for you." I reached for my drink and nearly spilled it all over the table when a warm hand slid over my thigh, alarmingly close to my crotch.

"You weren't thinking of getting another drink without me, were you?" Dill crooned in my ear, causing my dick to twitch. Given his hand placement, there was no way he'd missed the reaction either. He gave me one of those smiles intended to be innocent that missed by a mile.

"No," I squeaked, then cleared my throat and repeated firmer. "No. Think I'm caffeined out, actually."

He lightly squeezed my thigh, but didn't remove his hand as he turned back to Marcus. "You already know how we met. What about you two?"

"No, it's too embarrassing," Marcus groaned while Beth leaned forward eagerly, her coffee conundrum forgotten.

She batted him playfully on the arm. "Hush, it's sweet."

"Now I've got to hear this," I said with a chuckle, studiously ignoring Dill's nails scratching the fabric over my inner thigh.

Marcus let out a heavy sigh. "I went to her for tutoring in chemistry. Not a big deal, really."

"He was failing," she deadpanned.

"That's an exaggeration," Marcus mumbled, to which Beth subtly shook her head.

She took his hand, positively beaming. "Poor man couldn't distinguish between a covalent bond and an ionic one." She tsked at the shame of it all and I laughed.

"That makes two of us. Guess that's why we're in finance, eh?" Dill said to Marcus.

"So true," he echoed.

I scoffed and gave Dill a wry look. "Please, your chemistry is fine." He certainly never needed a tutor.

"Aw, thanks, babe." He smiled and planted a kiss on my cheek.

My face flamed, and to my dismay, I had nothing at hand to hide it. "That's not what I meant," I grumbled half-heartedly.

Beth chuckled. "Mai was right. You two are absurdly adorable."

"We're alright." Dill's hand slid along the inside of my thigh, reigniting my face.

"So what happened then?" I piped up. "You started tutoring..."

Marcus gave his wife an adoring look. "She's still the smartest woman I've ever met. How she puts up with me, I'll never know. I did end up passing Chem."

"Barely," Beth chimed.

"Barely," Marcus echoed. "In my defense, my tutor was very distracting. But by then, I couldn't imagine *not* seeing Beth every day. So, I asked her out."

Beth leaned forward. "It was the cutest, sweetest thing. He drew out a picture of bonds, but replaced the element names with ours. Naturally, I said yes."

The two beamed at each other, and my heart swelled for them. Could Dill and I ever have that? People kept calling us cute and adorable and "goals", but it was all a show. Except it wasn't. Not for me, anyway. I couldn't even pinpoint when it had stopped being an act. All I knew was that waking up with Dill, sharing kisses that melted my insides, and even the casually intimate touches were now something I couldn't imagine not having in my life anymore.

I glanced at my empty cup, taking in the swirly letters spelling out its name, and huffed a laugh. Jace really knew how to pick 'em. I was in love with Dill and if I didn't tell him, I'd regret it for the rest of my life.

"What's so funny?" Dill asked, giving my leg a light shake.

"Just thinking about the drink names. I wonder how they come up with them."

"Personally, I think it's darts on a board. But Carol assures me there's a method to the madness."

The four of us glanced up at the cheerful voice. It belonged to an equally cheery person with fair skin, a petite build, a pixie cut, and the usual apron complete with a pronoun pin that read "they/them".

"Sorry to interrupt. I'm Ash, the owner. How are you finding everything?"

"Marvelous," Beth said.

Marcus nodded and added, "Quite the establishment you have here. Ever consider franchising?"

"The thought may have crossed my mind." They glanced back at where Jace was managing a sudden rush. "Is there anything I can get you?"

"I'm good," Dylan replied, and the rest of us replied in kind.

Ash nodded. "Hope you have a colorful day!" they said, then joined Jace behind the counter.

"Guess that's our cue." Marcus stood and shifted to pull Beth's chair out. "Promised the missus we'd tour a farm on the outskirts of town that specializes in custom cheeses." Dylan and I mirrored them and stood as well.

"Please, dear, as if you aren't just as interested in checking out their operation. Especially since—"

"The baby goats," Marcus interrupted.

Beth's eyes widened briefly, and she darted a glance at Dylan. "Right. Baby goats. I hear they do goat yoga. Maybe I'll finally talk Marc here into giving it a go."

Marcus shook his head. "I gave regular yoga a chance, but I draw the line at having goats treat me like a mini mountain when I can barely maintain enough balance not to fall over as it is." He held out a hand to Dylan. "I've really enjoyed getting to know you better at this retreat. You're a real stand-up guy with a sharp mind."

"Thank you. That means a lot coming from the guy who single-handedly salvaged the Kepler merger."

"Nothing is ever single-handed at Infinity. IF it's not teamwork, it's not happening." Marcus gave a wry smile, and Dill chuckled.

Meanwhile, Beth groaned. "No work puns. You promised."

"Yes, dear," he said, shifting to shake my hand. "And you have been quite the surprise. I can see why you two are together. You complement each other admirably. Just like me and my Beth." He released my hand to beam at his wife once more.

She rolled her eyes, but it didn't diminish her radiant smile. "We'd best get going or we'll miss our tour time. And goat yoga!" she added, waving to Dill and I before making her way toward the door.

"No goat yoga!" Marcus shouted after her. "That woman. Anyway, we'll see you two tonight if we don't bump into you again before then."

We followed them out and paused in a sunny patch of the sidewalk. I turned to Dill. "So... what now?"

"Well," he began, surprising me by looping his arms around my waist so we were face to face and close enough to make my heart skip. "I have a quick errand I want to run, and I know you're still on the hunt for a commemorative magnet. What do you say we split up and I'll text you when I'm done so I can meet you wherever you're at?"

I wanted to ask him why we needed to split, but at the same time, it wasn't a bad idea. A little time away from him might be for the best. Give me a chance to clear my head and figure out how to break the news that I was bi. "Okay, sounds good."

"Excellent." He flashed me a smile that was doing shit all for my heart, then leaned up to press his lips against mine. I expected a chaste kiss; a quick peck and nothing more. What I got was a lingering tease that tasted like a promise. Our breath mingled as he slowly pulled away, highlighting the way our lips had fused together. "I'll see you in a bit," he whispered.

I nodded. "Yeah."

He released me and stepped back with a wry smirk. "Only one magnet, Jimmy."

"You're not the boss of me." I stuck out my tongue, and he laughed.

"Just remember, you have to get whatever you buy onto the plane." He gave me a pointed look, then turned to walk down the sidewalk while I mumbled to myself.

"It's my money. I'll buy what I want." But where did I want to get my magnet from? I checked my watch. Almost noon. Maybe the Twisted Pine had magnets. I hadn't checked when we'd been there before. Now that I had a heading, I spun on my heel and got to walking.

The journey, however, did not produce any inspired ideas on how to come out to my best friend or how the hell I was going to ask for a *relationship*. To top it off, I didn't have any better luck finding the door on my own, as I had with Dill. It took somebody walking out with a couple cases of beer to locate the damned thing. I held the door for the guy since he clearly had his hands full and to make sure I didn't lose the entrance the second it closed. He gave me an appreciative nod and walked toward a pickup in the sparsely populated lot.

I was surprised to find more patrons inside than vehicles in the parking lot. But then, what else did I expect on a Saturday in a small town? Smiling, I made my way toward the bar. About halfway there, I was waylaid by a familiar face.

"I was wondering if I'd see you again," Cassie said with a bright smile, tucking a now empty tray under her arm. "What can I get you?"

"I was wondering if you guys carried magnets with your logo. A keepsake to take back home."

"You're in luck." She led the way toward where a register sat perched on the bar top. Beside it was a modest display of koozies, pins, lanyards... and magnets. "There you have 'em. Where's home?" she asked as she absently began wiping the counter with a rag from her apron.

"Uh, Charlotte. North Carolina," I elaborated as I peered at the designs. I hadn't counted on having to *choose* one.

"That's quite a trip. When do you leave?"

"Umm..." I plucked up a magnet and compared it to another. The logo was the same, but where one was all logo, the other was smaller and had a bottle opener on it. *Fuck it. I'll get both. Dill doesn't need to know.* Decision made, I glanced back to where Cassie was leaning on the counter, still waiting for a reply. "Sorry. We head back tomorrow."

"Bummer. Just these two, then?" she asked, taking the magnets to ring them up.

I chewed my bottom lip and glanced back toward the door—which was obvious to spot on the inside—and recalled the guy with several packs of beer. What better way to break the news to Dylan than over a bottle of a new favorite? I turned back to Cassie. "Any chance of getting a six-pack of that oaky amber from the flight?"

"Shouldn't be an issue. Anything else?"

I glanced at the magnets already wrapped on the counter and the cardboard bottle holder Cassie was popping into shape. Dylan's obnoxiously astute reminder that I'd have to get any purchases I made on the plane back home rang in my ears. "Actually..." I grinned sheepishly. "What are the chances of getting that six-pack shipped? I'm wanting to surprise my boyfriend." I'd meant to say "friend", but clearly my brain was operating on a different frequency.

She ducked her head and appeared to be laughing at herself. "Sure thing. Let me grab Joe for you."

"I don't mean to be an inconvenience."

She flapped her bar cloth at me. "It's not a bother. We ship things all the time, though Charlotte might be farther than usual. Joe will get it sorted, though."

"Thanks. I'm hoping they'll get to be celebratory."

By the way her eyes brightened, it was clear she'd jumped to the conclusion of a very particular kind of celebration. "That's wonderful! I'll be sure Joe knows to give you the *special* discount." She winked and was gone before I could correct her assumption.

I turned and rested against the bar while I waited for Joe and wondered how perturbed he'd be to learn it was a promotion, not a proposal. But, then again, it kind of was? I was going to propose dating for real. I'd always believed we could be good together, but this retreat had opened my eyes to just *how good*. My dumb crush was out of control, and I didn't think I'd ever be able to stuff it back into its box.

Dylan was a fantastic boyfriend. I was honestly at a loss as to why he couldn't keep one longer than a couple of weeks. He was considerate, affectionate, and fucking incredible in bed. Maybe it really was his preoccupation with work that drove them all away. Not that I was complaining.

The fact that he was single was how we'd gotten to this point in the first place and why I thought there was even a minuscule chance he'd take me up on the offer to date. Except, maybe he *liked* being unattached. It was entirely possible that he didn't have a steady boyfriend because he didn't *want* one. And if that was the case, where did that leave me? I dropped my head back and released a frustrated sigh. Why couldn't this be simple?

"Sorry to have kept you waiting."

I straightened and spun around. "Oh, no, that's not why–"

"Relax," Joe said with an affable expression. "You look like a guy with a lot on his mind."

"You could say that." I rubbed the back of my neck. If virtual strangers could tell I was a mess, how would I hide my confusion from Dill?

"So Cassie says you're looking to have some of our craft beer shipped for some kind of *special* celebration?"

I chuckled at the way he mimicked Cassie's enthusiasm. "In the interest of being honest, it's not for the big proposal, if you catch my drift. Though it would be a pretty monumental step in our relationship." I hoped. Fuck, did I hope. What the hell would I do if he said no? Could our friendship even survive that? Suddenly, my big idea didn't seem so great.

"Hey."

I looked at Joe, taking in his serious expression.

"Whatever it is, I'm sure it will work out. If life's taught me any-thing, it's trusting your gut. If this feels right, then don't question it."

I took a deep breath and drummed my fingers on the counter. "You're right. Okay. What'll it take to get a six-pack, or two, of the oaky amber to Charlotte?"

Joe took a moment to consider it, stroking his beard thought-fully. "North Carolina's not the farthest we've shipped bottles, though it might be the fewest to go that far. I'll make you a deal. Make it a case instead of two six-packs and I can get it to you in a few weeks. Plus, I'll throw in the magnets and a set of koozies."

Twenty-four beers were significantly more than the six I'd planned on, but it was also a pretty sweet bargain. After another moment of deliberation, I caved. Whether or not I came out to Dill over beers, they were still damn good and would be drunk. "Done."

Joe's grin nearly split his face in two. "Great!" He reached be-neath the bar for what appeared to be an order pad and unclipped the pen from his shirt. "Name and the address where you want it shipped."

I stalled, not having thought that far ahead. "Uh…"

"Mind if I offer my two cents?"

"Please," I responded, sounding every bit as desperate as I felt.

He rested on his burly forearms. "Seems like the whole point is to drink them *with* your boyfriend, right? And I'm assuming you don't live together. Yet," he tacked on as an afterthought.

I nodded. There was an idea that hadn't occurred to me.

"Then I'd have them sent to you. That way he doesn't end up enjoying them without you and you're guaranteed to be there for the surprise. How's that sound?"

"Sounds great." I sagged with relief at having a more solid plan, at least where the beer was concerned. Once Joe finished ringing up the order with shipping and handling included, I understood better why he'd thrown in the freebies. Craft beer could be pricey in the best of circumstances, and Charlotte wasn't exactly *close* to Oak Haven. I did my best not to cringe as I paid and pocketed the magnets with a request to send the koozies with the case.

I was debating grabbing a beer when I checked my phone for the time and found four texts and a missed call. All from Dylan. Too late, I realized my phone had been on silent the whole time.

"Shit," I hissed to myself as I stepped outside into the sunshine and dialed Dill.

He picked up after the first ring. "What the hell, man? I was starting to think Stephan really had abducted you." He paused. "He hasn't, has he?"

"No. Sorry, I put my phone on silent yesterday and apparently never turned it off. Um, where are you now?"

"Where are you?" he fired back. If it hadn't been for the hint of humor, I might have been worried. "Wait, don't tell me. Outside the Twisted Pine."

I frowned and glanced around the parking lot. "How do you know that?"

"Because I know you. Also, I'm to your right under the big ass oak tree."

I spun, phone still pressed to my ear, and squinted against the glare off the windshields. Finally, I spied a figure waving by a tree. I waved back, hung up, then made my way over. "How long have you been there?" I asked as I joined him in the shade.

"Not long. I passed a nice-looking diner on the way over. Wanna check it out?"

"I could eat."

"That makes two of us." We fell in step and made our way toward the sidewalk that would lead us to the diner. We hadn't gone far when he glanced at me with a smile. "So, how many did you get?"

High above, a cloud lazily moved across the sun. When it cleared, pure light shone unhindered down upon us, and I was struck with how ridiculously handsome Dylan was. His sandy hair and tanned skin were nothing compared to his smile or the way his eyes seemed to reflect the blue sky. "Huh?" I asked, vaguely realizing he'd asked a question.

He stopped walking and faced me.

I followed suit, though the diner was only a little further, its fifties-style neon sign blinking in welcome. Maybe I could just tell him now. Blurt it out and be done with it finally. For the longest time, it hadn't *felt* like I was hiding my sexuality from him, but it did now. I was lying to my best friend and the man I was completely in love with. And I couldn't do it anymore. He deserved the truth. We both did.

"Dill—"

"Yeah?" he stepped closer, and my heart thudded painfully.

I'm bisexual. And I'm in love with you. It wasn't even ten words, but I couldn't push them past my lips. What if... What if the truth destroyed our friendship? Was I willing to sacrifice over thirty years of friendship on the *chance* of more?

"Hey, you two," Stephan said as he bounded up to us like an overeager puppy. "Jimbo, you missed out on the antiquing. They have some wild finds here." He glanced past us. "You headed to the diner?"

"Uh, yeah," Dill said, taking a step back, and my opportunity to confess.

I was going to strangle Stephan. Mentally, my fingers were already around his throat as I throttled him for his unwitting sabotage.

"Cool. We can all sit together. I believe Rafe and his wife have already snagged the event room for any IF people." Stephan leaned in close to Dill, then said in the worst whisper I've heard in my life, "If the rumors are right, Chase is here too."

Dylan's demeanor noticeably brightened after our almost intense moment. "Guess it works out that we were going there anyway. Right... Jimbo?"

I showed him my teeth in a fake smile.

Completely oblivious that he'd interrupted something important, *and* that Dill was teasing me, Stephan resumed his happy puppy routine. "Well, what are we waiting for?" He wrapped an arm around Dylan's and my shoulders, then steered us toward the hopping diner.

Chapter 18

Dylan

J IMMY'S REMINDER TO "M INGLE, mingle, mingle" played in my head as I tried desperately to focus on the conversation around me. But my focus just wasn't there. My gaze slid past Chase to where Jimmy was talking animatedly with Colleen. She laughed at something he said, and I found myself mirroring his grin. I didn't need to hear the joke. Jimmy was damn funny.

"I hate to be the party pooper, but I have a late flight to catch if I'm going to make it to the London office in time for tomorrow's meeting," Chase said, drawing my attention back.

A chorus of dismay at his leaving early rippled around me. I did my best to echo them, but I was relieved. As stunning as the final event was with all of its glitz and glam, I was ready to be back in the room. And if Chase was bowing out early, then I had one less reason to linger.

Chase extended a hand to me, much like he had to the others in our little circle. "It's been a pleasure to get to know you better, Wells. Put the man to the work, as it were," he said jovially as we shook hands.

"Same, sir. It's been an honor to meet you, and I'm truly humbled to have been included in this year's retreat."

He clapped me on the shoulder. "What did I say about all that humility? Own your successes. There are many of them. And hopefully, I'll get to see you before next year's retreat. Heads up, invest in sweaters and brush up on your snow skills. Nancy's angling for a winter getaway." He winked. "Right. I'm off. Keep in touch, Wells." With that, Chase made his way toward the exit, getting waylaid every few yards with more handshakes and farewells.

Not sure what to make of the interaction, I made a beeline for Jimmy. He'd wandered to the fringe of the crowd, but had a clear view of the dance floor, which was still bustling with happy dancers despite the hour. A shout caught my attention, and I turned to offer a wave without stopping. Jimmy's insistence on me mingling on my own might have made sense, but I'd grown used to having him right by my side, of being able to reach out and place a hand at the small of his back.

I faced forward, intent on rejoining my friend. Not for the first time since we'd gotten ready in our room, I caught him staring. It would have been easy to dismiss it as nothing, if he hadn't looked away so fast every time I caught him. Smiling to myself, I eliminated the last of the distance between us and called him out like I'd wanted to do the other half dozen times. "Do I have something on my shirt?"

"No, of course not." He took another sip of the beer he'd been nursing, his gaze noticeably straying.

Smiling, I slid a little closer so I could finally touch him. His brown eyes snapped to me, widening slightly as I placed one hand on his hip and stole his beer with the other. "Then what?"

"I don't know what you mean." His gaze flicked down to where we were nearly pressed chest to chest.

I downed the last of the now warm beer and set it on a nearby table already decorated with other empty glasses. "Yes, you do. You keep starring. I'd like to know why."

He swallowed, and while the slight pink in his cheeks could have been from the alcohol, considering how warm the beer had gotten, I seriously doubted it. He was blushing, and it was kinda making my night. "You just look really good in a suit."

I laughed and squeezed his hip. "You see me in a suit all the time."

"And it never changes," he said with a sigh.

Thankfully, he looked away again so he couldn't see the massive smile splitting my face and betraying the little cartwheels my heart was currently doing. "Hey." I placed a finger on his jaw and turned his head back to me. "You clean up pretty well yourself." I didn't bother hiding my appreciative gaze. When he'd laid out the clothes earlier, I'd initially been relieved that he'd remembered to pack a formal suit, then he'd gotten dressed and all I'd wanted to do was peel him right back out of it.

"Thanks," he mumbled, his cheeks darkening. Suddenly, he let out a big breath. "Dill, could we talk about something, please?"

"Mmm," I hummed. "I think I have a better idea."

He blinked. "You do?"

"I think we should blow this popsicle stand."

He leaned to the side to look past me at the room, still full of people. I knew exactly what he was going to say before he did. "What about the party? You're supposed to be mingling." He shoved his hand against my chest. I caught it and held it there.

"Chase already bounced and if I schmooze anymore, I'll die."

He chuckled, but didn't try pulling his hand away even when I started rubbing my thumb along his palm. "You could always say you're out of spoons instead of being so dramatic."

"Who says I'm out of spoons? Let me be clearer. I think *you* should head back to the room and... freshen up." His lips parted, and I resisted the urge to tease them further apart. I leaned closer and dropped my voice. "Don't pretend you haven't been dying for me to taste that sweet ass again." When I pulled back, his face was full-on lobster red.

He cleared his throat and took back his captive hand. "I guess I'll, um, head back to the room." He stepped to the side, and I let him go, letting my hand linger on his hip as long as possible. The things I was going to do to this man the second we were behind closed doors. He looked at me and I could practically *feel* the nerves rolling off him.

I reached for his hand again and gave it a quick squeeze for reassurance. "Go on ahead. I'll finish saying goodbye and be right behind you."

His tongue darted out to wet his lips, testing my ability to exercise even an ounce more of patience. Having him naked and moaning had all but filled my mind for the better part of the day. It had also made it damn near impossible to mingle effectively. He searched my face for another moment, then began the arduous process of extricating himself from a room of his adoring fans.

Rather than start my goodbyes like I promised, I watched him as he stopped periodically to have mini-conversations with one group after another, slowly working his way toward the door. Not that I could blame them. Jimmy had always had a gift with people. It was one of the things that made him so special. Finally, he slipped out of the ballroom.

I counted to thirty, then began my round of goodbyes, see you at the airport, and promises to keep in touch. By the time I made it to the hallway leading to our room, my heart was pounding in anticipation and my fingers were tingling. I keyed open the door, sending up a mental prayer that I had given him enough time.

"Oh, hey. I was about to text you," Jimmy said as I stepped inside.

Eager as I was, I couldn't help but take a moment to appreciate how truly incredible he looked in the crisp navy suit. It transformed his natural lankiness into a statement, and the pop of spring green from his button-down enhanced the earthy brown of his hair and eyes. Was it weird that I was glad he hadn't taken it off yet? That *I* wanted to be the one to strip it off him?

His eyebrows pinched together, and he looked down. "What?"

"Just you." Without further preamble, I crossed the distance between us. He released a muffled sound of surprise as I cupped the side of his face. Our mouths fused together, and I teased the seam of his lips with my tongue until he opened up. I rubbed my thumb along his five-o'clock shadow while he gave a soft sigh and pressed back. There wasn't a doubt in my mind that he could feel how hard my heart was pounding as he placed his hand against my chest. I shrugged out of my jacket and tossed it haphazardly toward the chair before pushing his off his shoulders.

We continued to trade long, indulgent kisses as I guided him toward the bed. Two months ago, I'd never had so much as a stray sexual thought about my best friend. Now, I couldn't remember the last time I'd wanted someone so much. But I didn't want to just claim every last part of him. I wanted to savor him. Wanted to make him squirm, and moan, and sigh my name. This was our last night. Tomorrow, things would be back to business as usual between us, and I'd be damned if I wasn't going to relish every last second.

I continued kissing him as I lowered him to sit on the bed, following his mouth with a passion. I pressed against him for a moment as I tangled our tongues. When I finally pulled up for air, he'd somehow undone all of my shirt buttons. With a soft chuckle, I straightened to let it slide from my shoulders, then reached over my head and pulled off my undershirt. Positively drunk with want, I braced myself on either side of him and tasted his lips once more. His fingers threaded through my chest hair as they coasted up my torso to cup my neck and encouraged a deeper kiss.

I left his mouth to lavish kisses on his neck and was immediately rewarded with a needy sigh that went straight to my dick. Fuck, I loved how much his sensitive neck turned him on. While he was distracted, I worked on popping his buttons loose, then freed his arms and helped liberate him from his undershirt.

I shifted my stance so I could press my lips down his torso, pausing to suck in each nipple, making him moan and wiggle. I groaned hard and moved on to his quivering stomach. I took my time freeing the button on his pants and sliding down the zipper, before palming his straining cock through his boxers. That there was already a damp spot had me dizzy with desire. I moaned right along with him, then began pulling off his pants so I could taste the prize beneath.

He lifted his hips to help, leaning back on his arms and arcing up. I slowly tugged the fabric down to reveal his beautiful cock, with its perfectly swollen cap and slit already pearled with pre-cum. When it was free, I couldn't help but run my tongue slowly up the shaft. He let out a strangled sound, and I finished working his pants off so that his legs fell into a perfect invitation.

I settled to my knees between them and leaned forward to trail teasing kisses on the inside of each thigh, then wrapped a hand around his swollen cock. I gave it a firm stroke before bringing my lips to the crown. His head fell back with a deep moan as I swirled my tongue around the head, then guided it into my mouth.

Never in a million years would I have thought I could crave the taste of Jimmy's cock on my tongue so much, but right now, that's what I was living for. His hips rose to meet my bobbing head, and we moaned in unison. Even with as slow as I was working him, it didn't take long for his sighs to turn into heavy pants.

"Dill," he gasped, his fingers threaded through my hair. "Please—" His words broke off into a groan as I sucked harder. Then his grip tightened, threatening to loosen a few strands. "I want you to fuck me. Please... please tell me you got more condoms."

I stood, pulled one free of my wallet, kicked my pants aside, then leaned down. "I've got you, baby."

His answering whimper could have been real or pure imagination. Whichever it was, I surged forward to kiss him hard. He fell back, taking me with him until eventually our bodies lined up and our cocks rubbed together.

I rocked my hips and moaned at the way he jerked beneath me. I shifted to snag the lube on the stand, then returned to find his ass already perched on a pillow and waiting for me. I quickly rolled the rubber on and slicked my covered cock. Then leaned forward to tease a kiss from him and stroke his cock as well.

"Dill," he huffed, sounding strangled.

I dallied another moment at Jimmy's neck, making him writhe with pleasure, before bringing my attention to his eager hole. I smothered a moan as it tightened in anticipation and rubbed a lubed finger along the quivering rim before sliding my middle finger deep in a single smooth thrust. He bucked into my hand as I gently massaged his prostate.

After a few measured thrusts, I added another digit, dizzy with the way his ass pulled me in. I wanted nothing more than to drive my cock fast and deep into that ass, but I was determined to take my time and draw this out as much as possible. The fantasy we'd found ourselves in would end tomorrow. Then it would be like none of this had ever happened.

"I'm getting close," he said through harsh pants.

I pulled my fingers free and lined up my sheathed cock, then with agonizingly slow strokes worked my way inside, his tight heat threatening to undo my resolve. I roved my hands over his thighs and sides as I lazily thrust, pulling almost all the way out before slowly sinking back in. "Still with me, baby?"

"Fuck yes," Jimmy moaned, one hand tangling in the sheets while the other tightened around the base of his cock and stroked in-time to the rocking.

I struggled to keep my movements unhurried, but the sight of my best friend sprawled before me, completely lost in the moment, was the sexiest thing I'd ever seen. I lowered to connect our lips in a deep kiss and started picking up the tempo until my pelvis was snapping against his tight ass and we were panting into each other. He gave up his hold on his cock to wrap his arms around me and pressed the heels of his feet into my ass, urging me deeper.

I dropped my head to his sweat-slicked shoulder while my hips pumped frantically. "Fuck," I groaned, not ready for this to end.

"God, Dill... I'm so close," he said so huskily the words were almost unrecognizable.

"Me too, baby," I admitted. I gripped his thigh like it was the only thing that could keep me tethered to the earth and a little terrified of what would happen when I let go. The tingling at the base of my spine intensified and my balls tightened. "Come with me," I panted.

All it took was the mere mention of coming to have both of us grunting out our releases. I gave a few more faltering thrusts, riding the wave of my orgasm and lost in the way his ass squeezed me. When I was completely spent, I sagged against him, peppering his shoulders, pecs, and wherever else I could reach without moving with soft kisses.

"Yes," he sighed several times while he stroked my forearms and shoulders.

Finally, I had to move from our cocoon of bliss. He groaned his dissatisfaction, and I decorated the side of his neck with kisses that turned the aggrieved sound into a ball-tightening moan of pleasure. If it were possible to stay exactly like this, I'd have done it in a heartbeat, but nature had other plans.

Regretfully, I pulled my softening cock free, then disposed of the condom, took a quick piss, and returned with a warm damp cloth. He shuddered when the cloth touched the cooling cum on his chest and let out a small whine when I moved it down to his hole. Once I was satisfied, I crawled back into bed and gathered him against me beneath the covers.

He snuggled in closer, gracing my chest with a kiss while I rubbed my hand up and down his back, trying to commit the contours to memory in a new way. I'd never begrudged Jimmy his ever-present need to cuddle, though I'd rarely cuddled with any of my partners in the past. Maybe I'd been doing it wrong. This... this felt different, and I wasn't entirely sure what I was going to do when it was gone.

Chapter 19

Jimmy

The plane landed, and Dill jolted awake. He immediately straightened, stretching his arms overhead and leaving my shoulder to cool. He glanced at me as he unsuccessfully attempted to stifle a yawn. "You catch any Zs?"

"Yeah," I lied, mimicking his yawn, because those fuckers were contagious. I *wish* I could have passed out like he had, but my head had been too much of a mess. Still was. The retreat was over and… What? What now?

"Good." He smacked my leg before standing awkwardly to wait for an opening to exit. "Then you can carry your own shit."

"No one asked you to carry it. You just took it."

"You were taking too long."

I rolled my eyes and pushed up to join the impatient queue to leave the plane. Contrary to his teasing, he pulled out my carry-on the moment there was room enough. It wasn't until we emerged in the terminal that he handed it over.

"Why does baggage claim have to be so far away from the terminal?" I griped, mostly to myself.

He chuckled and took off toward the distant baggage claim. On the upside, by the time we finally got there, bags were making the rounds. Just like on the plane, he grabbed my luggage.

I huffed, none too quietly.

"What's up with you?" he asked as he reached for his suitcase, still holding mine captive.

"You. First you accuse me of not being able to handle my stuff, then you won't even give me a chance." I all but snatched the handle from him and wheeled the case to my side.

Confusion flashed across his face. "Okay, my bad. You sure you're okay?" He extended his hand until the tips of his fingers grazed my cheek. My heart preemptively melted at the promise of the caress. Then he withdrew his hand, taking the much-needed touch with it. His cheeks darkened, and he cleared his throat. "Sorry, guess it will take longer than I thought to get back in the groove of things."

I opened my mouth, fully prepared to tell him right here in the airport lobby I didn't want things to change back.

"I vote we grab something to eat on the way back to your place. Traveling always makes me hungry," he said before I could. He tightened his grip on his carry-on bag like it would try to escape... or like he didn't trust his hand not to reach for me again.

I sullenly followed his lead to long-term parking. I didn't need him making excuses for my poor attitude, even if I *was* hungry. Food wouldn't fix what was wrong as well as his touch would. Had it really only been twelve hours since I'd been content and wrapped in his arms?

We settled in the car, and he glanced at me. "What are you thinking?"

I was thinking that I should have come clean at any of the countless opportunities I'd had on the retreat. But that wasn't what he was asking. "How about barbecue? Give ourselves a proper welcome home."

"I like the way you think. That joint by your place still open?"

"Last time I checked."

He flashed me a grin that made my heart skip and my stomach a little queasy. "Excellent."

Thankfully, when we pulled up, the hole in the wall was open and not too crowded. The day had cooled as we drove, so we opted to eat on the patio and enjoy the early evening breeze.

I plucked at my pulled pork sandwich while Dill tucked into his ribs with a relish I couldn't muster. Not interested in being called out again, I filled the void. "When will you find out about the promotion?"

"It's not a guarantee."

I snorted. "It's a guarantee. Everyone loved you."

He ducked his head to hide his grin. "I did seem to make a good impression." When he glanced up again, my heart skipped at his surprisingly shy grin. He stretched his hand across the table, where it hovered above mine. Maybe I wasn't the only one who didn't want things to return to exactly how they were before. I was milliseconds away from intertwining our fingers and letting him know exactly how I felt. Before I could act, he curled his fingers inward, retreating from me yet again, then awkwardly reached for my napkin, despite having his own. "Couldn't have done it without you. Thanks again."

"You act like I got nothing out of it," I said to hide my disappointment.

He finished wiping his mouth and hands with a chuckle. "Those questions were something else. Did you get all of them out of your system? Any last-minute additions?" The glint in his eyes gave me hope I wasn't brave enough to pursue. "Come on, I'm sure you've got at least a couple lurking."

Could you ever love me the way I love you? The question filled my head until it felt like I was drowning, but I couldn't bring myself to voice it. "Nah, I'm good." He gave me a skeptical look, but didn't pursue it.

We finished disposing of our trash and returned to the car. Before I knew it, we were pulling up to my complex. I stared up at the stucco exterior that had been modern twenty years ago, loath to go inside to my sad, tiny apartment. Alone. My heart squeezed painfully as the reality that I wouldn't be sleeping cuddled around Dylan tonight, nor would I get to wake up to his grizzled face in the morning, settled into my bones.

"For the record," Dylan said as he put the car in park and lurched me out of my melancholic spiral. "If you end up having other burning questions—even hella inappropriate ones—maybe *don't* wait to use them as a bargaining chip. Just ask."

"Really?" That ridiculous hope that refused to be extinguished burned a little brighter.

"Of course. We're best friends and, as you've pointed out *countless* times, we don't have secrets." He shook his head with a wry laugh as we stepped into the elevator. "We certainly don't anymore."

Except I did. But I didn't want it to be anymore. I couldn't bear the thought of going through life the same as before. I wasn't the same after the retreat. *We* weren't the same. And, fuck it all, if he didn't stop "almost" touching me, I was going to scream and punch him in the face.

"Though I'm surprised you never asked about Kennedy." He glanced over his shoulder at me and nodded for me to unlock the door.

I bit back a snarl. I didn't want to know why the longest relationship he'd ever had, that seemed fucking perfect on the outside, hadn't worked out. Especially not when I wanted him for myself. But I couldn't very well say that without sounding like a bitter asshole… even if right now I was one. "It's a sensitive topic for you. I get that." I shrugged and pushed inside. I gave the suitcase a shove, and it rolled a few feet toward the bedroom before stopping.

He slapped me on the back hard enough that I wheezed and stumbled a step. "It'll take some time to get back into the swing of things, but we'll manage. Before you know it, things will be back to normal."

Fuck that noise. "About that." I turned to face him as he lowered the carry-on to slump on the floor.

"Yeah? You finally going to tell me what's been bothering you?" He raised his eyebrows expectantly.

I rubbed the back of my neck and took a deep breath, suddenly anxious, despite having tried to get to this moment for *hours*. "Actually, yeah."

Worry sparked in his eyes so fast I almost missed it. "Did I do something?"

"No! No," I said again at a more reasonable volume. "It's, um, definitely a *me* thing."

He frowned and tucked his hands into his back pockets, which had the unfortunate side effect of pulling his shirt tight across his chest. "Okay. What's up?"

"What if… what if I don't want things to go back to normal?" I chewed on my lip, fear tangling with hope and the conviction that if I didn't come clean now, I never would and I'd regret it for the rest of my life.

His forehead crinkled as he frowned. "I'm not following. It's not like we can *stay* on vacation indefinitely. We have jobs. You probably have a hundred messages from clients."

"I think you're exaggerating my popularity, but that's not what I mean." I wasn't ashamed of my sexuality. I wasn't even worried he'd reject me. Then why did telling him feel so impossible?

"Then what?"

This was it. Moment of truth. Why the hell was it so difficult? I swallowed hard as years of keeping this huge part of myself locked away from my best friend battled to get out.

"Jimmy?" He took a step closer, and the final dam broke.

"I love you," I blurted, then quickly added, "romantically," before he could explain it away as friendly or, heaven forbid, brotherly.

His smile took on a strained edge, and he looked away. "I'm sure it feels like that. We, uh, crossed a lot of lines. Which maybe we shouldn't have." He released a long sigh, then finally returned his gaze to me. "But we're adults. More importantly, we're still *us*. We'll get through this like we've gotten through everything else. You'll see. Things might just be a little awkward for a while."

I shook my head. "You're not hearing me. I'm *in* love with you, Dylan. The retreat just opened my eyes to what was right in front of me this whole time. If you're up for it, I'd like to try dating for real. If it doesn't work out, like you said, we're adults and we can get through anything."

"I don't really see that working out. Especially not once we've gotten some distance from our very convincing act during the retreat. Give it some time. You'll realize the way you're feeling now is just..." He waved his hands in the air. "Temporary. Not real. We're great friends. It's understandable things got muddled."

"Are you really patronizing me right now?"

"No, of course not. I just think we maybe committed to our roles a little too much and pretend feelings are getting conflated with real ones."

My disbelief intensified, and I frowned. "Don't tell me how I feel. I know exactly what my feelings for you are. I'm in love with you and I have been for a long time. The retreat simply made it impossible to keep ignoring."

He let out an exasperated huff and rubbed his forehead as he walked deeper into the living room. "Except you're not."

"Yes, I *am*." His shoulders tightened, but he didn't turn around. "Dylan." I stepped toward him, and he held out a hand.

"No." The definitive tone cut me to the quick. "We crossed boundaries, had fun, that's *all*."

"No, it's not. Why aren't you listening to me?" I asked, getting increasingly frustrated. "Yeah, we pushed the boundaries of our friendship, and we're good enough friends that we could go back to the way things were. But *I. Don't. Want. To.* Dill, I loved everything we did. Loved it. As in, want-more-of-it, loved it. Specifically, with you."

He spun back to face me. "Stop. Just... stop. Do you even realize what you're saying? It's been—what—six months since your last relationship? I get it, you're lonely and things got... confusing." He glanced away again.

"I am perfectly capable of seeking out a relationship if and when I want one. Which is exactly what I'm trying to do. With you."

"Jesus, Jimmy. Stop. You think I haven't been here before? That I don't recognize what's happening? Trust me, I know the signs. And *you* know how I feel about that gay-for-you shit. It's an excuse to experiment without consequence."

"Or it's a way for people to sidestep their truth," I countered.

"This is *not* the time for you to therapize. The bottom line is that you're not gay and you never have been."

"I never said I was," I shot back, my exasperation increasing. We'd taken a hard left somewhere, and I had no clue how to get us back on track.

"Exactly! So stop making this something it isn't." He crossed his arms, his jaw ticking as his scowl worked on becoming a permanent part of his face.

"Ah!" I threw my hands up. "Just because I'm not gay doesn't invalidate how I feel about you."

"I told you—"

"I'm bisexual," I all but shouted over him.

He scoffed and rolled his eyes. "Since when?"

"Since—are you fucking for real? Since always."

He raised his eyebrows. "Yeah? Because this sounds like news to me. Which makes it 'gay for you' with better terminology. So, please enlighten me. How did you know you were 'bisexual'?" he asked with air quotes.

"Probably has something to do with the fact that my first ever crush was on a boy. You, in fact," I snapped, shaking with anger, frustration, and a whole host of other emotions I didn't have a prayer of parsing out right now. Of all the people in the world, I never would have expected to face bi-erasure from my best friend.

Confusion eclipsed his righteous indignation. "What? When was this?"

I sagged, exhausted from fighting and having held onto this secret for so long. "I realized I had a crush on you the summer before you came out. If I'm being totally honest, part of me hoped that your sexual awakening was because of me."

"Honest? Where was this honesty then? Why didn't you tell me? Did you think I wouldn't support you?" Hurt mixed with anger in his words, making each question feel like a gut punch.

I winced. "I didn't... I didn't want to steal your thunder. Coming out was big, and I didn't want to take away from it by being like, 'me too.' Well, not 'me too,' but you know what I mean. I figured I'd wait for a better time."

His glower returned in full force. "So instead, you lied to me. Let me believe you were straight and just carried on."

"I didn't lie, per se. I always *meant* to tell you, I just couldn't find the right time."

"There *is* no right time!"

I rubbed a hand over my face. "I was worried if I came out right after you it would look like I expected you to be into me. Which, yeah, saying that out loud sounds terrible, not the least of which because I *did* hope you would be. So, I waited. Figured I'd focus on supporting you. Then a couple of years went by and it felt weird to tell you then. So, I waited a little longer, thinking it would come up organically. But it didn't. Then more time passed and... And it was too much time. It would have been weird to say anything. And... and... I don't know, coming out is hard, in case you forgot."

"I have *not* fucking forgotten. Does your family know? Did your other partners know?"

My stomach sank as our hard left turned into a deep dive into the Mariana Trench. "Well, yeah."

His cheek twitched and his lips pursed, while anger fought to dominate his face. "So, you're telling me that literally everyone else *but me* knew you were bisexual?"

Fuuuuuck.

Something dark flashed in his eyes. "Have you been with other men?"

"I mean, yes. Fooled around mostly, dated a little, but nothing lasting."

"You're a fucking hypocrite," he snarled, bypassing anger and sliding into open fury.

"Excuse me?"

He advanced on me, and I took an anxious step back. "You spend *days* lecturing me, making me feel guilty for not sharing everything about my dating life with you, and you've been going out of your way to hide the fact that you're dating men. Some open book you are. A fucking redacted one."

"I..." Okay, I'd done that, but it hadn't seemed nearly as awful as when he said it.

"Fuck you, Jimmy." He pushed past me and stalked to the door.

"Dylan."

He opened the door with enough force that I feared for the hinges. Then he was in the hall, and I was rushing to catch up.

"Dill!" I shouted down the hall, but he didn't so much as slow down. To my horror, the elevator opened right as he pressed the button. I sprinted down the hall to stop him. We could fix this. Talk it through with cooler heads. I skidded to a stop in front of the elevator just in time to catch a final glimpse of his furious expression before the doors closed. "No!" I slammed my fists into the metal, but they didn't magically open. "No," I whispered softer.

With heavy feet, I made my way back to my apartment and snatched my phone from the counter where I'd dropped it.

> Dill, I'm sorry. Please come back. We can talk about this. I get it. I fucked up. Don't lock me out.

I waited a moment, but no bubbles popped up. After another minute of staring at the screen, it went dark. I squeezed my eyes shut, but the burning only intensified behind my eyelids. What had I done? Why had I waited so long to tell him the truth? Forget being together as a couple, I may have just irreparably sabotaged our friendship.

The phone slipped from my numb fingers and clattered on the floor. Was there any coming back from this?

Chapter 20

Dylan

MY PHONE BUZZED, BRIEFLY disrupting the financial commentary that filled the background. I glanced at the device, but couldn't bring myself to pick it up. It was likely Jimmy, just as it had been the other fifty times. A mix of guilt and anger sliced through me as I continued to stare at the now silent device. The red notification above the messages icon increased by one.

I turned back to my monitor, ignoring the message like I had all the others. From what I'd gathered reading the notification banners, they all said about the same thing. Apologies. Pleas for a chance to explain. Regret. More apologies.

At ten days, this was officially the longest we'd ever gone without talking. I hated it. I hated that he'd lied to me more. With grim determination, I focused on the analyst report displayed before me. What would I even say? I couldn't even bring myself to open the damn messages and had only made it through one painful voicemail before deciding not to bother with the rest.

I was hurt, but it was also more than that. What had I done to make him believe I wouldn't support him, wouldn't be there for him like he'd been there for me? We shared *everything*, or at least I thought we had. The retreat had certainly disabused me of that notion. Which was exactly why I'd promised myself to be better. I'd spent most of the flight back weighing the consequences of telling him that the retreat, being with him, had surprised me. Admitting that our "fake" relationship hadn't felt fake at all, that it actually felt like the most natural thing in the world, wouldn't have been easy, but he deserved the truth. We both did.

Except he'd been off, not his usually chatty or energetic self. His persistent melancholy had worn at me until doubt wormed into my heart. Getting back to our usual routine was going to be difficult enough without me complicating things by confessing I'd gone and caught feelings. Then he'd dropped his own truth bomb. For a tiny moment, I'd actually dared to hope that this was some kind of kismet, that he wouldn't have to help me move past my sudden romantic interest in him, because we'd indulge the fuck out of it. Then the sheer hypocrisy of his confession—his betrayal—registered, and my world imploded.

I leaned back in the chair and pinched my nose, willing the headache to ease. Not that I was optimistic anything I did would alleviate the pain of my tired, over-strained eyes. Because, of course, like the workaholic I was, I'd focused all of my energy on getting caught up rather than confronting the issues currently blowing up my phone and my life.

"Mr. Wells?"

I lurched so hard in the tilted chair I nearly fell out of it. I cleared my throat and glanced up to find Simon hovering in the doorway. "Hey, what's up? I'm just going through the reports," I added, as if I needed to justify my actions.

"Sorry. I knocked. When you didn't respond, I figured I should check in on you."

They had? Wait. Respond? Respond to what? I frowned and darted a glance at my desk phone. "Did you call?"

Simon's dark eyebrows climbed up their forehead. "Actually, I emailed yesterday and sent a reminder through chat. When I didn't hear anything, I texted your personal phone and then tried calling."

I shifted my gaze to the cell phone I'd been pointedly ignoring, despite it sitting a mere foot away. "Oh."

They gave me a curious look. "Yeah... So you should probably head to the meeting."

Still frowning, I quickly pulled up my calendar to see what they were talking about. I didn't recall any pre-existing meetings, but then, I also couldn't remember when I'd last checked my calendar. The moment it pulled up, I hissed a curse. Sure enough, there was a meeting that started fifteen minutes ago, with none other than Marcus Abernathy. I quickly pushed away from the unusually cluttered desk and did a pat-down inventory. Keys. Wallet. Keycard. I tucked the neglected phone into my inner jacket pocket. "Are we in the Havana Conference room?"

"I told Mr. Abernathy you got stuck on a call with a rep. He decided to go on ahead and asked that you meet him on the twentieth floor."

I breathed a sigh of relief. "You're a lifesaver." Simon stepped aside to let me exit, but I only made it a few steps before I ground to a halt. "Wait, isn't the twentieth floor under construction?"

They shrugged. "Last I heard, but I'm just the messenger."

I gave myself a good shake. "Right. Thanks again for having my back. I owe you." I spent the short trip up doing my best to dispel my anxiety. Why was Marcus here, and why was he on the twentieth floor?

The elevator dinged, and the doors slid open with a low mechanical whisk to reveal plastic sheeting, cardboard walkways, various ladders, and other equipment. No sooner did I register that the floor was in fact under construction than Marcus stepped out from behind a plastic sheet with a man in work gear. Both wore construction helmets, heightening my confusion.

Marcus caught sight of me, and a broad grin stretched across his face. "Wells! At last!" He reached into a cardboard box and pulled out another bright yellow helmet. "Here, you'll need one of these."

I accepted the helmet, still uncertain what we were doing here. Or, hell, why Marcus was in Charlotte at all. "Sorry, I'm late, Mr. Abernathy."

"I won't hold it against you. Not like you had a lot of heads-up to rearrange your schedule." Well, that was one relief. "And none of that 'Mr. Abernathy' nonsense. It's Marcus."

"Yes, sir," I said with a tentative smile as I put on the helmet.

"Good. Wells, I want you to meet Javier Guttierez. He's the lead contractor on this project and has a fabulously dry wit."

I extended a hand to the man. "Nice to meet you."

"Nice to finally put a face to the name. I thought you'd be taller."

Marcus laughed, and I joined him awkwardly. "You and Javier can get to know each other better later. Right now, I want to show you around." He turned to the contractor. "Thank you again for helping an old man out."

Javier snorted. "If you're old, then my papa is the undead." His face remained perfectly deadpan, then he cracked the smallest of smiles. "We'll be in touch. I look forward to working with you." He shook my hand again and made his way to the elevator.

I waited for the doors to close before turning to Marcus. "Uh, not to be impertinent, but what was he talking about? And why are we up here?"

"I'm so glad you asked." He clapped me on the shoulder and guided me around the edge of the room toward the vast expanse of windows. "Normally we wouldn't be so hush-hush about this, but I convinced Chase it'd be more…" He waved a hand in the air as he searched for the word. "Impressive, I guess."

"Okay…"

"Upon your advice, we looked into the options you recommended and decided that you were right about the Charlotte location being underutilized. Thus," he held his arms out to encompass the renovations in progress around us. "We've acquired the floors and the remodel should be completed by the end of the month. We lucked out there. The corporate announcement will go out first thing in the morning, but I wanted you to hear it from me first."

I couldn't help but brighten, though I was still lost as hell. "I'm so glad I was able to provide valuable insight." We stopped in front of the floor-to-ceiling windows. If the view downstairs was stellar, this one was jaw-dropping.

"Oh, you'll be doing much more than providing insight."

I turned away from the incredible, unobstructed view of uptown Charlotte. "What do you mean?"

"Dylan Wells, I'm here to officially offer you the position of District Manager for the Northeastern division of Infinity Financial."

I staggered back a step. This wasn't some promotion that bumped me up a few rungs. This was life-altering, career-defining, jump on a new ladder. Finally, my tongue caught up with my brain. "Wow. I mean *wow*. But wait, isn't that *your* position?"

"Not anymore. Never thought the day would come, but the missus and I have decided we're over city life. We're ready for a fresh adventure." He got a wistful look in his eye and a small smile quirked his lips as he stared out at the cityscape. Then it clicked.

"The farm in Oak Haven."

"And the goats," he said with a wink.

I couldn't help but chuckle. "This is an incredible opportunity, thank you. And congratulations on the early retirement. But…"

He raised an eyebrow. "But?"

"Don't get me wrong, I'd be a fool if I didn't jump at this like a skydiver, but aren't the northeastern headquarters in New York? When I spoke with Chase at the retreat, I told him I wasn't interested in relocating. My life is here." *Jimmy* was here. Not that we were on friendly terms at the moment, but I couldn't imagine being that far away from the man who'd been my best friend my entire life.

Marcus' expression turned sad as he nodded. "Chase mentioned that, but I assured him that for this kind of promotion, an exception could be made."

"I'm sorry to disappoint you, Marcus, but I meant what I said. My life is in Charlotte. If turning this position down means that I have to submit my resignation, I understand." My gut twisted. First Jimmy, now my career. How had the retreat fucked up so much of my life? And how would I ever make it right? I didn't *want* to leave IF, but I would if I had to. As for Jimmy, I may not know how to fix things yet, but I at least wanted to be close enough to try.

Marcus continued to give me a considering look, but I stood my ground. Then his face split into the same massive grin that he'd greeted me with at the elevator. "A man of conviction. I admire and respect that. I told Chase there wasn't a better person for the job. You'll make an amazing District Manager."

"Wait, so you *don't* want me to resign?" I asked, brow furrowed.

"And risk all your talent going to another firm? Of course not!"

"Forgive me, I'm still a little lost here. The northeastern head-quarters is still in New York, and that's a deal-breaker for me."

Marcus clasped his hands behind his back and turned to face the window once more. "Did I forget to mention that we'll be relocating the headquarters to Charlotte? This very building, in fact. Guess we'll have to call it the Eastern District now." He glanced at me, a decided twinkle in his eye. "You really were right about the prime location."

I opened my mouth to say something, but the words wouldn't form. The northeastern headquarters would be *here*, and they wanted *me* to run it.

"I take it those terms are more amenable to a yes?"

I nodded, still unable to find my voice.

He clapped his hands together. "Excellent! The official offer for you to sign is already being prepped in one of the conference rooms downstairs. We can order lunch and go over it in detail." He stepped toward the elevators, then pulled himself up short. "I understand if you'd like to speak with James first. Take your time. I'll order some of that fine ass barbeque everyone's always bragging about and meet you in the room."

"Thank you, sir." He gave me a stern look, and I quickly correct-ed myself. "Marcus. Thank you. This is... this is more than I could have hoped for."

He clapped me on the shoulder with a genial smile. "It was well-earned. You've made quite the impression, not just on upper management, but on your local team as well. But just to be clear, if that food gets here before you're finished speaking with your partner, I'm eating without you."

I laughed. "Understood." He spared me another grin, then left me to call my partner. *Jimmy.*

I waited until I heard the telltale chime and the clunk of the doors closing before pulling out my phone. A host of notifications greeted me, including the several Simon had sent. I leaned against the glass and stared at the screen. Seventy-five text messages. Not all of them were from Jimmy, but the majority were. My thumb hovered over his name. Did I read the messages first? Would it help? Was I even ready to talk to him?

I sank down to the floor and rested my head on the warm pane. It wasn't that I didn't want to tell him about the promotion; he'd helped me get it after all. But I didn't think I could handle hearing his voice, and news like this deserved a phone call. Even if I sent him a message, it would require seeing all the previous unanswered ones. I *missed* him. So much. But he'd broken my trust—something I didn't even know was possible—and I didn't know how to forgive that.

Finally, I straightened and tucked the device back in my pocket. As luck would have it, the food was just arriving as I stepped into the Havana Conference room. Marcus waved me over enthusiastically.

"Perfect timing." He eyed the spread being unloaded. "I think I might have gotten a little carried away. In hindsight, I don't think there are quite this many people in this office."

I forced a smile and stuffed the rest of my emotional upheaval back into its box to be unpacked later. Hopefully, it looked authentic and not as pained as it felt. "I assure you, it won't go to waste. Since it's set up here, why don't we invite the office in to eat first, then we can go over the offer?"

Marcus pointed a wrapped set of utensils at me. "That right there is why you'll make an outstanding district manager. Always putting people first. Will Jimmy be able to join our little celebration?"

I did my best to hide a wince. "He's, uh, busy with clients."

"Shame. Better luck next time."

Yeah, next time. If there ever was a next time.

Chapter 21

Jimmy

I LEANED AGAINST THE door for support as I fished out my keys. *Everything* hurt. My arms, my legs, my ass... and not in a good way. The door finally swung open, and I shuffled inside and directly to the sink, where I filled a glass with water and chugged it like my life depended on it. Joining a gym had been a mistake. I was sweaty, miserable, and turns out hurt quads did *not* distract from a hurt heart. If anything, being at the gym only made things worse. Every time I saw sandy blond hair in the mirror, I spun around in search of Dill, even though I *knew* it couldn't be him. I'd intentionally chosen a gym he didn't attend for that very reason. Shame my heart refused to read the memo. At this rate, I didn't know what would kill me first, fucking chin-ups or the way my heart surged with hope every ten minutes.

The cup rattled on the faux granite linoleum countertop as I placed it back in the line of other empty cups beside the sink. I pushed the pizza box, precariously stacked upon another, to a more secure position. On a whim, I peeked inside. I couldn't decide if I was relieved or disappointed that there weren't any slices inside. With a huff, I glanced around the rest of my apartment. Where the kitchen was littered with empty boxes, cups, and utensils, the living space was faring no better.

Clothes lay discarded in haphazard piles that mostly hid the worn blue fabric couch. The small chest that made up the coffee table now bore water rings along with its assortment of dead game controllers, work papers, and unopened mail. I contemplated kicking off my tennis shoes, but couldn't recall the last time I swept, or did the dishes, or did laundry, or, fuck, had a salad.

Irritation prickled at the back of my neck. This wasn't like me. I may not keep the neatest house, but I wasn't a slob. Fueled by anger, mostly directed at myself, I launched into a cleaning frenzy. I may not be able to control my best friend acting like a fucking child, but I *could* control the state in which I lived.

The dishwasher door squealed in annoyance as it flopped open. I unceremoniously piled in every dish cluttering the counter, including a few that I was pretty sure *weren't* dishwasher-friendly. I set it to start, then began sweeping off all the crumbs and bits of shredded napkins, along with the empty boxes, into the trash. In hardly any time, the bin was overflowing. I yanked the bag free and continued to stuff it until the stretch was maxed out. The thin plastic strands bit into my hand at the sheer weight of it and reminded my aching muscles just how sore they were. I'd cancel that ridiculous membership later. Right now, I was on a roll. I tied it off and chunked it into the hall to deal with later, then stomped into my room, which was equally a mess, to retrieve the laundry basket.

Only a couple of articles had actually made it into the basket, while the rest seemed to be trying to escape the room altogether. Muttering to myself, I shoved every piece of clothing I could see into the basket without distinction whether it was clean. From there, I dragged the basket into the bathroom and gave it the same treatment. By the time I made it back to the living room, the basket was in danger of overflowing, and I still had the disaster on the couch to deal with.

My quads twinged in protest as I squatted down to retrieve odds and ends poking out from under the couch. The fact that there was yet another empty pizza box underneath only added to my irritation. I slung it out into the open, letting it slide across the worn decorative carpet and onto the linoleum "hardwood". The gritty scrape of cardboard on dirt was unmistakable. With a grunt, I shoved off the floor and grabbed the broom, then swept not just the scuffed linoleum but the shabby carpet as well. Though the amount of dirt that actually made it into the dustpan, given my overly aggressive sweeping technique, left a lot to be desired. At least I could *see* the floor and my sad excuse for furniture now.

My frantic movements slowed, and I took more care clearing the rest of the coffee table and putting things away with mindless focus. There wasn't much I could do about the rings at this point beyond sanding the entire piece down and re-staining it. I frowned as I tried to recall what had happened to my coasters. I'd definitely had some. Three drawers later, I found them stuffed under some outdated coupons. I tossed the coupons out along with several menus for restaurants that hadn't been open for years.

It wasn't until I placed the coasters back where they could be of use that I remembered why I'd put them away. Dylan had given them to me as an apartment-warming gift. I could still hear his laugh as he teased that since I wasn't one for "fancy" things, he'd found the most ridiculous *nice* ones he could. My bottom lip quivered as I ran a finger over the collection of iconic movie scenes. I didn't think they were ridiculous then, and I didn't think they were ridiculous now. They were thoughtful.

I gasped and turned away from yet another painful reminder of our close friendship. "They're just fucking coasters. They probably cost all of ten bucks." But I wouldn't get rid of them, even if I doubted I'd ever be able to look at them with the same level of joy again. I shoved down the wave of emotion with a savagery that probably should have startled me and moved onto the shit that had accumulated in the corner between the chair and sofa. To my surprise, I found the suitcase from the retreat.

"Oh, for fuck's sake, I *know* I washed this shit." I pulled it out and set it on the couch. Fortunately, it didn't weigh like it had a bunch of six-week stale clothes, but there was definitely still something inside. I flipped the lid open and froze. My hand shook as I reached for the orange jacket I'd packed for Dylan, even though I knew he hated loud colors. Except he'd looked great, amazing even. I loved seeing his self-conscious smile as he received compliment after compliment.

I flashed to the struggle to get him to wear it. The warmth of his chest beneath my hand, his eyes bright from the tussle, his chest hair tickling my palm, his quick breaths that matched my own. I'd wanted so badly to kiss him at that moment, outing be damned. But like so many opportunities I'd had during the retreat and the last twenty-odd years, I didn't.

Finally, my fingers curled into the parachute fabric. I pulled it out of the suitcase with the full intent of tossing it into the basket, but only made it as far as clutching it tightly to my chest. Faint whiffs of Dill's cologne clung to the fabric, bringing back not just memories of the retreat but of our life. The riot of emotions that had plagued me surged forward as I buried my face in the fabric with an aggrieved sob. I missed him *so fucking much*. I was also furious with him for ghosting me like I was some sort of clingy hookup. While I could appreciate his hurt, what about mine? Had he forgotten how hard coming out could be? He said he hadn't, but he'd also twisted the whole argument to be about him. What about me? I'd waited literal decades to tell him I was bisexual—albeit, not intentionally—and he couldn't spare five fucking minutes to be supportive?

I stalked over to the near-bursting basket and shoved the jacket forcefully down. I didn't care if it broke. Or if everything spilled out. I didn't care about any of it. I wanted my best friend back, and He. Was being. A fucking. *Child.* The characteristic sting behind my eyes made a reappearance, and I snarled at the bulging laundry.

While I'd never been one to judge anyone for crying, I was also so tired of it. I felt wrung out and shriveled, like jerky left to bake in the sun. One hundred forty-two messages, twenty-two voicemails, and a draft folder of thirty-seven emails. While I couldn't be certain of the voicemails, I knew for a fact that he hadn't opened a single text. A couple of weeks, I could understand. We hadn't had a fight this big since... Well, ever. It made sense and was probably for the best to take time to cool off, gather our thoughts, so we could come back to the conversation with clearer minds.

Six weeks was ridiculous. I'd been his best friend for thirty-three years. He at least owed me a conversation. We were adults. We could handle this like *adults.* If he didn't or couldn't reciprocate my romantic feelings, fine, but *tell me* that. I wasn't some one-night stand he'd picked up at a club. I was his ride or die. And I fucking loved him!

Clinging to my increasing anger like it was a lifeline, I kicked over the basket with a furious shout that captured my fractured heart better than words ever could. The sound was still ringing in my ears when a familiar pounding came on the wall.

"Yeah, yeah! I'll quiet down when you stop watching porn in surround sound!" I yelled back, earning myself another round of banging.

Breathing hard, I glared at the tumped over basket and spill of clothes on the formerly clean-ish floor. *Of course,* the damnable orange jacket was sitting on top. I had to get out of this place. Thank *God* my lease would be up in the next couple of months and I could finally say goodbye to this shitty shoebox excuse of an apartment. Maybe I'd leave Charlotte altogether. Move somewhere new that didn't have memories of Dylan at every turn. Somewhere like Denver or Seattle, or hell, Hawaii. I could live in paradise for the rest of my life and leave this unbearable misery behind.

I pressed my palms into my eyes and took a shaky breath. Leaving wouldn't solve anything. It only sounded good now because I was hurting, grieving. I let out a derisive laugh. I couldn't even hurt like a normal person. Except I didn't want therapy, even if I did need it after this mess. I wanted my best friend to talk to me, even if it was to yell some more. Anything would be better than this stonewall. Could we really not talk about this? Evidence pointed to the contrary. Maybe I was wrong and our friendship had never been as resolute as I believed. Maybe we *weren't* friends anymore. I shook myself, refusing to go down that path... again. It always ended the same–a whole pizza, a pint of ice cream, yet another crying jag, and a slew of desperate messages that would go unanswered.

As I stood in the middle of my sad apartment, I stared up at the ceiling and admitted the truth I'd been running from since I was fourteen. I'd put off telling Dylan that I was bisexual and into him because I was terrified he'd reject me. Not because he couldn't accept my sexuality, but because he couldn't accept my love for him. Couldn't return it. The bubble of pain I'd tried so hard to deal with—work through, ignore, transform—welled up, threatening to burst.

My phone vibrated in my back pocket, and I scrambled to answer it, my heart surging with hope. I glanced at the caller ID, and that same traitorous heart fell with an unpleasant squelch to the pit of my stomach. Not Dylan. Of course not.

I shoved my heartache away, swiped to answer, and brought the device to my ear, a forced smile already on my face. "Hey Tina, long time no chat."

She laughed on the other end. "I know you're saying that teasingly, but it certainly feels like it, doesn't it? Always takes a bit to adjust after coming back from the retreat."

"Yeah," I agreed half-heartedly. I'd already spent far too much time thinking about the retreat—dwelling on the good, dissecting every moment, trying to convince myself I'd never had any reason to hope he'd return my feelings.

"Any who," she said, ignoring my lackluster response. "I was calling to see if you'd like to get together. We could do lunch, dinner, whatever. Catch up."

"Uh, I don't know if you've forgotten, but I'm in Charlotte. North Carolina," I added, because of course there was more than one Charlotte in the states.

Her uninhibited laughter lifted my spirits a hair, and my smile became more genuine. "Oh, Jimmy, I do miss chatting with you. *Yes*, I remember that you're clear across the continent. It's unfair, really. You're *way* better than my shopping friends here. But I digress. No, I'm actually going to be in town for the grand opening of the new IF East District office."

Rather than admit I had no clue what she was talking about, I played along. "Forgive me. My calendar is a mess. When is that again?"

"I know exactly what you mean. I've already transposed the dates for two other events, including one I had to reschedule to attend the grand opening. But I couldn't very well miss it, not when it'd give me a chance to see you again. Not to mention congratulate Wells in person. You must be so proud," she gushed.

I racked my brain for any reason I'd be proud and vaguely came up with Dill mentioning Charlotte as an alternative site for the office. He'd told me about it while we laid in bed, devising our plan of attack for the next day. A familiar flash of pain stabbed through me as I recalled his bright eyes and excited smile, the warmth of having him near, and his energetic voice. "Um, yeah, of course." My voice cracked, and I willed it to firm up. "It's pretty cool that Infinity took Dylan up on his suggestion to relocate to Charlotte."

"James Wallace," she deadpanned. "Do not be coy with me."

I frowned and glanced at the phone, not sure what I'd missed. Maybe I'd guessed wrong? "Beg your pardon?"

Tina let out an exasperated cry that had me pulling the phone away again. "Come on. You've got to be bursting at the seams with pride for your man."

My brain flatlined. *My man.* Except he wasn't. Probably never would be. At this point, I wasn't sure I'd even get my friend back.

"Seriously! Why aren't you bouncing off the walls and talking a mile a minute? Wells is replacing Abernathy as the East District Manager! Gah. That's *huge.* I don't know what world you live in, but that's pretty big, life-altering news where I come from."

"Right, that." I struggled to resuscitate my brain, but it refused to give me so much as a blip. Her words tumbled over and over like they were stuck in the spin cycle, but I couldn't get them to process. Dylan was going to be the East District Manager?

Tina scoffed. "Fine, be all cool. I get it, you're an independent man with a thriving career of your own to manage. Your honey's success doesn't define you. Please, at least tell me you celebrated. Better yet, give me all the details. Knowing you, I bet it was sensational."

My brain finally latched onto the information being lobbed at it. Yeah, the celebration *would* have been sensational... if I'd known anything about it. "I–"

"Oh shoot, I'm getting another call. One I sadly can't ignore. I'll see you on the fifteenth!" Before I could clarify the fifteenth of which month, the call ended, and what was left of my heart imploded.

I staggered back as if I'd been gut-punched. Needing space was one thing. But not telling me he'd gotten a promotion? And not just any promotion either, a massive, life-changing, holy-shit-is-this-real promotion. Shit like that warranted an in-person meeting, or at *least* a phone call. And not so much as a text?

The last of the hope I'd been stubbornly nursing died as the unforgiving reality crashed over me. Dylan wasn't just avoiding me. He was never coming back. We'd never talk things through. Never be more than friends. Never be anything. I bit down on my knuckle in an effort to stifle a sob. The tears I'd fought so valiantly streamed uninhibited down my face. My greatest fear had come true: my feelings for Dylan had completely and irrevocably destroyed our friendship.

As if to underscore my heartbreak, the happy chime of the doorbell rang through my apartment. A knock followed when I didn't immediately respond. I grabbed a shirt from the heap and used it to clear what I could of my meltdown. The doorbell rang again, and I croaked, "I'm coming."

I opened the door to find a young courier outside, dressed in a crisp uniform with wide eyes. His cheeks colored slightly as he took in my appearance. No doubt picking up on my puffy eyes and red nose. "S-sorry. I'd have just left it, but it requires a signature."

I nodded and rubbed my nose with a sniffle. "Not your fault. I should have responded sooner."

He opened his mouth, then promptly closed it, clearly at a loss for what to say. He passed me the electronic pad with a sheepish expression.

I confirmed it was addressed to me and glimpsed something about alcohol before signing. He tucked the pad into a pouch on his belt, then reached for a dolly. As he did, he noticed my confused expression.

"It's, uh, kind of heavy and says 'fragile'. Would you like me to bring it in?"

"If you're allowed to, yeah, that'd be a big help." I stepped to the side, and he wheeled in the box. "Anywhere will do."

His purposeful pace slowed as he glanced around for a suitable spot, his gaze tripping over the toppled basket and the spew of clothes. Finally, he angled toward the now mercifully clean kitchen and carefully tilted the box free. Mission accomplished, he dragged the now empty dolly back into the hall.

"Thanks again," I said, somehow sounding even worse than I had when I'd answered the door.

"No problem. Um, I hope your day gets better."

I offered him a weak smile and waited for him to start toward the elevator before shutting the door. Once everything was locked, I ran a hand over my face and approached the mysterious box. I didn't recall ordering anything recently—besides way too much pizza—and didn't typically order things that might be labeled fragile anyway. Curious what might be inside, I didn't bother searching for the box cutter, opting instead for a readily available paring knife. A smart man would have read the shipping label to get a clue as to the contents, or at least the sender, but today I was *not* a smart man.

I sliced through the packing tape with the efficiency that comes with having recently had to unpack a lot of boxes and pulled the flaps apart. Immediately, all the air went out of my lungs, and I collapsed to the floor beside the unexpected package, much to the despair of my abused body. Except it *was* expected. It was the beer I'd specially ordered to surprise Dylan when he got his promotion. The one he hadn't deigned to tell me about, despite how hard we'd both worked to make sure he'd gotten it.

The logo of the Twisted Pine stared up at me as I crumpled in on myself. How had things gone so horribly wrong between us? Was he really so hurt as to throw away three decades of friendship without so much as a conversation?

I resisted the temptation to smash all the beer and pushed the box away. Not that it slid very far, given how heavy it was. Whatever stubborn motivation had propelled me through the last month and a half vanished. My aching sobs rebounded off the walls while I curled in on myself, lacking the energy to relocate. I didn't care that my asshole neighbor would likely complain about the noise or that the floor was extremely uncomfortable and still gritty. My best friend in the entire world and the man I was completely in love with had forsaken me without a second thought. Much as I didn't want to, I had to face the facts: it was time to let him go. And as unbelievable as it was, that hurt more than anything else.

Chapter 22

Dylan

I LOOKED UP AT a knock on the door and, of course, looked in the wrong direction. Getting used to the new office set up was more of an adjustment than I'd anticipated. Not that you'd catch me complaining about the killer view or the automatic shades that shifted to counter the afternoon sun. IF had spared no expense in making this the new East District headquarters.

I pulled my gaze across the mid-century modern motif that felt both inviting and modern in the actual sense. It was comfortable, but with purpose. I had yet another rogue thought about how much Jimmy would love it, along with a less-than-friendly vision of standing behind him with my arms around his middle as he appreciated the kick ass view. Finally, my gaze fell on Simon. It still felt weird to have an executive assistant of my own, but I couldn't imagine a person better equipped for the position.

"Is it time for the review meeting already?"

They nodded and gave me a commiserating smile as I let out a long-suffering sigh. The grand opening of the office was only a couple of weeks away, and there was still a mountain of work to do. Even with Javier completing the renovations in record time with a proficiency that earned him whatever recommendations he could want, it still felt like time was slipping through my fingers. I pushed away from my innovative, albeit sparse, desk. Eventually,

I'd have to add some personal touches, ideally before the big event. But that was a problem for another day. Today I could afford to procrastinate a little longer.

Simon fell in step as we made our way to the new conference room. While I'd seen the plaque designating the room several times now, I still chuckled and shook my head. When the design team approached me about a theme for naming the rooms, I floundered. I was a numbers guy, not a creative. No doubt Jimmy would have come up with something amazing, but I still hadn't figured out what to say to him. So I'd passed on the decision to Simon. I only had myself to blame for the galactic-themed names. Currently, we were conferencing with the New York team during the transition in the cozy Milky Way Conference Room. Once we were officially open, however, we'd likely have to shift to the significantly larger Beetlejuice Conference Room.

I slid into my usual seat, grateful for the cushiony chair, right as the wall-sized projector screen came to life. After a few seconds, Simon gave me the thumbs up to signal we were live. I plastered a smile on my face and turned to greet Marcus and his EA.

"How go things on your end?" Marcus asked, skipping the small talk.

I leaned forward to pull the folder and notepad Simon had set out closer. "They're going. We finally got the furniture snafu sorted, and they're nearly done installing the smart boards for the advisor offices and meeting rooms."

"Ugh, I always hated dealing with interior designers," he groaned.

Simon ducked their head to hide a laugh while I shook my head. "They're not all that bad."

He snorted. "Tell that to the one my wife found for our rural escape. The rate they're going, we'll end up featured in Architectural Digest." It was hard not to laugh at his morose expression of defeat.

"Sorry, I can't help you there," I said with a smile that I almost felt. Maybe it was the whirlwind of it all, or *maybe* it was because I hadn't been able to share any of it with the number one person in my life, but I struggled to find joy in my new role. "Speaking of interior design, did Corporate decide what to do with the existing furniture at the location? It seems a shame to just toss it out."

Marcus gave me a wry smirk. "I may have made a convincing case to donate the usable furniture and office equipment to non-profits and local startups."

My smile was definitely genuine now. "When I grow up, I wanna be like you," I teased.

"You already are."

I let out a heavy breath. "Sorry, it still doesn't feel real."

"It'll take time. Luckily, you have an amazing support system. Simon is an absolute gem." He pointed at the camera with a serious expression that dissolved into a jovial grin. "You're lucky I'm retiring, or I'd be stealing them away from you." His executive assistant, who was still sitting next to him, coughed politely into her hand. He turned his bright smile on her. "Not that you're even remotely replaceable, Ebele."

She arched a dark eyebrow and made a note on her tablet. "I will let Mrs. Abernathy know you prefer the rustic barn design."

Marcus winced. "Okay, I deserved that. Anyway, back to the agenda. How are things going with the preparations for the grand opening?"

Details and plans filled the rest of the meeting, making my head whirl. Chase and Marcus were right. A good executive assistant was essential. Simon's steady note-taking and ability to roll with sudden alterations gave me hope we could actually pull this off. Now if only I could get my heart into it as well.

By the time I slunk back to my office, lunch had come and gone, I was bone-tired, and ready for a vacation. As I logged back into my desktop, I diligently reminded myself that it wouldn't always be like this. The only reason things felt so chaotic was because we were in the middle of a major transition—new leadership, new location, new everything.

I debated going out after work to let off some steam. A hot, sweaty body and an eager mouth would go a long way toward releasing my stress. But just like all the other times I'd contemplated hitting up a club or hooking up with someone from the app, I dismissed it just as quickly. I didn't want a random hookup whose name I either wouldn't get or wouldn't remember. I wanted... It didn't matter what I wanted. There was work to do.

With a resigned sigh, I returned to responding to the emails Simon had flagged as urgent. From there, it was on to reviewing the list of transfer requests and potential new hires. I was still poring over applications when Simon poked their head back into my office.

"Please tell me I didn't miss another meeting memo."

"Not today, boss." They swanned in, the bell sleeves of their exaggerated jacket swaying with each step. Then I realized they were carrying... a pot?

I frowned and straightened. "What's that?"

"A courier just dropped it off for you at the front desk. I know you're busy, but figured you wouldn't mind a minor interruption."

They narrowed their gaze as they got closer to the desk. "I see you didn't find the sandwich to your liking."

I blinked and swiveled to see what they were talking about. Sure enough, a perfectly wrapped sandwich from my favorite deli sat on the edge of the large desk. Poor Simon had been working so hard to go above and beyond for their new position, and here I was completely ignoring such a thoughtful gesture. "I'm sorry, Simon. I've been a little out of it." Distracted was more like. I couldn't help but think how much *easier* all of this would feel if my head and my heart were on the same page. And, fuck if that didn't sum up my life lately.

"Perhaps this will lift your spirits." They set down the potted plant in a space not currently occupied with paper with a flourish.

The spiky leaves and round, fuzzy ones tugged at recognition, but I was at a loss. "Who's it from?" And what the hell is it?

"Oh! There's a notecard." They swiveled the plant around, and my heart lurched into my throat at the familiar handwriting.

I swallowed past the lump and croaked, "Can I... can I get a minute?"

"Of course." They turned to leave, but stopped after a few steps. "Is there, um, anything I could take for you?"

"Yeah, could you pass these along to Nancy?" I pushed the short stack of applications and requests I'd sifted through without taking my eyes off the note.

"You've got it, boss. And, uh, try to eat something. 'kay?"

I made a noncommittal noise. The empty pit in my stomach had nothing to do with being hungry. Left alone with my thoughts, I read the note all the way through, then read it again.

I know you're the worst with plants, and flowers are cliché. So I went with succulents. Figured they'd be a lot harder to kill. They don't take much, promise. Anyway, congratulations on the promotion. Told you you didn't need me.

~Jimmy

I tentatively touched the variety of plants clustered together in the shallow pot. Each leaf was a different texture and shade, everything from soft tines and velvet leaves to vibrant greens tipped with a rosy pink. The lump in my throat returned with a vengeance, and I released a stuttering breath as I leaned back in my chair. I should have known Jimmy would find a way to reach me when I didn't respond to any of his calls or messages. To be honest, I'd half expected him to show up at the office. If I was being more honest, part of me had hoped he would. But how had he known about the promotion? Did it matter? He did. And instead of coming here, he'd sent... a plant.

Thirty minutes later, I was still staring at the message, having officially committed it to memory, and trying to figure out why it was so upsetting. What right did I have to expect him to show up here? Make a scene? It wasn't as if I'd given him any sort of encouragement over the last two months. Yet I was still upset and getting more so with each minute that passed. I forgot all about the urgent emails still dinging as each came in, the bustling office beyond my doors faded away, and the sandwich remained untouched.

Then it finally hit me what was wrong with the note. It didn't read like congratulations. It read like a goodbye. Fuck *that*. What the hell was wrong with me? Wallowing in self-pity wouldn't fix anything. What it *would* do was cost me my best friend, a man I refused to live without.

I surged out of my chair, grabbing my blazer as the chair rolled away to smack into the window with a hollow thunk. "Simon!" I shouted, forgetting that the phone had a more appropriate intercom function to contact them.

They skidded to an abrupt halt in the doorway as I finished slipping on my blazer. "Is something wrong?"

I yanked open the desk drawer to retrieve my phone and keys. "Whatever appointments I have remaining today, cancel them." I paused. "Tomorrow's too. Make whatever excuses you need. I'm taking a personal day." I considered adding to contact me if there was an emergency, but didn't want to put that out there. Simon was more than capable, as was the rest of the team here. They'd be fine without me for a day or so.

"Yes, sir." Their lips tilted up in a small, knowing smile.

"Yeah, yeah," I said as I walked past them.

They attempted to smother their grin. "I don't know what you're referring to."

I hesitated and glanced at them. "Does the entire office know?"

They raised their eyebrows. "That you're completely in love with your best friend? Don't know what you mean," they said, but their persistent smirk belied their supposed innocence.

I rolled my eyes. "Wish me luck."

"Good luck. You're gonna need it."

Oof, I felt that in my bones. Just how badly had I fucked things up? Short answer: A LOT. I just prayed I wasn't too late.

Chapter 23

Jimmy

I MANEUVERED THE BOX to my side and kicked the car door shut. Thank heavens it was the last one. Maybe I *shouldn't* have been so hasty to cancel that gym membership. My arms were killing me. Then again, that was money I could use toward a new apartment. I groaned at the thought of the apartment listings waiting for me. Since when had everything gotten so damn expensive? Not to mention small. I might have tackled my student loans, but I wasn't made of money. At this rate, I'd be moving from one shoebox to a slightly more updated shoebox.

Guilt flashed through me for the hundredth time. I really couldn't afford to take a week off from seeing clients. Except I wasn't really any good to them while I was a total mess. The time was necessary for me to get my life back together. My manic cleaning and organizing of the apartment had led to a massive purge of nonsense I'd accumulated over the years, and now my office at the new clinic was getting the same treatment. Taking the week off was best for everyone. Now all I had to do was hold on to that conviction for five more days.

The box I'd neglected to tape shut shifted, threatening to slide from my grip. I scrambled to get a better purchase and made my way to the door, where I got to do some impressive contortions to get the damn thing open. A blast of warm air hit me and would have been welcome after the chill outside if I hadn't already been sweating from hauling boxes here and there.

"Hey, Courtney," I said, after blowing a huff of air to free the strands of hair sticking to my forehead.

Our receptionist gave me a cautious smile. She was sweet in that nosey-yet-dependable aunt sort of way, and I was immensely glad she'd agreed to move with me and my three colleagues to the independent clinic. "Now, don't get mad."

I halted my awkward trudge to my office at the end of the hall. When I glanced at her with narrowed eyes, she somehow appeared even more sheepish. "What is it?"

She worried her lower lip. "You have a client waiting in your office. I was just about to call you."

"Courtney," I hissed, lowering my voice, though I knew the insulation in the building was above par. "What part of no appointments this week says let one in my office? How long have they been waiting?"

"I know. I know! But he said it was an emergency, and I know your stance on that. He hasn't been waiting too long. Twenty minutes at most, but he said he was willing to wait."

I set the box down on the counter and rubbed a hand over my sweaty face. "And there wasn't anyone else who could see him?" Luckily, my colleagues shared the same opinion as me when it came to mental health emergencies—all hands on deck.

Courtney shook her head, causing her tight brown curls to bounce. "Sabrina is booked for the rest of the day. Darius is with a client now. And Ezequiel is at his daughter's dance recital."

"Okay, okay. I just..." I let out a heavy breath, then squared my shoulders. I could do this. A standard session was only an hour long. I could put on a brave face and be the counselor this guy clearly needed. "Did he say what it was about, by chance?"

Relief flooded her face, and she quickly referred to her notes. "Um... looks like something about losing a loved one."

Fuck me sideways, it would have to be about grief. I dug deep for my professional face and picked the box back up. It wasn't until I was opening the door to my office that I realized I'd forgotten to get the client's name. So much for being a professional. Sighing to myself, I used my foot to push the door open wide enough for me and the box. Rather than carry it across the room where I'd originally intended, I opted to set it on a decorative side table. After a quick glance into its contents to confirm no sensitive material was visible, I dusted my hands and shifted my focus to locate the client.

"Thank you for your patience. I've been working on some reorganizing. Hope you haven't been waiting too long."

The client stood at the far end of the room, studying the sole framed picture I'd hung before going on the retreat and subsequently going off the deep end. Otherwise, the office was depressingly bare. Hence the box. As far as art went, it was nothing spectacular, but it was a favorite of mine. The vibrant hues and impressionist style lent the Charlotte skyline a fantastical quality that always brought a smile to my face. But I wasn't looking at the picture. The man held all my attention. He slowly turned around, confirming what I already knew.

"I'd wait as long as it took," Dylan said.

I stared at him for a long minute before finally finding my voice. "What are you doing here?"

He took a deep breath that pushed the lapels of his suit jacket apart. "What I should have done two months ago."

My stupid, stupid, traitorous heart lurched into my throat. "And that would be?" I asked thickly.

He glanced down at his perfectly polished loafers and rocked back on his heels. "You never did ask why Kennedy and I broke up."

It took every ounce of restraint I had not to snap at him. Why the fuck would I want to know that now? Months of nothing, and *this* is what he wanted to talk about? "We already established that it's not something you're open to discussing."

He finally glanced back up. "I think you should."

"Fine," I huffed and crossed my arms. Normally, I was much more mindful of my body language with clients, but Dylan *wasn't* a real client. "Why did you and Kennedy break up?"

He turned slightly to look at the painting once again, taking his hand from his pocket to trace the frame. It seemed safe to assume he'd come straight from his office, since he was still dressed in his usual business professional attire. His *new* office. Anger, I thought I'd conquered, flared back to life.

"Well?"

"Did I ever tell you that Kennedy and I were planning to move in together?" He flicked a glance my way.

A fresh wave of hurt washed over me. I knew he'd loved Kennedy, knew they were getting serious. But he'd never once contemplated living with a partner. "You know damn well you didn't," I snapped, praying the harsh words hid how much what he'd said wounded me.

His shoulders slumped. "I deserved that. The point is, we were." He glanced wistfully up at the ceiling. "Had deposits all saved up. Had even toured a few apartments and houses. The houses were my idea, not his."

I tightened my arms around myself. I didn't give a shit whose idea it was. I just wanted this awful trip down memory lane to be over.

He shoved his hand back into his pocket and resumed his study of the carpet. "Anyway, it was exciting and terrifying." He chuckled to himself. "I even turned down a few places because I knew you'd hate them." His face became somber. "Guess that's how it started. It wasn't much at first, but as time went by and we got closer to deciding, he would get—I don't know—upset anytime I mentioned you."

I frowned, not liking where this was headed.

"Then one day he sat me down and told me I needed to choose. Him or you."

I gasped despite myself. That was *not* where I'd seen that going. "That's really fucked up, Dill."

"No shit. A little jealousy we could have worked through. But an ultimatum? Like, who does that?"

"An insecure asshole," I mumbled. Apparently not quietly enough, because he shot me a sour look. I shrugged, refusing to apologize for my views on his ex's shitty behavior.

"The thing is, I didn't even have to think about it. Sure, I took a day because that's what you're *supposed* to do, but I already knew my answer. You. Kennedy and I may have been together for a few years, but we'd never have the history you and I did, the connection. Ultimately, I think he saw something I wasn't ready to see." He squeezed his eyes shut while a parade of emotions danced across his face.

My stance relaxed, and I took a step toward him. "Dill?"

"Fuck, Jimmy," he said, his voice completely raw. He drew a haggard breath and looked at me with glassy eyes. "I'm so sorry.

There's no excuse for my behavior these last few weeks. I was so busy letting my hurt define me that it got in the way of everything else. You came out to me, for fuck's sake. It's none of my damn business why you waited. You're my best friend. It's my job to support you." He sniffed and gave me a wan smile. "So, you know, congratulations, by the way. To think we could have been talking about guys this whole time."

"Forgive me if I didn't want to talk about other men with you."

He huffed an ironic laugh. "I know the feeling. I just… didn't know why."

I plucked at the pilling on my sweater that was definitely not client-facing appropriate. "And you do now?"

"Don't you? At a time when I thought I was the most in love, I chose you. I *choose* you. It was always going to be you."

I bit the inside of my cheek to distract from the stinging in my eyes. "Why not say anything sooner? And, yes, I'm aware of how hypocritical that sounds."

"I don't think it's hypocritical at all. Why would you put yourself out there like that when I'd never given you any incentive? As for not telling you, I was scared." His eyebrows lifted. "Terrified. The last thing I wanted was to be that stereotypical gay guy pining after his straight friend. So, I refused to think about you like that. That sounds pretty ridiculous to say out loud, but it's like I developed some kind of brain-block."

"Okay…" I wasn't really sure what to do with that.

He shook his head. "I'm not doing a great job of explaining any of this."

"You have always been pretty shit at expressing your feelings."

"Asshole," he said with a wry smirk. "What I'm trying to get at is, as great as I thought my relationship was with Kennedy, it was nothing compared to our fake one. It was natural and felt *right*. And the more of you I had, the more of you I wanted. I let my fear of what would happen if we didn't work out blind me to what could happen if we *did*." He paused, and I held my breath, uncertain of what came next. "I won't let fear keep me from you ever again. I feel like I've been waiting my whole life to love you."

Well, shit. I stomped over to the door. I couldn't deal with this. It was too much. He'd torn my heart out and now... My chest tightened. I picked the box up from the side table, not really sure what to do with it, though throwing it at him was starting to look like a reasonable option.

"Jimmy, please. Wait. I know I fucked up. You deserve so much more than how I've treated you. I'm begging you. I get that I'm stupid late to this, but can we please at least talk about it?"

I dropped the box in front of the door without thinking and whirled to confront him. "*Now* you want to talk about it? After weeks, *months*, of giving you a chance to be a fucking adult and get your head out of your ass, *now* you want to talk? You've got some nerve."

He at least had the decency to wince. "You're right. To say I acted like an immature brat doesn't really cover it."

I crossed my arms and glowered at him. "You can do better than that. I can understand and even respect needing time to process. I'm not exactly without culpability. But what you did..." I trailed off as raw hurt clogged my throat. "Jesus, I was ready to give up. Let you go."

His small gasp snagged my attention. "So I was right. The note with the succulent was a goodbye. You were really going to let our friendship die without a fight?"

"How fucking dare you! *I* wasn't the one dodging calls and ignoring texts. I may have been in love with you for most of my life, but I'm not desperate. I won't fight for something the other person clearly doesn't want."

He raked his hands through his hair, his face contorting with pain. "I never said I didn't want you. I just—"

"No," I cut him off, "you didn't say shit. Instead, you let your silence do the talking, and it said plenty." I wrapped my arms tighter around myself and looked away. "You really hurt me. And while you were out living your best life, I was falling apart."

"Jimmy." His voice broke. He took a deep breath and tried again. "I've been a wreck, an absolute shell. I thought... I thought getting lost in work would help. That I'd eventually figure out what to say. And then that damn cactus showed up—"

"Succulent," I corrected.

"The green things in a pot, and I realized I'd waited too long. That falling into old habits when a relationship got hard wouldn't fix this."

I gave a derisive snort. "If I'd known all it took was a damn plant to get you to talk to me, I'd have sent one sooner."

"It wasn't some plant. It was a thoughtful gift from my best friend and a note that showed me how close I was to losing the person I love most in this world. Because I do. I love you, Jimmy, and I hate what I put you through to figure that out. I'll do whatever it takes to make it up to you. I'm not above groveling for your forgiveness."

"Tempting."

"I'm begging you, Jimmy. Give me a chance to show you how truly sorry I am, how much I care about you—love you. I've hated every second we've been apart since the moment I got on that elevator. The retreat was the reality check I needed to see what life with you as a partner and not *just* my best friend could be like. And I *wanted* that. Then, when I learned it was actually a possibility, I... panicked. My brain broke, and I latched onto the hurt to stay afloat. But I was wrong. So very, very wrong."

My arms finally fell to my sides. This was all I'd ever wanted from him, and while we still had a shit ton to work through, I wasn't about to make the same mistake he had. I stormed over to where he was still pleading for a chance. "Shut the fuck up, Dill." His endless tide of apologies cut off, and I grabbed his face. Despite all of my anger and hurt, the moment our lips touched, something settled inside me. I hungrily devoured his mouth and relished the fierceness of his return. By the time I pulled away, my lungs were screaming for oxygen. I released the sides of his face and coasted my hands down his chest to rest on his lapels. "Tell me again."

"I'm so sorry."

My lips twitched with a smile. "We'll come back to that. The other thing."

His blue eyes briefly widened with doubt, then softened as he cupped my jaw. "I love you, Jimmy. I love you so fucking much it hurts."

The stinging behind my eyes returned with a vengeance, but before they could escape, he captured my lips once more. I wrapped my arms around him, pulling him close, as he continued to deepen the kiss.

"Fuck, I've missed you," he rasped between kisses.

"Feeling's mutual," I said as I slipped my hands beneath his jacket.

He rested his forehead against mine, panting for breath. "I plan on spending the next however many years it takes making it up to you."

My heart fluttered, and I smiled. "I like the sound of that."

"Good, because I'd like to see you try to stop me."

I snickered. "Oh, babe, I'll never stop you from groveling. If you want, I have a whole workbook dedicated to the art of apologizing I could loan you."

"Shut up." He kissed me again, teasing my bottom lip before moving on to the sensitive spot on my neck. I couldn't help but moan. "Fuck, that sound has been my undoing."

"You're welcome," I gasped as his teeth raked over the thin skin, then made a put out sound when he stopped and pulled away. "What gives? Making up is the *only* good part about fighting."

He chuckled, but didn't resume the tortuous kisses. "When's your lease up again?"

"End of September," I replied as I tried unsuccessfully to snag his lips.

"Found a new place yet?"

I huffed my irritation. "No. I still have an ungodly pile of brochures to go through. Can we get back to the making out now?"

"Don't."

"Don't what? Keep kissing you?" What the actual fuck? Dill could give lessons in how to blow hot and cold.

"No." He rubbed his thumb along my cheek, tickling the stubble I hadn't bothered to shave that morning, or the day before. "Don't go through the brochures."

"Uh... why?"

"Because I don't think I can bear one more day of waking up without you."

I stared at him, not entirely sure if I was hearing him right.

"Move in with me."

Doubt eclipsed my previous joy. "Are you sure? We've never really lived together. What if we can't stand each other?"

His laughter went a long way toward brightening my disposition. "Jimmy, if I didn't kill you when we were fifteen and I woke up to you drooling on my face, I think we can survive any quirks that might creep up. Not that I expect any will, for the record."

"Wow, so you're serious. You really want to move in together?"

"The sooner the better," he said with a smile that erased any lingering doubts. "We know each other better than any two people I've ever met. I'm yours, Jimmy. If you'll have me."

I grinned so wide my face hurt. "Oh, I'll definitely have you. More than once if I have anything to say about it."

"That so?" He teased my lips before snaring me with a kiss while his other hand drifted down my backside to grab my ass.

I moaned and ground against him, elated to find him equally aroused. "Damn right."

"I think I can accommodate that." He continued to snatch at my lips as he guided me backward.

"Mm, not there," I mumbled against his lips, halting our trajectory toward the couch.

"Why not?"

"Clients sit there."

He nipped at the side of my neck, and I shuddered. "Okay, then where?"

I glanced around for a reasonable alternative while his hands roved over my body. "The desk," I said breathlessly, then snagged his hand and dragged him over to my chair, where I shoved him down.

He smirked, and I didn't hesitate to straddle him, though the chair squeaked in protest at our combined weight. He leaned forward to resume licking and nipping at my neck.

"Hold up." I quickly vacated my not exactly comfortable position and swiveled around to search the desk. The chair squeaked again and suddenly he was pressed against me, his hands on my hips and mouth on my neck. I did what I could to muffle another groan as I scrambled for the stereo remote. Finally, I got hold of it and switched it on, turning up the volume to the highest level that wouldn't be too disrespectful to my colleague a couple doors down.

He barked a laugh as the playlist I'd been rocking started. "All-Star? Really?"

I turned around as best I could, given that I was now sandwiched between him and the desk. "Shut up. It's my feel-better playlist and, in case you hadn't guessed, I haven't exactly been in the best spirits. Plus, there's not a chance in hell I'm going to be quiet."

Sadness flooded his blue gaze despite my lighthearted comment. "I'm so, so sorry, Jimmy. I—"

"Nope, you can keep apologizing later. We're doing other things right now." To emphasize my point, I turned the volume up a little more and yanked my sweater over my head. The walls had amazing insulation and were surprisingly sound-resistant, but I wasn't taking any chances.

"Understood." He slipped his fingers beneath my undershirt, lightly brushing my fevered skin as he pulled it up, then tossed it aside. His mouth closed back over mine and he palmed my dick, which was already straining for freedom. His tongue fucked into my mouth while he undid my belt, then released my fly and pushed my pants down, taking my boxers with them.

I moaned into him, even as I flinched when my ass kissed the cold desk. I reached for his belt and fly, stopping once I could round my hands over the swell of his bare ass. He moved to take off his jacket, and I grabbed his tie, pulling him down for another searing kiss. "Leave it on."

"All of it?" he asked with raised eyebrows.

I stole a moment to appreciate how fucking incredible he looked with his sharp navy jacket, pale pink button-down, and beautiful cock jutting toward me from his open fly. "Yeah," I replied huskily. "You look fucking *hot* in a suit."

He gave me a wicked look as he situated me more firmly on the desk and positioned himself snugly between my legs. "And how many times have you fantasized about fucking me in a suit?"

"Way too many." I used my hold on his tie to pull him back down, licking into his mouth and borderline vibrating with the erotic feel of the fine fabric of his suit against my bare skin. Then he angled his hips and our cocks brushed together. My head fell back with a truly indecent moan. As much as I would have liked him to be bending me over the desk instead, I wasn't exactly in a condition for that. He wrapped a hand around our cocks and I jolted at the overwhelming flood of sensation. But it could be better. I flapped my hand around for the drawer handle and could just barely reach inside. Finally, I pulled out the lube and shoved it at him. "Here."

"James Wallace. What happened to 'I see clients here'?" he teased.

I scowled at him. "I'm a professional, not a saint."

Chuckling, he popped the cap and poured a healthy amount of the liquid on his hand. I hissed at the cold when he resumed his hold on our cocks. "Sorry, too impatient," he muttered before attacking the side of my neck, the scruff of his beard a delicious contrast to the silky glide of his suit pants on my thighs.

I bucked into his fist and writhed in tortured ecstasy on a desk I'd never be able to look at the same way again. Meanwhile, the playlist kept going, switching from one loud, upbeat song to another. Thank God I'd been listening to the music like this for weeks between clients, otherwise someone was bound to investigate, and the box sitting in front of the door wasn't *that* heavy.

"That's it, baby. I love making you feel good. Let me hear it." He captured my earlobe between his teeth, and I about came undone. "You're so amazing. I was a fool not to see how much more you are to me. I love you." With each panted praise, I got closer and closer to the point of no return. My release danced right at the edge and, much as I wanted to watch the bliss blossoming on his face, I could barely keep my eyes open under the tide of mounting pleasure. "Fuck, Jimmy, you're so beautiful. I love everything about you."

I buried my hands in his hair and twined my legs around him as best I could, needing him closer. His hand pumped faster, and stars danced behind my vision while my imminent release coiled in my gut. I wouldn't last much longer, but I didn't want it to end.

"I'm close," he growled beside my ear.

I whined my agreement.

"You gonna come with me, baby?"

"Yes," I gasped, already dangerously close to spilling.

"You're so damn perfect. That's it, baby, come with me."

"Yes," I said again.

On cue, he grunted, his motions becoming erratic as he came onto my chest. His cock pulsing against mine was all it took to send me crashing right along with him. Cum hit the underside of my chin as I arched against the wooden desk and spurt rope after rope. Finally, my body relaxed into a sated pile of Jimmy-goo. I blinked the world into focus and found Dill with his sweaty hair plastered to his forehead, his face stunningly flushed, and a shimmer in his blue eyes I'd waited my whole life to see.

"I love you, Dylan," I said on a spent exhale.

"I love you too, Jimmy. I'm sorry it took me so long to see it." He leaned down, and I shoved a hand between us. He looked at me in confusion. "What?"

"You'll get your suit covered in cum."

"Fuck it. I'll get another one." He tried once again to reach my lips.

"But I like *this* one. Plus, every time you wear it, I'll think of this moment," I argued.

He smirked and leaned back. "Hard to dispute that logic."

I sagged onto the desk, feeling more relaxed than I had in weeks, more whole. "That. Was. Amazing."

"*You* are amazing," he countered.

I smirked and turned off the music, then pushed myself up to a seated position. "I am, aren't I?"

"Mm hmm, and so humble."

I finished cleaning myself off with some wet wipes from my drawer and accepted my clothes back from Dylan. When I hopped free of the desk, my stomach gave a loud rumble. I chuckled. "I don't know about you, but I could eat."

"Pizza?"

"No!" I said too quickly. "Uh, no. Something else. Not too heavy, though. You're fucking me properly when we get home."

A dazzling grin spread across his face. "I like the sound of that."

"Fucking me?" I asked slyly, with an arched eyebrow.

"That too," he said, stepping close, "but I was referring to the 'we get home' part."

My face heated, and I ducked my head. "So, we're really doing this? Dating? Fucking? Living together?"

He nodded. "Going furniture shopping, arguing about who's doing the dishes, fighting over the covers. The whole nine yards."

I launched myself at him, nearly sending both of us to the ground, and peppered his face with kisses. "I love you so damn much."

He stroked my cheek. "I love you too. Now, what do you say we get some food in you, then fuck ourselves into a coma?"

I laughed and followed him to the door. "Don't you have to get back to work or something? I imagine there's still a shit ton to deal with at the new office, especially now that you're in charge." I narrowed my eyes at him. "Still pissed you didn't tell me about that, by the way."

"You have every right to be angry. It was a dick move. I wanted to call and tell you first thing, but I..." He glanced away. "I don't think I'll ever be able to express how truly ashamed I am for the way I acted." He reached for the door handle, and I stopped him. "What?"

"Need to move the box first. I'm horny, not stupid."

He snorted. "No one in their right mind would ever think you're stupid. You're fucking perfect and the best man I know." I'd scarcely opened the door when he tugged me back to him to nuzzle then kiss the back of my neck. I squirmed in his grasp, failing miserably at keeping my laughter to myself.

"It's about damn time." Courtney's exasperated tone snapped both of our attention to the desk where she, along with Darius and Sabrina, were standing.

Dylan chuckled behind me and let me go. "Your office too?"

My face flamed hot enough to fry an egg while I did a quick mental inventory to make sure we didn't look exactly like what we'd just done. "Uh, hey."

Sabrina rolled her eyes, then walked back to her suite.

"Glad to see you two finally worked things out," Darius said with a smirk. He hiked a thumb at me. "He's been moping for *weeks*."

"I have not," I replied indignantly.

Dylan's arms once more circled my middle. "It's okay, baby, I have too."

I glanced at him over my shoulder. "Really?"

"Babe, I started moping our last night at the retreat."

My jaw dropped. "That would have been nice to know. You could have told me, saved us this whole mess."

"You're right, I *should* have told you. No more secrets. I promise."

I smiled back at him, my heart impossibly full. "No more secrets."

Dylan

THE ELEVATOR DOORS OPENED, and a wave of cheers washed over us. Smiling, I exited with an arm wrapped around Jimmy's waist. The babble of voices combined with the press of bodies was a tad overwhelming, but as Jimmy had proven repeatedly, I could conquer anything with him by my side. We managed a few steps before a joyous screech pierced through everyone else's well wishes.

"You're finally here!" The crowd parted, allowing Tina to pass unencumbered. Despite the party technically being for the new office and my promotion, she made a beeline for Jimmy.

He chuckled and took a half step away in order to catch her exuberant hug. "Like I'd miss it." He glanced at me over her shoulder, his eyes shining with pride.

I smiled back at him, my chest fuzzy with joy. My hard-headed obstinance had nearly cost me the greatest love of my life, but between profuse apologies and mind-blowing sex, we were in a good place.

He pushed Tina back by her shoulders. "Damn, woman, you look great. I *told* you the fitted vest would look incredible."

"And don't forget the pants! Finally found a decent occasion for them." She did a little swish, and I couldn't help but laugh when

I realized they were the same emerald trousers she'd worn on the retreat. "But what about you? You clean up pretty well yourself."

I stepped in close again, replacing my arm around his waist and planting a kiss on his perfectly smooth cheek. "That he does."

Tina turned her beaming grin on me and extended a hand. "I know I've said it a dozen times on the phone and on video calls, but congratulations, Dylan. The new Eastern headquarters looks amazing and is already running like a dream. Your remarkable attention to detail has truly done wonders."

"Thank you, but I couldn't have done any of it without the incredible team here. If this office is a success, it's because of them," I replied, shaking her hand.

"Now, what did I say about that modesty?" Chase said gruffly as he joined our little trio. His serious expression melted into a grin. "Congratulations, Wells. I'd say I'm impressed, but that would imply I didn't know I had it in you. So, instead, I'll say I'm glad you accepted the position and gave the rest of the world a chance to appreciate your brilliance."

"Chase." I hid my face against Jimmy's chest to hide my blush, but I was pretty sure even my ears were burning after that praise.

Jimmy rubbed my back, and I glanced up at him. "He's right, babe, you're brilliant and I'm so freaking proud of you."

I caught sight of a server carrying a tray of sparkling flutes and broke away. "Nope. I am not tearing up. Not tonight." Their laughter chased me, with them not far behind.

The evening quickly became a blur of faces and bubbles. I wasn't normally such a fan of champagne, but every time I finished my glass, someone replaced it. I'd resorted to sipping them so slowly that they got warm.

A cluster of IF corporate heads from the West Coast drifted away to marvel at the Charlotte skyline. I shook my head, mentally berating myself. Technically, I was a corporate head now and every bit as much of a "big wig".

"What's up with you?" Jimmy asked as he sidled up next to me.

I took advantage of his proximity to lean against him. "Nothing. Just... still getting used to it, I guess."

"And there are a lot of people here."

"A *lot* of people," I echoed with a light laugh.

"Brought you something." He plucked my half-full champagne flute from my fingers and set it aside. Then he handed me a glass filled with dark amber liquid and cream foam on top. "Figured you could use a reprieve from the bubbles."

"Aha! I knew there were supposed to be other drinks besides champagne."

He chuckled. "And not just any drinks. Seems like we're not the only ones who are fans of the Twisted Pine. At least it's not the same lager we have at the house."

I gratefully accepted the drink and downed nearly half of the blissfully cold beer. I let out a satisfied sigh and tilted my head back to look at him. "I love you."

"Aw, babe. I love you too." He brushed his lips briefly over mine and gave me his clownish grin.

"Ham," I scoffed before turning back to appreciate the sheer number of IF people that had come out to celebrate. Marcus and Bethany were by the south-facing windows, regaling their latest cluster of well-wishers about their new farm... with goats. Simon was busy flirting with a rep from the Midwest. Even Stephan and Mai had made it, though they were currently trying to one-up each other in a random game of company trivia.

"You really do look hot as sin in a suit," Jimmy whispered in my ear while he subtly grabbed my ass.

"James Wallace, are you checking me out?"

"Maybe."

I laughed under my breath. "This mean I'll be keeping this penguin suit on longer than I originally planned?"

"Tempting, but I haven't decided yet. I might not have the patience to appreciate it properly."

I angled to face him and fully embraced the way my heart swelled every time I looked at him. I'd been running from those telltale swoops in my stomach and the way my heart raced for so long. But not anymore. Never again. I leaned up, and he met me halfway, sealing our lips together in a sweet kiss that made me want to sigh with contentment.

"Oi, you two. You can moon at each other later. Your adoring public is waiting for you," Tina said, cutting through our tender moment with the grace of a freight train. She certainly hadn't gotten to where she was by being subtle.

We laughed and separated. Then I caught Simon, now hovering a pace behind Tina, and groaned. "No, no speech."

"Damn right, you're giving a speech." Tina rubbed her hands together with malicious glee.

I gave Jimmy my best puppy-dog eyes, though his were way better. "Please don't let them make me."

"You've got this, Dill." He gave me a helpful push toward the pair. "Don't worry, I'll be right in the front waiting for you. Always."

"Always," I repeated with a smile.

I have enjoyed writing Dylan and Jimmy's story more than I can say, and I'm so sad to let them go (for now). But I couldn't have done it without the incredible help from my critique group, the MM Huddle. Evie McGlynn, Sam Drake, Cyd Sidney, Court Stephens, and TA Nieman, thank you for helping me make these guys shine!

SAM BOLANOS (SHE/THEY) IS a genderqueer author and founder of Chaotic Neutral Press LLC. They believe in love, equality, and the Oxford comma. When not playing with her three dogs or spending time with her incredible husband, she's probably agonizing over edits or escaping into her latest fantasy.

NEWSLETTER: SUBSCRIBE

WEBSITE: SBOLANOS.COM

FACEBOOK: @SBOLANOS

READER GROUP: SAM'S SUNBEAMS

INSTAGRAM: @SBOLANOSBOOKS

TIKTOK: @SBOLANOSBOOKS

www.ingramcontent.com/pod-product-compliance
Lightning Source LLC
Chambersburg PA
CBHW020753190726
48285CB00006B/2017